About the author

Susan Parry began writing when she was a university professor at Imperial College. Her work included forensic studies and archaeological investigations that form the basis for her writing. She lives with her husband in Swaledale, where the views from her house provide inspiration.

website: www.susanparry.co.uk
facebook/instagram: susanparryauthor
twitter: @susan_parry

PROOF TOXIC

A YORKSHIRE DALES MYSTERY

SUSAN PARRY

Viridian Publishing

First published in the United Kingdom in 2023 by
Viridian Publishing

Viridian Publishing
PO Box 594
Dorking
Surrey
RH4 9HU

www.viridian-publishing.co.uk
e-mail: enquiries@viridian-publishing.co.uk

ISBN 978-0-9567891-9-8

For Ian

Chapter 1

'I'm leaving NOW!'

Mills froze in the doorway. Simon wasn't alone. He was sitting upright with his hands resting on the desk in front of him. The figure seated opposite was twisting a crumpled cotton handkerchief in his hands. Mills couldn't see his face but his straggly white hair and curved shoulders suggested he was elderly.

'Sorry, I didn't realise you were busy,' she muttered, turning to leave.

'Don't go on my account,' the old man called, struggling to get up.

Simon glared at Mills as he helped his visitor to his feet, supporting him as he ushered him towards the door. Now she could see his reddened eyes, unshaven chin, his chapped lips. She stepped back automatically as the bent figure walked past her unsteadily and wandered off down the corridor.

'Let me know how it goes with the police,' Simon called after him.

Mills followed him back into the office. 'Who was that?' she asked, sinking into the chair that the old man had vacated.

Simon ignored her while he fiddled with his computer

then shoved files into a desk drawer noisily.

'A customer – I hope,' she teased, unsure why he was ignoring her.

Finally he sat back with a sigh. 'If you must know he's an old colleague. He's retired but still potters around in the Biology Department from time to time. Professor Robert Benson, or should I say Professor Emeritus Benson? He's upset because his wife has just passed away.'

Assuming he must be a close friend of Simon's, she made sympathetic noises, but that only caused her partner to smile.

'I hardly know him, Mills. When I say he's an old colleague, I mean he's a colleague and he's old. He came to see me in a professional capacity.'

'I see. Have you started a counselling service?'

Simon grimaced. 'It's not funny, Mills. In fact it's quite tragic really. His wife had secondaries following breast cancer from years ago. She was receiving treatment but the prognosis wasn't good. He says she was in a lot of pain most of the time, so it took a while before he realised how rapidly she was deteriorating. By the time she reached hospital she had organ failure and was dead within hours.'

'It was the cancer that killed her?'

'Prof Benson's waiting for the post mortem but meanwhile he has an appointment with the police tomorrow morning.'

'Why?'

'Because they have some questions for him. He's worried they're going to accuse him of assisting with her death.'

'And did he?'

'Definitely not.'

'So why did he come to see you?'

'He knows we run a forensic service so he thought I could tell him about the post mortem.'

Mills laughed, amused by the thought of Simon attending a post mortem. He was quite squeamish when he'd quizzed her about them in the past, and had been impressed that she was able to sit through the procedure.

'No, listen,' he continued. 'He was asking about what tests they would do for any foreign substances, other than her medication.'

'Are you sure he's not worried about getting caught?'

Simon frowned. 'I don't think so. He seemed devastated by her death and was more interested in whether the PM would establish if his wife had taken her own life. It's been a shock for him so he's looking for an explanation.'

Changing the subject, Mills reminded him that it had been snowing in the past hour, suggesting they should get going if they didn't want to spend the night at the university.

There was little sign of snow on the roads for the first part of their drive home but, as they arrived in Swaledale, the scene suddenly changed. A thin layer of white had settled on the fields, broken by the darker lines of the drystone walls. The lights were on in the cottage and Harris was waiting behind the front door to greet them.

'Sorry we're late. Did you have a nice day?' Mills asked the lurcher.

The dog let her tickle him behind the ears before rushing off to the kitchen where Simon was filling his dinner bowl. Mills warned him not to overdo it because, although Muriel was an excellent dog-minder, she was also a good cook and Harris was filling out noticeably since he'd begun spending time with their next-door neighbour.

Mills heated up half a leftover flan and microwaved a tin of beans while Simon lit the fire. They ate at the tiny kitchen table while Simon went over the details of Professor Benson's visit. The old man had been distraught and spent over an hour talking about his wife, who had been twenty years younger, so he hadn't expected her to go first. It was a huge shock because until a year ago she'd been in reasonable health, despite the cancer. They had told her it was incurable but she'd been receiving treatment up to a few months ago. She had become weaker since then, confined to bed, in pain and breathless most of the time. He felt bad that he hadn't noticed how quickly she'd deteriorated.

'So what happened to her?' Mills asked.

'Her breathing became weaker, gradually losing the use of her limbs. He eventually had the sense to call an ambulance and they whisked her straight into intensive care, where she quickly died of heart failure.'

They sat quietly until Mills asked whether he would see the professor again.

Simon wasn't sure. 'When I explained it was impossible for me to attend the post mortem, he suggested getting a blood sample for me to analyse.'

'Poor man. I hope you said no?'

'Of course. I'm sure the post mortem will show up underlying complications of her illness that explain her death, which will be the end of it.'

'Let's hope so, he looked so desperate.'

By the time they'd tidied the dishes away, the tiny sitting room had grown comfortably warm. Harris had already taken up his usual position on the sofa, where Mills settled down next to him, determined to return to the unfinished discussion from yesterday.

'So what do you think we should do, Simon?' she asked.

He was scrolling through his phone. 'About what?'

'You know what.' There was no response. 'I think we need to raise the profile of the company. How do people know we can offer forensic services if we don't tell them?'

When she moved Yardley Forensics to the University of North Yorkshire the plan was to expand the business to include a range of specialities. Simon's toxicology laboratory was already the star attraction, bringing in some valuable work but she needed income to support the chemistry facilities, Donna's salary in particular.

'You mean advertise?' he asked disapprovingly.

Mills sighed. 'No, I mean make contacts, talk to the companies that need our services: lawyers, barristers…'

Finally he looked up. 'Don't you mean forensic service companies.'

'I suppose so.'

He went back to his phone. 'There are plenty if you want to approach them but it would need to be for the techniques that they don't have in-house themselves.'

Mills didn't consider it would be difficult. Simon had an international reputation with the toxicological research he undertook on drugs, and the instrumentation she had at the university was state of the art. She was proud of what they'd set up. Yardley Forensics did cutting-edge work, it was just unfortunate they had so few customers.

She carried her laptop to the kitchen to begin searching for companies advertising forensic services. Some had long lists of tests, including toxicology, but she focussed on those with limited capabilities. Several covered only the basics, such as searches for body fluid and DNA, relying on external consultants for more sophisticated testing. One specialised in digital forensics, something they had no expertise in themselves.

She had found ten target companies by the time Simon came through to see what she was doing. She showed him her list, telling him she planned to send them a copy of their fancy brochure that had cost so much to produce.

'Can't do any harm I suppose,' he conceded when he'd examined the websites.

'I think it's a great idea,' said Mills, getting up to make coffee. 'We can't compete with the large organisations. You've seen how flashy their websites are. I bet they spend thousands on publicity.'

Next morning Mills was up early to walk Harris. More snow had fallen in the night, forming a blank canvas as they wandered up the lane. The lurcher investigated any tiny tracks that crossed their path, stopping to mark the route then bounding forward to find the next interesting spot. Mills pulled her coat tighter and shoved her gloved hands in her pockets. Her wellington boots leaked so inevitably she soon felt the cold seeping into her socks. It wasn't long before she was calling Harris as she turned back towards Mossy Bank. The village looked picturesque with the sun rising above the opposite fells, casting long shadows. Mills decided the snow would be a good excuse to work from home, giving her time to get in touch with the companies she'd identified as potential future associates.

Back indoors, Simon had already finished his porridge and disappeared upstairs. Mills was still eating when he returned dressed in his thick padded jacket.

'I'll warm up the car. It might be slow getting along to Reeth. Will you be long?'

When she explained her plan to stay in the cottage, he said he had lectures so had to dash. The door slammed followed by the sound of the engine running as he scraped the windscreen. Harris was sitting up with his ears alert.

'I'm sorry,' she told him. 'You're staying with me today, so there won't be cake I'm afraid.'

He lay down in his bed with an audible sigh as Mills opened her laptop to begin work. Although it was early, she reasoned that people were often by their phones at the start of their day, so it was a good time to catch them.

Her first call was a disaster. When the phone was answered on the first ring, she assumed she was speaking to the receptionist and asked to be put through to the laboratory manager.

'I *am* the laboratory manager,' the woman replied irritably. 'What do you want?'

Mills, flustered, didn't explain herself well. She was almost relieved when the woman told her she was too busy to chat.

She consumed two mugs of coffee while she worked on her pitch, keeping it brief but highlighting the key points: the fact they had accreditation, they had a dedicated member of staff and modern instrumentation. She would finish by offering a tour of their facilities. After a brief practice she started on the next name on the list.

It wasn't taking long to work through the companies she'd identified. Some hadn't answered her call and she'd not always been put through to the relevant person when she did get through. One unhelpful man said he didn't think they would be interested but would ask around, another said he would get back to her. It was time for another coffee before one last set of calls.

Finally she put a line through the companies that didn't require her services, despite what Mills thought. She also ruled out places where they told her they would be sticking to their own specialisms, although one woman did wish her the best of luck with her venture. That left a short-list of the three possible leads who said they would be in touch.

'Which probably means we won't hear from them again,' she told Harris. 'Come on, let's get some fresh air.'

Simon found a note on his desk when he returned from lecturing the third-year students. The message, in the departmental administrator's handwriting, asked him to ring a mobile number he didn't recognise and wasn't in his contacts. It rang several times before a female voice said hello.

'Simon Pringle from the University of North Yorkshire. You left a message for me to ring you.'

'Oh thanks for calling back. Dad asked me to speak to you. I'm Rachel Clark. My father is Professor Benson.'

'You're Prof Benson's daughter?'

'Yes, I'm at the police station with him now. They're questioning him. He said to let you know.'

Simon was unsure how to respond.

'Dad said you were helping him, is that right?'

'He asked me about the post mortem but it's not my area. I can't really help, I'm afraid.'

'Professor Pringle, I'm really worried about what's happening. They want to talk to *me* next, I've no idea whether I should be getting legal advice. Dad is scared they think he killed my mother. It sounds ridiculous when you say it out loud but that's what he told me.'

Simon reassured her that things weren't as bad as they sounded until she finally calmed down sufficiently to agree.

'I wonder, Professor Pringle, whether I can ask a huge favour. Would you have the time to see my father? I know you must be very busy but he begged me to ask you.'

How was he supposed to respond to such an emotional plea? He suggested they come to his office once they'd finished at the police station. She thanked him several times before ending the call. He was considering how best to deal with the situation when Mills rang to tell him about her busy morning. Eventually she stopped in mid-sentence and asked him what the matter was.

Simon apologised. 'Sorry, it's just this business with Prof Benson.'

He told her that he would be seeing him with his daughter that afternoon, although he had no idea what to say to them. When Mills suggested they'd do better to consult a lawyer not a toxicologist, he thought that was getting everything out of proportion.

He took a solitary lunch in the cafeteria then went back to his office to wait for his visitors. He answered emails, marked a few practical reports and wrote a brief reference for a PhD student. All the while he was checking his watch, his phone, and his emails. It was getting dark and he was wondering whether to ring Rachel Clark when a call came through from the departmental office announcing her arrival.

The woman was younger than Simon had expected. The professor had been retired for years but the woman in front of him couldn't be over thirty. Her suit looked expensive, her blonde hair was smooth and shiny, her nails long, and there was a subtle perfume in the room.

'I'm so sorry. It's been a bit… fraught. Dad's gone to his office to check on things so I thought it might be useful to catch up before you see him.'

The administrator grinned at Simon as she left.

'Professor Pringle,' Benson's daughter continued, seating herself on the other side of Simon's desk, 'my father is being accused of helping my mother commit suicide… which is still illegal in this country, apparently.'

Chapter 2

Simon sensed that Rachel was struggling to control her emotions but eventually she paused to regain her composure. She explained that jet lag, lack of sleep and the loss of her mother was catching up with her. She was trying to answer his questions but he soon realised she understood little of what had occurred.

'I'm sorry but my father has been vague about his interview. He was very upset when he came out but I was asked to go straight in, so I didn't have time to talk except in the car coming over here. He's really overwhelmed. They didn't give me any information, but I can tell you what they asked me.'

She went through her entire ordeal while Simon sat stroking his beard and nodding. She explained how they'd asked about her mother's cancer, how bad it was, how long did she have left?

'I told them she wasn't dying. No-one said she was dying. Ask her doctor. So how was she in herself, they asked, was she depressed, in pain, suicidal? I couldn't tell them because I wasn't there. I've been working in Japan for the last two years, so we only talked over the internet.'

Simon coughed but said nothing, so she continued.

'Their questioning was very intrusive. They asked about my parents' relationship. I told them, it was the same as anyone else's, generally they got on well. Dad is a workaholic, as you well know.'

That was when Simon explained he didn't know her

father well at all. 'I'm sorry, Rachel, but your father only came to see me yesterday for information about your mother's post mortem because of my forensic work. I told him it wasn't my area so I couldn't help him.'

Unsure what to do next, he accompanied her to the Biology Department. Professor Benson's office was untidy, with piles of paperwork on the floor and a strange 3D model on the desk, where he was sitting with his head in his hands. As they entered, he looked up in surprise.

'Hi Dad,' Rachel said, switching on the light. 'I've come to take you home.'

But the professor was keen to give Simon details of the post mortem report. 'I don't have a copy but they gave me the bare bones,' he said. 'They talked about toxic shock, which I'm sure you know all about.'

'Time to go, Dad,' his daughter said but he ignored her.

'Her organs failed, they said. That's why it happened so quickly.'

'Do they know what caused it?' Simon asked.

'Not yet but they are getting further tests done. They want to identify the toxin.'

That was when Rachel realised why the professor might be able to help them after all. She'd looked him up and discovered he was a very clever toxicologist, which presumably meant he knew all about toxins.

'Toxic shock is caused by bacteria getting into the body,' Simon explained for Rachel's benefit. 'Did she have any open wounds?'

'No,' replied her father.

'Had she had any surgery recently?'

He shook his head. 'Not for a couple of years. Why?'

'As you know, toxic shock can be caused by the

Staphylococcus bacteria, and Staphylococcus aureus is usually found in hospitals.'

Rachel gasped. 'You mean she had MRSA?'

'Until we know the nature of the toxin, we won't be able to determine where it came from. The toxicology will establish its origin.'

'You know, Dad, I really think we should be getting back. It's almost dark and Janine is coming this evening. She's my stepsister,' Rachel explained to Simon.

She thanked him and helped the old man into his coat before guiding him back down to the entrance. Simon noticed her eyes were wet with tears as she turned to leave.

Breathing a sigh of relief as he closed the door to his office, Simon picked up the phone to call Mills, closing his eyes as he waited for her to pick up. She listened while he described his meeting with Benson and his daughter.

'It was awful. They're in such pain and all I did was sit there like a dummy then give them a scientific lecture on Staphylococcus aureus. It was horrible.'

'I'm sure you're exaggerating. I suggest you come home before the snow really sets in.'

'Is it bad over there?'

'Not yet but it looks as though it might get worse.'

He went back to the office to clear his desk, shoving his laptop in its case before making for the door. Mills was right, it was already sleeting as he left the campus and when he reached the road over to Swaledale, the fields were turning white. He had only just parked the car when the door to the cottage opened.

'You made it,' Mills called.

'It wasn't that bad.'

'I was worried,' she said, closing the door behind him. 'The forecast isn't good.'

Harris was hurling himself down the hall so it was a few minutes before Simon followed Mills into the kitchen. 'Did you have a good day?' he asked.

She laughed. 'Oh yes, wonderful. I've had one response to my calls so far.'

'A forensic firm?'

'Yes. One single company willing to risk its reputation with us.'

'You mean they want to send us work?'

'Not exactly. They said they'd bear us in mind.'

'It's a good start,' he said, giving her a hug.

'Yeah, right.'

She pulled away and opened the oven door. 'I thought we could celebrate with a shepherd's pie and, before you ask, it *is* lamb.'

Mills had been gradually decreasing the number of meals they cooked with meat but Simon was never going to be persuaded to become totally vegetarian.

'With cabbage, I suppose?'

'I'm afraid so.' She slammed the oven door. 'So tell me about Benson's case. Did he show you the PM report?'

'No, he wasn't given a copy, they're running further tests. I can't comment without knowing the details.'

'He's entitled to demand a copy of the post mortem.'

'Really?'

'Sure. Particularly if they think there's something dodgy. There will be an inquest, I guess.'

'You don't really know, do you?'

'I can ask Nina.'

'Here we go again, consulting your buddy in the police.

No, it's none of our business, Mills. I really don't want to get that involved.'

'But just think, we'll be able to see where they get the analyses done. If he poisoned his wife…'

'Which he didn't.'

'But if he was accused of doing so, you could ask to run a set of confirmatory tests for his defence.'

'I think you're blowing this out of all proportion. I'm going up to change.'

Mills called after him, 'At least you should get a copy of the results to find out who provided them!'

After dinner Mills went over the scribbled notes she'd made during her conversations with the forensic service companies. She would follow up the remaining few that hadn't yet replied but she wasn't optimistic about them responding. She told Simon they needed a big break to bring them to the attention of the world, like a criminal case that turns on the forensic evidence they provide. When she suggested that Benson's wife might be just the thing, Simon ignored her and switched on the television. It was his typical way to avoid an argument, leaving Mills annoyed and irritable. She went off to make coffee but while she was in the kitchen, she checked something on her phone. When she returned, she reported that the penalty for assisted suicide in the UK was as high as fourteen years imprisonment, so Professor Benson might want to look for a lawyer as well as a good toxicologist.

The road out of Swaledale was treacherous next morning with warnings of black ice. Mills was hanging on to the door handle as they sped close to the stone walls that bordered the lane. Simon was still being unreasonable and they'd not spoken since breakfast, when he told her to talk to Benson herself if she wanted to know the results of any further tests on his wife's body. As they approached the university, Mills decided it was probably quite a sensible suggestion, since *she* had more experience of what a post mortem involved and how forensic investigations were carried out than he did. When she told him so, he mumbled that he would let her know if Benson or his daughter got in touch.

Mills found Donna in the lab, helping a student with his research. The agreement to house Yardley Forensics in the Chemistry Department came with a commitment to academic support for a proportion of the time. Currently the university was getting more than its fair share of Donna's time because she had little else to do. Mills left her technician with the student and made her way back to her office in the Archaeology Department. Unlike Donna, she had to spend half her time on academic duties. Today she would attempt to concentrate on marking while she waited for a call from Simon about the Bensons.

When lunchtime arrived, she called Simon but he was "up to his eyes" in work, so she went to the cafeteria alone. The place was packed so she perched on a stool at the window with her sandwich, looking out across the lawn.

'Hi Mills! All alone?'

Nigel Featherstone balanced his tray on the narrow ledge next to her while he struggled out of his jacket, tossing it on the floor beside him. He smoothed his unruly hair before balancing himself on the stool beside her.

'I thought you'd be with the Pringle,' he said, attacking a plate of fish and chips.

Despite sharing an office with Nige, Mills often didn't

see him for several days. He was a senior academic in the department, working hard juggling work with care of his three kids. He continued to ask her about Simon but it was only in fun and because he wanted to hear her news to report back to his wife, Nina. She and Mills were best friends.

'So how's the family?' Mills asked.

'All fine thanks. The kids are already getting excited about Christmas.'

They discussed their plans for the holiday, or rather the lack of plans in her case. Simon's son was not coming over from the States, so it would be their first Christmas together. Mills wasn't keen on taking Simon to visit her family but was equally nervous about meeting *his* parents. When she told Nige about the problem, he sympathised but offered no advice. This year he would be spending Christmas with his in-laws who, despite being born in India, had fully embraced all the Christian festivals. Nina had already described to Mills how the outside of their house was decorated with lights and the tree laden with baubles.

'It sounds wonderful, Nige.'

'I'm off to the boys' school now,' he said, picking up his empty plate. 'It's my turn attend the nativity play this year.'

Mills sat for a while looking out of the window. She had her own happy memories of Christmas from when her mother was alive but since then she wasn't completely comfortable with family celebrations. She left the warmth of the cafeteria to wander down to the lake and sat on a bench beside the water, watching the ducks glide towards her in search of food. Soon, growing cold as well as miserable, she started walking back to the department when she heard a familiar voice.

'Mills, wait!'

She turned to see Simon striding across the grass towards her, accompanied by a blonde woman in an expensive-looking camel coat. He was introducing her as Prof Benson's daughter, when the woman interrupted him.

'Technically I'm his stepdaughter. Mum met him after my biological father died. Anyway, I'm pleased to meet you, Simon says you know all about post mortems so I've managed to get a copy of my Mum's.'

Mills didn't know how to respond. She offered to help if she could, suggesting they went back to her department, leading the way until Simon stopped her.

'Look, I've got a meeting now but I'll be back in my office in about an hour if you need me.'

He said goodbye to his visitor before hurrying away.

Mills apologised. 'I didn't realise he'd be going.'

'Please don't worry. I'm just sorry that you've been left to look after me but he has already given up too much of his time, he must be very busy. I'll try not to keep you too long.'

Mills assured her it was no bother while silently cursing Simon for assuming she wasn't working equally hard.

'So,' she began when they were settled in her office. 'Did Simon say you had a copy of the PM?'

'PM?'

'Sorry, the post mortem report.'

Rachel produced an iPad from her handbag. The report was in a format familiar to Mills so it didn't take long to get the gist of its contents. There were many questions she wanted to ask about Mrs Benson's death but didn't like to. Instead she explained what the report said about the effects of her ongoing cancer and the treatments she had been receiving. The big question left unanswered was why she had deteriorated so suddenly. The signs pointed to a deadly toxin taking over her body so rapidly that she died within hours of reaching hospital. Further tests were being carried out to identify it. Meanwhile, the post mortem simply stated that death was due to septicaemia associated with failure of several organs, including the heart.

'Basically all it says is that your mother died of a blood infection that caused her heart failure,' Mills explained.

'And it was MRSA?'

'They haven't identified the specific bacteria yet.'

'And will that confirm it?'

'I suppose so.'

Rachel put the iPad back in her bag. 'I read the details,' she said at last, 'but I couldn't understand some of the jargon. The wording is so formal, you wouldn't know it was about Mum. I hadn't realised she was so ill or I would have come back sooner.'

She sat with her hand over her mouth.

Mills couldn't imagine what it would have been like to read her own mother's PM report. 'I'm sorry. It must be very hard for you.'

She then learned that Rachel had lost her father when she was nine and somehow Mills found herself talking about her own loss as a teenager, even admitting how hard she'd found it when her father met Fiona and they had eventually married. Rachel understood, but she'd had a different experience because she was very fond of her stepfather, Robert.

'Mum worked here at the university for years as his secretary, so I'd met him a few times before they began to socialise. That was about a year after Dad died and after Robert's divorce. I was thrilled when they eventually got married. I was thirteen and longed to be a bridesmaid. I even thought it was cool to have a stepsister, although she was twenty-one and had left home. Thinking about it, she didn't come to the wedding, so I guess she felt a bit like you did about her father remarrying. And I suppose her mother wouldn't have approved.'

They sat in silence for a short time so, assuming their conversation had reached a natural conclusion, Mills asked, 'Do you know when the results of the toxicology tests will be available?'

Rachel looked surprised. 'Didn't he tell you? They said they would be back this afternoon. That's why I'm here, so I can show them to Professor Pringle as soon as they arrive.'

Chapter 3

Mills had taken Rachel over to the cafeteria, thinking it would provide a more relaxing environment while they waited for the toxicology report. But the woman kept checking her phone, muttering impatiently about bureaucracy. Simon eventually joined them when he'd finished his afternoon practical session.

'Any news?' he asked.

Mills shook her head.

Rachel stood up. 'I'm going to find out what's holding them up,' she declared. 'Excuse me.' She picked up her phone and walked over to the window.

Simon smiled across at Mills. 'Sorry about earlier. How's it going?'

She sighed. 'It's fine but she's very upset by her mother's death and worried for her stepfather. Hopefully the toxicology results will draw a line under it all.'

'Did you get anything from the PM?'

'Nothing we didn't already know. She was suffering from a recurrence of her cancer but her death was the result of organ failure from septicaemia, hence the further tests.'

Rachel was making her way back to their table with a grim face. 'They say they'll send the report right over. I think they forgot about my request to see it, although they wouldn't admit it.'

They sat in silence while Rachel watched her phone. Minutes ticked by while she scrolled back and forth. Finally she let out a small cry. 'It's here. It's downloading now.'

She tapped a few buttons then pushed the phone across the table. 'Will you read it for me?'

Simon looked at Mills before struggling to remove the spectacle case from his jacket pocket. She knew he found reading text from a phone screen quite challenging these days. He sat quietly scrolling down the document before suggesting they decamp to his office. On the way he muttered to Mills that he couldn't read a damn thing on such a tiny screen and, when they arrived, he asked Rachel to email him the document. They sat in silence for several minutes while Simon concentrated on his computer screen. Mills, who was sitting on the other side of his desk so couldn't see what he was reading, was becoming frustrated.

'What does it say, Simon?'

'The laboratory has made several attempts to culture the bacteria but their results are not conclusive.' Simon looked back at the screen before continuing. 'Unfortunately the material they received was in poor condition because of the necrosis.'

He turned the screen towards her, looking at Mills for support.

'What he means to say is that your mother's organs were badly affected by the bacteria so they probably found it difficult to get a good sample for analysis.'

Rachel looked as though she wanted to ask further questions but bit her lip,

Simon turned the screen back to continue reading. 'They seem to be suggesting that in the absence of confirmatory evidence, the cause could also be due to Neutropenic sepsis which is a complication of anticancer treatment which can be fatal.' Then he added, 'They mean your mother's chemotherapy.'

Mills broke the silence by asking Simon to print two copies of the report. She gave Rachel one and put the other on his desk.

'Does that help?' he asked.

Rachel was shaking her head. 'No, but I need to get back to my father. He'll want to know what's going on.' She stood up. 'Can I ask you something?'

'Of course.'

'Do you think it's still possible that my mother contracted MRSA from the hospital, even if they can't find evidence of it?'

He shook his head. 'It's impossible to say without further tests but it is common for someone to be a carrier without any symptoms.'

'But why would it have such a devastating effect on my mother?'

'Perhaps because she was in an immune-suppressed state after having chemotherapy.'

Rachel looked close to tears. Mills was having difficulty maintaining her own composure. To her relief, Rachel slipped her coat back on, and picked up her bag while thanking them both for their help. Simon rushed to open the door, offering to walk her to the entrance hall.

'No, I can find my own way, thank you,' she said.

Once she was gone, Simon sat back at his desk. 'Thank goodness that's over. It was doing my head in.'

Mills picked up her jacket. 'Let's get out of here,' she suggested. 'We've both had enough for one day.'

Mills checked her phone on the way to the car park but there was nothing from any of the forensic service companies she'd contacted. Simon said he wasn't surprised but that she shouldn't worry, something would turn up.

'Anyway,' he asked, 'shouldn't you be concentrating on your research work? When's the deadline?'

He was referring to her research on teeth from the seventeenth century. It was part of a much bigger project where her small contribution was to study the fatty acids found in the dental calculus of inhabitants of the Yorkshire Dales. Simon had agreed to help her with the methodology since it required the use of the equipment in his toxicology lab. Mills thought it would be a great way for him to instruct Donna in how to operate the equipment.

'It must be finished by March. We're ready to start on the old teeth but I've got to source some modern equivalents for comparison.'

'I still don't understand why you want to scrape the plaque off a load of old rotting teeth.'

'I suppose it's fine to mess about, as you call it, with bits of fresh body like you do?'

'Yes, but that's only blood and tissue.'

It was a discussion they'd had many times. Mills knew he was only winding her up but he really didn't get excited by archaeological remains in the way she did. Despite all her modern forensic work, she would always feel a buzz when working on a dig with the students. She was already planning her field trip with the second-years at Easter when they would venture abroad, instead of visiting the university site on the North York Moors yet again.

The snow had partially melted then frozen on the lane up to Mossy Bank. She could hear the rough surface of the ice crunch under the wheels as Simon drove slowly up the hill and felt the wheels slide to a stop at the side of the lane.

There was a welcoming light falling across the path from inside the cottage. Mills could see that the way was clear but stepped gingerly up to the front door.

'I think Muriel must have swept the snow away,' she commented, letting herself in.

Muddy footprints led down the hall into the kitchen, where Harris lay flat out on the floor under the table. A few seconds passed before he woke and leapt up, nearly knocking over a chair in his attempt to stand. Once he'd greeted her and run off to see Simon, Mills read the note propped up on the table. Muriel had given him a long walk so he would probably be very tired this evening. Judging by the pandemonium in the hall, he'd already recovered pretty well.

It was Simon's turn to cook, allowing Mills to spend time online checking on local volunteers who had offered to provide her with modern teeth for comparison in her research. She was about to close her inbox when a new message appeared. The name was unfamiliar but she recognised the forensic service company she had contacted in Newcastle. The subject was 'Your enquiry' so she opened it expecting a polite negative response, but as she read the long message, she called to Simon to come and see.

'They want to meet us,' she told him. 'Shall I invite them to see the labs or should we go there?'

He shrugged. 'I don't know, it's your call. You're the business manager. I've got to watch the rice.'

He returned to the kitchen, leaving Mills frustrated at his obvious pretence of indifference. Exasperated, she replied immediately, saying she would be delighted to visit them at a date and time that suited them.

'I've told them I'll go over to Newcastle to see them,' she reported to Simon.

'When?' he asked, serving out the risotto.

'When it suits them, I suppose.'

'It had better be when I'm free.'

'I thought you weren't interested.'

'Of course I am, it's just…'

'Just what?'

He placed the bowls on the table. 'I suppose it's a big step. We were supposed to be working for ourselves not for someone else.'

'It will be our work, Simon, but someone else will have to find it for us, that's all.'

Mills spent most of the rest of the week in the lab with her technician, showing her how to take samples from the precious seventeenth century teeth. Donna was so excited about the opportunity to learn a new skill, that Mills was convinced she'd made the right decision in taking her on. Even Simon was impressed by how quickly Donna was learning how to use the sophisticated equipment. She was showing Mills the results of her first test run when Simon appeared, looking harassed.

'Have you got a minute?' he asked Mills.

They withdrew to the room that served as both the office and a kitchen. While Mills made them both a coffee, Simon told her that Rachel Clark wanted to see him yet again. She had some information that she wanted to share.

'Couldn't she have told you over the phone?' Mills asked, putting a mug down in front of him.

'Apparently not. She says it's very important and confidential.'

Mills thought the needy woman was seeing Simon as a shoulder to cry on, so when he asked her to please come to give him moral support, she refused.

'I'm busy this afternoon, Simon. Sorry.'

He sat brooding for a while then offered what he obviously thought was an incentive. 'I'll come to the meeting in Newcastle if you help me.'

'It's already booked. I'm going on Monday, in the afternoon, are you free?'

She already knew he wasn't because she'd checked his diary online before offering the date. He shook his head.

'I'll tell her I can't see her,' he said, pushing back his chair.

Mills laughed. 'That's silly. I'll come if you're scared to see her alone. Do you really think you need a chaperone?'

'Don't be daft, I'm just worried that she might be a bit unhinged.'

In truth, Mills was intrigued to find out what further development there could possibly have been in the death of Mrs Benson. So at precisely two o'clock she was waiting in Simon's office while he went to meet Rachel Clark at the entrance to the building. When he reappeared, perfume accompanied their entrance. She was dressed in tan trousers and tweed jacket, looking the real country lady. Her hair was in the sort of neat French plait that Mills knew she could never have achieved.

Simon offered their visitor something to drink. 'Tea, coffee?'

'No thank you. I know you must be busy and I don't want to take up your time, but something has happened. I hoped you might know what to do. I can't tell Dad, not until I'm sure, you see.'

She was fiddling with a fine gold necklace with a tiny letter R hanging from it. Mills waited to hear what she had to say.

'Right, how shall I put this?' She held her hand to her cheek for a couple of seconds before taking a deep breath.

Mills thought she was being rather melodramatic and looked across at Simon, who appeared hypnotised by the woman.

'Here goes then,' she continued, her cheeks reddening. 'Janine, my stepsister, came to see her father last night. It was rather awkward because she never got on with my mother so we didn't have much to do with each other. Apparently, she started visiting the house very regularly when Mum was in treatment. I hadn't realised. She seemed surprised to find me staying with Dad and made little effort to show sympathy for my loss, being much more interested in how *he* was coping. I did my best to be friendly but she almost ignored my presence.'

Get to the point, thought Mills, we know she didn't like you. She looked at Simon but he was still mesmerised.

'It must have been awkward,' said Mills, hoping to jolt her into telling them her news, if there was any.

'Yes. I hadn't seen her since I was in my teens or thought about what she'd been doing all these years. I just knew she was training as a nurse when Mum and Dad married. It turns out she works in a big teaching hospital, specialising in infectious diseases!'

She looked at them in turn, seemingly expecting some reaction. Mills raised her eyebrows at Simon who returned her gaze with a puzzled look.

'So…' His comment hung in the air for a moment.

'Don't you see?' she demanded. 'You know already of

course but I had to look it up to see what it entailed. She would be an expert in that infection Stapho...' she stumbled over the word.

'Staphylococcus aureus,' Simon corrected her.

'Exactly. But when I asked her to explain how Mum could have got infected, she feigned ignorance. Don't you think that's odd?'

Mills waited for Simon to answer her. After a long pause he said, 'Perhaps it just isn't her area of expertise.'

There was an awkward silence.

'Maybe it was difficult to discuss your mother's death with you,' offered Mills.

Rachel was fiddling with her necklace again. 'She had been in and out the house for months before Mum died,' she said at last. 'She could have...' She stopped.

Simon looked anxiously across at Mills so she finally took control of the situation. 'You're not suggesting your sister, sorry, stepsister, had something to do with your mother's death?'

'She bore a grudge ever since Dad left her mother, who incidentally died a few years ago. She hated Mum. She didn't hide it.'

'So what are you suggesting happened?' Mills asked, looking over at Simon, who still hadn't looked up.

Rachel appeared to be gathering her thoughts. 'Well, I suppose she might have brought the infection into the house with her, on her hands or her clothes if she'd been at work. If she knows she was responsible she'd want to keep quiet about that.'

Simon finally looked up. 'So not deliberate then?' He sounded relieved.

'We don't know do we?' Rachel replied with a shrug. 'We

won't ever be able to prove it was MRSA, unless you know a way of testing for it properly?'

So that was why she was here again, thought Mills. Simon seemed to be considering the question, as if he thought there might be a way. Mills tried to attract his attention by shaking her head very slightly.

'I can look into it,' he said slowly. 'There might be a more sophisticated test than the one the lab used.'

Rachel sat up straight, looking excited. 'Would you, Professor Pringle? That is so good of you. Just let me know what you need, I can afford whatever it takes.'

Simon looked embarrassed, as he always did when payment was discussed. As Rachel gathered her things together, Mills warned her that there might not be a positive answer to her question. She said she understood but was wanting to explore all avenues to find out what happened to her mother. As soon as she left, Mills turned on Simon.

'Why on earth did you say you would look into it for her?' she cried. 'The woman is loopy, can't you see. She wants to prove MRSA was a reason for her Mum's death when it was probably that other thing caused by her cancer. If anything she should be looking to sue the hospital for not saving her mother's life or the doctor for not identifying sepsis sooner.'

Simon ignored her outburst. 'I said I would look into it and I will,' he said, pulling on his coat. 'Now I'm going to get my lunch.'

Chapter 4

Nothing was said about Rachel Clark's visit during the weekend because Mills was far too busy preparing for her meeting with Rogerson Forensics to discuss it with Simon. He didn't appear interested in knowing what she was planning to say to the company in Newcastle.

'They might not want a presentation,' he'd remarked, peering over her shoulder at her laptop screen.

She'd slammed the lid down. 'Too bad, they're going to get one.'

Sitting on the train on Monday morning, she rehearsed her speech, checking her notes when she got in a muddle. She wanted her pitch to be perfect, so much was riding on it. The journey was over too quickly, so she still didn't feel adequately prepared to meet the people at Rogerson Forensics as she made her way to their offices. In the impressive old building that might once have been a bank, Mills was told by the receptionist that she should go up to the first floor. She climbed the grand staircase before entering a corridor through heavy glass doors, where she was met by a middle-aged man who introduced himself as Derek MacDonald. He opened the door behind him to usher her into a small office containing a large table with four chairs. The rest of the room was empty.

She took a seat, declining his offer of coffee. While they waited for his colleague to join them, he explained the history of the company. Strangely it had begun as a small business specialising in gathering evidence for divorce cases. Derek assured her they were a very different company now, with a wide portfolio of forensic competences. Mills told him that she had been impressed by the range of activities on their website and hoped to extend their capabilities with her own company's expertise. They were interrupted by a young man opening the door carrying a mug in one hand.

'This is my colleague, Damien. He's our technical guy, here to take notes,' Derek explained.

After the introductions, he spent a long time explaining that their company specialised in criminal defence for solicitors, barristers, and independent investigators. Some areas were familiar to Mills, such as blood patterns, footwear impressions, fibres, fingerprints and drugs, but they also had experts in firearms, arson, and motor accidents.

'But you don't cover toxicological evidence?' she asked, knowing the answer.

'No,' Derek responded, 'which is why we were interested when you contacted us.'

It was her cue to give them the pitch she'd spent most of the weekend polishing. She pulled her laptop out of her bag and powered it up while Damien chatted quietly to Derek about a case they were working on. Her presentation lasted fifteen minutes and when she'd finished, Damien produced a handwritten list of questions, several of which she couldn't answer. That was when she wished she'd asked Simon to accompany her after all.

'Why don't you come down to our laboratory to meet Professor Pringle?' she suggested. 'He's an international expert in toxicology and would love to discuss details with you.'

When Mills asked whether they could show her their laboratories, she discovered they were in places as far afield as Durham, Leeds and Birmingham.

'We subcontract all our laboratory work to external companies like your own,' Damien admitted. 'We rely on expert witnesses from a range of organisations. I assume you are used to giving evidence in court?'

Mills nodded. She had appeared as an expert witness on several occasions but Simon had not. His professorial status would be invaluable for the defence's case but she wondered whether he would be willing to train for the task. It was something they would have to agree on sooner rather than later. Damien was leaning back in his chair, pencil poised above his notebook.

'And now, do you have any questions for us?' he asked.

Mills wanted to find out which laboratories carried out their routine forensics, thinking she might know them. But when she asked about the companies, he seemed cagey, leaving it to Derek to respond.

'I'm afraid our subcontractors are confidential,' he replied with an apologetic smile.

It was time to go but before she left, they arranged to visit the university to meet Simon. Mills suggested the end of the week when she knew all his teaching would be over.

'Let me show you out,' offered Derek.

Mills followed him down the corridor, checking the name plates on the closed doors on either side as she went. The individual offices belonged to a number of different organisations.

'There are quite a few different companies in the building,' she commented casually as they descended the grand staircase.

There was no response. When they reached the entrance, Mills could see a board listing the occupants of the offices, but Derek was already ushering her out. They shook hands, agreeing that they were looking forward to meeting again.

She used the train journey back to check on the occupants of the building she had visited, confirming that it contained dozens of individual companies. There were several meeting rooms that could be booked for the day and presumably Rogerson's office was also somewhere inside. She checked their smart website again, offering a range of services, with contact numbers and a registered office address in London, but no address for where Derek and Damien actually worked. She began to wonder if she'd made a mistake asking them to meet Simon, when she really didn't know who they were.

Fortunately, Simon was too distracted when she got home to ask for details of her visit. He had spent several hours contacting colleagues, trying to answer Rachel's question.

'So have you found a better way to look for the toxin?' she asked.

He scratched his neck. 'I'm not sure yet. It's not really my area so I've been talking to the microbiologists. They tell me that distinct strains of bacteria can be identified using something called PGE, or was it PFE?'

'It's PFGE, short for pulsed-field gel electrophoresis.'

Simon looked surprised. 'Do you know how to do it?'

Mills laughed. 'I know what it stands for but that's about all. It's like a DNA fingerprint for bacteria.'

He seemed impressed. 'So where do we find someone to do that?'

'In the Biology Department, I guess. You'll need an

experienced microbiologist to do the work.'

It was then that she realised what she was saying. 'But what are you planning to tell her, Simon? That you can help her? You know she'll be running off to swab her stepsister's house or something equally outrageous? You must be careful what you say.'

He nodded gravely. 'I assume the infection was picked up in the hospital where her mother was being treated, in which case it could be a strain of MRSA. It would put Rachel's mind at rest to know that's where it came from.'

Mills agreed reluctantly. Anything to get the woman off their backs. They had more important things to focus on, like Rogerson Forensics. She warned Simon about the impending visit, telling him not to worry, explaining that Derek was very friendly and she'd got the impression that Damien didn't know much about toxicology, so it would be a breeze.

But later that evening he was still worrying about how to deal with Rachel Clark so she told him what to do.

'Call her tomorrow and tell her that you don't believe the cause of death was MRSA. But if she insists on seeking confirmation, we can put her in touch with someone in the Microbiology Department.'

Chapter 5

When Mills warned Donna that Rogerson Forensics was visiting the laboratory, she immediately began cleaning the benches. Mills tried to help but it was soon clear that her technician preferred to do it alone, so Mills excused herself and returned to the office she shared with Nige.

'Who was that elegant young woman I saw you talking to yesterday?' he asked before she was hardly through the door.

'Rachel Clark,' she replied, knowing the name would mean nothing to him. 'Robert Benson's daughter,' she explained, assuming he wouldn't know of the emeritus professor either.

'Looks too young to be his,' Nige remarked.

'You know him?'

'Of course, he's notorious, isn't he?'

'Really? How come?'

'He was in the press a while ago... quite a few years ago actually.'

Nige had worked at the university longer than Mills. He was a postgrad in the department over fifteen years ago, when Mills was just a student.

'When exactly?' she asked.

He considered for a moment. 'Must be over ten years because he was still active in the Biology Department. He was very well respected in his field until then.'

'What happened?'

'I don't know. The university tried to bury it at the time.'

'Bury what?' Mills demanded. 'What happened?'

'There were student demonstrations outside the department. Something about his work in the States.'

'Why, was it controversial?'

'I don't know the ins and outs, but it was during the Iraq war when there was all that fuss about the abuse of prisoners in Abu Ghraib prison.'

'So what did the students think he was doing?' asked Mills.

He shrugged. He didn't know. But Mills was intrigued and searched for the professor's page on the university website. Nige was right, the man was eminent, with several prestigious honours and awards for microbiology. It appeared he'd retired four years ago. Further searches brought up papers he'd published with colleagues and students over the years. His doctorate was in drug discovery and he'd worked for a large pharmaceutical company in the States before becoming an academic.

'You didn't say why Benson's daughter was visiting you,' Nige commented much later.

'No I didn't. And it's not really any of your business, is it?' she teased.

She settled down to catch up with her academic work and the office fell silent for the rest of the morning. At twelve o'clock Nige announced he was going to fetch a pie from the cafeteria if she wanted anything. She thanked him but said she was going to see how Donna was getting on.

As expected, the laboratory was spotless with everything in its place. There were new lab coats ready by the door, as well as safety specs and gloves. Donna explained that she had collected more overshoes and caps from the storeroom in readiness for the visit.

'Did you say they were from a firm called Rogerson?' she asked as they stood together surveying the lab.

'Yes. Did you come across them when you were at Wakefield?'

Donna had worked at the police forensic laboratories in West Yorkshire before joining Mills at the university.

'No, I didn't,' she replied. 'In fact I asked around but no-one had heard of them.'

Mills told Donna she would have a chance to quiz them when they visited, urging her to talk to them to find out anything she wanted to know about the company. They were interrupted by Simon, who expressed surprise and gratitude at Donna's hard work before whispering to Mills that they needed to talk.

'I've found a guy in the Microbiology Department who says he can examine a sample for us. He reckons he has some clever ways of growing staphylococcus if it's there.'

Mills sighed. 'You're always telling me not to get involved in other people's business but when the gorgeous Rachel flutters her eyelashes…'

'Seriously?' he asked. 'You think that's why I'm doing this?'

He looked more hurt than angry.

'I don't know,' she replied. 'Why *are* you doing it?'

'I thought that's what we agreed to get her off our backs. If you don't want him to go ahead, you'd better tell him soon because I gave him her number.'

'How will he get material to work on?'

Simon shrugged. 'I don't know. I assumed Rachel will ask for it.'

Mills shook her head in exasperation. 'Who did you talk to in Microbiology? Give me his name. I'll need to speak to him about how to deal properly with forensic material.'

He was grinning as he gave her the details. 'Thanks, I knew you'd want to help.'

'I do *not* want to help, Simon. I want it to go away but if it is going to be done, it had better be done properly. And, by the way,' she added as she made for the door, 'Donna wants a word about the state your lab was left in.'

Dr Martin Butterfield was a newly appointed lecturer in microbiology. Mills thought he looked no older than twenty-five. He listened carefully as Mills explained who she was and why it was important she instructed him in how to process forensic material.

Soon he was interrupting her. 'Hang on a minute. Professor Pringle didn't tell me this was a police investigation.'

'It isn't.'

'But you said it was forensic material, than means…'

'Don't worry, it won't go to court. It's just that the family want to get a conclusive result for the absence of MRSA. It will put their minds at rest.'

He looked uncertain but nodded. She told him to ensure the sample wasn't contaminated or confused with any other specimens. She waited until he'd finished making notes then said she would contact the family herself to arrange for collection of a sample of blood for analysis. He seemed pleased with the arrangement so she asked if he would explain the procedure he would be using. She was soon lost but didn't like to show her ignorance, pretending to follow his description. When she thanked him, he said that he should be thanking her because this was just up his street. It was one of his research topics to look for microbes under difficult circumstances.

'Such as out in the field,' he added with a knowing look.

Mills smiled at him but had no idea what he meant. When she got back to her office, she looked him up on the college system. Martin had only been a lecturer for a year. Previously he'd been working at somewhere with the initials DSTL, which she discovered stood for Defence Science & Technology Laboratory, with headquarters in Salisbury. It didn't take long to make the connection with Porton Down.

She spent most of the day on the phone and sending text messages. First, she alerted Rachel Clark that she was contacting the Microbiology Laboratory Manager at the hospital so she would need confirmation from her, or her father, that they were happy for her to proceed. Rachel replied with her consent an hour later. Next, she prepared a polite request to receive a suitable blood sample from the hospital, promising to disclose any results. She put her message on their official Yardley Forensics headed paper and emailed it as an attachment. Finally she called the hospital Pathology Department to check they'd received her message. The manager was concerned whether the material was still viable but said she would have it ready for collection by the end of week. After she put the phone down, Mills remembered that their visitors from Rogerson's were arriving to see the labs on Friday, so she would have to be back from Newcastle by eleven o'clock to greet them.

Simon arrived as she was shutting down her computer. She explained the arrangement she'd made with the hospital. 'If I get delayed, you'll have to look after the Rogerson people. I'm sure Donna will be ready with the coffee and biscuits.'

Simon wasn't happy to meet them on his own but, as she pointed out, it was his own stupid fault that she was having to race to Newcastle on a wild goose chase anyway.

Chapter 6

It was still dark when Mills arrived at the hospital to make her way down to the Pathology Department. She'd visited the lab once before, when Yardley Forensics was still in Harrogate, and the white-haired lab manager remembered her immediately.

'We've got the sample ready for you, Dr Sanderson,' she said, before disappearing down the corridor.

She returned with a yellow bag. 'It's been kept cool but I can't guarantee it's still viable. You do know that we couldn't culture anything recognisable.'

Mills said she understood and that she wasn't expecting to find anything new. 'It's just that the family requested we try,' she explained.

The manager gave her a sympathetic smile. 'I understand. We can only do our best can't we?'

Mills left quickly. She reached the university with time to drop the sample off and still be back in the lab to meet her visitors. She walked quickly up to Martin's office in the Biology Department. It was empty. She roamed the corridors until she spotted him alone in a teaching lab, hunched over a bench.

'I've brought the sample,' she announced loudly.

He eyed the yellow bag suspiciously as she thrust it towards him.

'You'll keep it cool, won't you?' she demanded, adding, 'Will you be able to start on it today?'

He nodded, taking the bag as if it was a bomb. 'Yes, I

thought I'd make a start this afternoon. I haven't got much on.'

Mills was relieved. The university term was over but Christmas was only a couple of weeks away. They stood in silence for a couple of seconds before Mills told him she had to dash.

'Keep in touch!' she called as the door slammed behind her.

She rushed down the stairs and out into the cold, running across the grass to the Chemistry Building. The door to Yardley Forensics was closed but she could see two figures through the glass. Simon was shaking Derek's hand, waving him through to the kitchen that served as their office. Donna took Damien's coat as he went to join his colleague. Mills knew Simon would be hoping for her to arrive to take control of the meeting, so she flung open the door, entering with a loud greeting as she pulled off her jacket.

'Good morning, Derek… and Damien,' she said as she shook hands with them in turn. 'You found us all right?'

Their journey had been fine, the map on their website was clear, they'd used the sat nav anyway. Formalities over, they took their seats round the table awkwardly, waiting for Donna to make their coffees.

'D'you want to start by giving some background?' Mills asked, looking pointedly across at Simon. 'Your role in the facility and the university more generally?'

He hesitated before launching into a prolonged account of his research activities in the department. Mills was about to stop him when Donna placed a tray of mugs and a plate of biscuits in front of them then slipped away.

'As you can tell,' Mills interrupted, 'Professor Pringle is

a true expert in his field. He is also very familiar with the sort of analyses I assume you will be more interested in, such as class A drugs, poisons, toxins, and other pathogens.' She hoped she sounded as if she knew what she was talking about because she couldn't tell from Simon's expression.

Over coffee, Mills explained how she'd worked at Yardley Forensics when it was based in Harrogate, supervising all kinds of analysis. 'That's where I first met our technician, Donna,' she said. 'She went on to work at the police forensics labs until I managed to entice her back.'

She thought they looked suitably impressed. 'Perhaps you'd like to tell Professor Pringle a little about Rogerson Forensics,' she prompted, leaning back to savour her coffee.

As Simon commented afterwards, they gave little away. Derek simply said that they covered most aspects of forensic work, using laboratories like theirs, as and when required. He didn't offer to say what their areas of expertise were so Mills didn't like to push them. As soon as everyone had finished their drinks, she suggested they take a tour of the labs, leading them down the corridor to where Donna was waiting with white coats, overshoes, gloves, and goggles. She could tell that neither of their visitors was used to wearing such outfits.

Mills found it easier to talk about their work once they were inside her section of the lab. They must have been there for half-an-hour before moving on to Simon's domain. Mills regularly asked if they had any questions but they said no. They seemed interested enough but Mills concluded that much of it was over their heads. Admittedly

Simon did go on a bit, insisting on using acronyms which she then had to ask him to explain. When Derek began to look bored, Mills suggested they return to the office for a sit down and a chat. That was when it got a bit surreal.

'Was that the sort of thing you were expecting?' she asked.

Damien laughed. 'To be honest I thought there would be more people working here. How many staff do you actually have?'

'You've met the permanent staff,' Mills replied, 'but we do have people we can draw on if required. Are you anticipating a larger amount of work than we could handle?'

She was rather pleased with her response as it seemed to shut him up. Derek reassured her it shouldn't a problem, provided it didn't affect turn-round time because when they had items, they would need the results quickly.'

Simon looked puzzled. 'Can I ask what sort of items?'

Damien pulled at the end of his tie. 'Class A drugs mainly,' he replied.

'Oh, right. Is this for the police?'

Mills guessed the answer before Damien replied, 'No, defence work.'

Simon raised his eyebrows. 'Are we talking cocaine, heroin?' he asked.

'Yes.' Damien was fiddling with his tie again.

'And what else?' Mills asked, hoping there would be toxicological tests that would interest Simon.

'That's all,' said Derek. 'Just the drugs.'

They seemed to be in a hurry to leave but Mills had one final question regarding money. She knew Simon wouldn't ask.

'We haven't given you a price list,' she said, which was silly because they didn't have an official one yet anyway.

'The price we pay is related to the quality of the drug,' Derek said sharply as he rose to go.

Mills wanted to ask what he meant but they were already standing to leave. They shook hands with Simon before Mills led them up to the main entrance. As she watched them heading for the car park, Joseph came round from the reception desk to stand beside her.

'Have you seen their car?' he asked. 'Great big Mercedes. They must be worth a bob or two.'

She agreed. 'Someone must be making money in forensics,' she muttered as she went back to the office.

Simon made his feelings clear immediately. He was not impressed with the men from Rogerson's. Mills told him that beggars couldn't be choosers and maybe the toxicology business would develop over time once they'd proved themselves with the drug analysis.

'Did you hear him, the older one with the greasy hair?'

'Derek.'

'He actually said "The price is related to the quality of the drug." He might as well have said the quantity.'

'I don't know what you mean. It's perfectly normal for defence lawyers to ask for a more lenient sentence if they can prove that drugs are less pure than they appear. I've been involved in that sort of work before.'

Simon looked unimpressed. 'Donna says no-one's heard of them.'

'I don't suppose many people have heard of *us* either. If we don't start getting customers soon, Donna will be out of work,' she snapped.

She returned to her office, where Nige was eating lunch

at his desk.

'What's up?' he asked her.

'What d'you mean?'

She didn't understand his reply.

'I beg your pardon?'

'I said that you have a face like a wet week.'

'Is that a special Welsh phrase?'

'My mam used it a lot. Is there something wrong?'

'No, I just need to do some due diligence.'

'Sounds important.'

'It might be.'

Mills began by checking Rogerson's website yet again, then went on to Companies House to find that they were indeed a legitimate business, in fact doing rather well judging by their assets. There were three directors listed, including one with the surname Rogerson. Derek MacDonald and Damien Pawson were also listed. So far so good, Mills thought.

'Nige, is Nina in the office today?'

As a detective sergeant, Nige's wife was often away from her desk. Mills needed a favour but she didn't want to interrupt her if she was out on a job. Nige, who was about to take a bite from a pork pie, asked why she wanted to know.

'I just had a quick question, that's all.'

Not wanting Nige listening to her conversation, she decided to send a message instead. She compiled a few lines asking about the children and their plans for Christmas, then mentioned casually that they were working with Rogerson Forensics, perhaps she'd heard of them? That was all. She pressed "send" then closed her computer.

'Good, I think it's time for something to eat,' she said.

Donna was washing glassware when Mills returned from lunch. To her relief there was no sign of Simon because she wanted to hear what her technician had made of their visitors.

'They don't know much about forensic analysis,' Donna remarked.

Mills defended them by pointing out they managed the company so probably had expertise in other areas.

'Such as?' Donna asked.

'I don't know, probably digital forensics or financial fraud,' she replied irritably.

She went into the office to sign off a report but once she'd filed it away, she could only stare at the empty in-tray and sigh. So much depended on getting work from Rogerson's that she couldn't be discouraged by her colleagues' lack of enthusiasm. She checked her phone but there was no response from Nina, so she tried calling her.

'Mills!' Her friend sounded cheerful.

'Are you busy?'

'No, I'm in the office getting my paperwork up to date.'

'Same here.'

She asked her friend about the kids, what they were doing for Christmas and they arranged to meet up in the new year. Just as Nina said she should be getting on with the pile of paper on her desk, Mills asked the question.

'Did you see my message?' Nina hadn't. 'I wondered if you'd come across a company in Newcastle called Rogerson Forensics. We're doing some work for them, at least I hope we will be soon. I'm just checking, for due diligence.'

Nina hadn't come across them and Mills knew it was a cheek but she asked if Nina did hear anything, could she let her know. Her friend, understanding exactly what Mills meant, said she would ask around but couldn't promise anything. Mills had just finished the call when Simon came in looking pleased with himself.

'I saw Martin in the corridor. He thinks he might have something.'

'What?'

'He's been incubating the bacteria in the sample you gave him already. He thinks he may have something to work with.'

Chapter 7

Mills agreed with Simon that they really had to finalise their plans for the Christmas break. It had become routine on a Friday to have fish and chips from the van but he suggested they book "The Punchbowl Inn" to discuss arrangements. She understood it was a diplomatic way of ensuring she didn't fly off the handle like last time, when he'd tried to persuade her that they spend the entire holiday in Canary Wharf with her father, his wife and daughter.

The busy bar had a festive feel, reminding Mills that they'd done nothing to decorate the cottage for Christmas.

'Is there still time to get a tree?' she asked as they stood waiting to order drinks.

'Do you have anything to put on it in the way of decorations?' he asked.

She admitted they hadn't and there certainly wasn't time to shop for baubles when they had last minute presents to buy.

'Maybe next year,' suggested Simon. 'We could invite your family up here and really go for it.'

She knew he was joking but even so, it set the tone for the evening. He wanted to spend Christmas in London. She didn't, not all of it anyway. The alternative was to visit Simon's parents, something she'd been avoiding so far, convinced they would compare her unfavourably with his ex-wife. Somehow both families had gained the impression they were staying with them over Christmas. She went off to find their table.

Simon brought the drinks over, sat down and looked across at her. 'I've made a decision,' he began. 'I think it will work. How about we drive down to be with your father and Fiona for Christmas Eve and Christmas Day? That way we can enjoy watching Flora opening her presents.' Mills began to interrupt but he held up his hand. 'We drive to my folks on Boxing Day, staying for as long or as little as you want. Mum and Dad are usually pretty relaxed after the big day so there's no pressure. We can say our plans are a bit fluid if you like. That way it's just two days in London plus one or two in Derbyshire. We'll take our walking boots to get some fresh air after the excitement of Canary Wharf.'

Mills disliked the fact that he had it all planned but could see how it would keep everyone happy. She sighed, picking up her glass to take a sip of wine before responding.

'OK, it sounds like a plan but you've forgotten Harris.'

'You said Muriel offered to have him.'

'He'll be spoiled rotten.'

Simon looked as though a weight had been taken off his shoulders. He picked up his beer glass, draining the contents. 'This calls for a celebration,' he said, 'I'll get you another.'

The bad feeling that had developed over the lack of holiday arrangements and Simon's suspicion about Rogerson's had dissolved as they planned a shopping trip to Leeds the following day.

The weekend was a great success. Simon had more experience of buying presents for children than Mills so she accepted his advice when it came to choosing a gift for

Flora. Knowing Fiona would have strong views about what was a suitable plaything for her daughter, they took great delight in purchasing a karaoke set with flashing lights and loud music.

'She'll be horrified,' exclaimed Mills with a laugh.

Simon wanted them to have a nice lunch out but everywhere was packed so they went to the Christmas market instead. They queued for a bratwurst which they ate as they wandered round the stalls. Mills didn't mind, it was more fun, she told him. Christmas shopping in the past had been a chore, one to be put off until the last minute. The festive season generally depressed her. She'd always anticipated spending time in the company of her father's wife with dread. Granted it had improved after Flora's arrival but she was still irritated by the way Fiona fussed over the child and ordered her father about.

'Well this year it will be different,' Simon reassured her.

She smiled, thinking it wasn't her family that now worried her but how his parents would receive her.

'I don't have anything decent to wear,' she declared. 'I'll need time to find something this afternoon.'

He grinned. 'That's fine, I've one more present to get. The most important one.'

Knowing that his son's gift had been posted to the States weeks ago, she blushed because she'd not looked for Simon's present yet. Consequently she spent most of her allotted time in John Lewis frantically searching for a suitable gift. With only twenty minutes left, she rushed to the fashion floor grabbing three dresses in her size. The best one was too tight so she found the next size up without trying it on and joined the queue to pay. As she left the department with her purchase, there was a message on her phone asking if she was ready. She replied that she needed another thirty minutes and rushed back to the "gifts for men". As she passed through the toy department, she had a brainwave. When Simon bought Lego for his son, he'd raved about the various cars that were available in the range. The stocks were limited but she found a Porsche that she was sure he'd be delighted with. Relieved that shopping was finally over, she quickly bought a supply of wrapping paper and found her way out.

She spotted Simon waiting by the entrance, his back towards her. He was loaded down with all their purchases, which meant she could see no clues to what he'd bought her. When she tapped him on the shoulder he turned, looking smug.

'All done?' he asked. 'Got everything you wanted?'

'Yes, I found a dress. I think it will be all right.'

He assured her she would look lovely in anything, before offering to take her bags.

'No it's fine, I'll carry these,' she insisted to his amusement. 'Let's get home, I'm exhausted.'

Despite enjoying the outing, Mills was relieved to leave the crowds behind, falling in and out of sleep on the drive back to Swaledale. As they drew up in Mossy Bank, she offered to make dinner if Simon went next door to pick up Harris and give him a quick walk up the lane in the dark. She instructed him to check that Muriel was still happy to look after the dog if they went away for a few days over Christmas. While she peeled the potatoes, she decided they should spend Sunday wrapping presents and calling their respective families to finalise arrangements. That would leave the week free to sort out any last-minute issues in the lab before they travelled to London on Christmas Eve. At last she felt comfortable with their plans for the following week.

Monday changed everything. Mills was in her office marking the last few end-of-term assignments before the break when there was gentle knock and Donna poked her head round the door. She looked over at Mills then spotted Nige.

'Oh sorry, I'll come back later,' she said, turning to leave.

'Don't go on my account,' called Nige as he picked up a pile of papers. 'I'm taking these back to the departmental office.'

'Can you spare a minute?' Donna asked once they were alone.

Mills told her to come in and shut the door. She was keen to hear why her technician, who was supposed to be on leave, looked so apprehensive.

'Sit down. I wasn't expecting to see you today.'

'It's probably nothing but I thought I should come and tell you anyway. I don't want to worry you.'

Various scenarios flashed into her head: unwanted attention from students or staff, a serious illness, another job offer, pregnancy? Mills urged her to tell her what was wrong.

'I went to Wakefield on Friday night,' she began. 'It was my old lab's Christmas party. When they asked if I wanted to go, I thought it might be fun.'

'And was it?' Mills asked anxiously.

Donna smiled. 'Yes, it was nice to see everyone again, you know, catch up.'

There was a pause in the conversation until Mills gave her an encouraging smile. 'So?'

'They were asking what I was doing now so I told them about the lab and everything. I said we were going to do work for Rogerson Forensics and...' She paused as if searching for the right words.

'...and they had heard of them?' asked Mills.

Donna frowned. 'Yes. At least this one guy had. I don't know him; I think he was new.'

Now Mills was getting anxious. 'And what did he say?'

Donna was tugging at the sleeve of her cardigan. 'He said he was a witness in a case where Rogerson's was acting for the defence. He reckoned they were what he called economical with the truth.'

'How?'

'He didn't say and I didn't have the chance to ask him.'

'Do you think you could find out any more details from him for me?'

She shrugged. 'I'm not sure. I don't even know his name.' She paused. 'I suppose I could call my friend; she might know.'

'Please do, Donna, and thanks for coming to tell me. Perhaps best not to mention it to anyone else until we get more information,' Mills added as her technician was leaving.

She was still staring into space when Nige returned to the office.

'All clear?' he asked.

'Yes.'

'Everything OK? She didn't look very happy.'

'No, she just came to say she's off home.'

'Well I'm going to do the same. I'm going to start my Christmas shopping.'

'Bit late.'

'Better late than never. I only need to get Nina's present. She does all the rest.'

'What are you buying her?'

He shrugged. 'What would you suggest?'

'No idea.'

'Perhaps you could get some hints? She won't give me any suggestions but I know her parents will want to see what I've given her.'

Mills laughed. It wasn't the first time he'd asked her for help. She promised to text him if she came up with any suggestions but as soon as he left for Darlington, she picked up the phone. She now had the perfect excuse to contact Nina again, she was calling to ask for ideas to pass on to her husband.

'Nige said he might go shopping this afternoon but I didn't know he was getting me anything this year,' her friend commented.

'I can tell him anything, Nina. Just say whatever you fancy, money no object!' Mills joked.

'Now I know he didn't say that, but I really don't mind what it is.'

'Nina, I think he's more worried about what your parents will think.'

She laughed. 'Seriously? That's so silly. In that case he'd better get me something eye-catching.'

'Jewellery?'

'Probably, but I'd have to choose it. Thanks, Mills, I'll look on line and send him a text. Where's he going?'

'Darlington.'

'Good, there's a little place where I got some earrings last year, I'm sure I can suggest something if I look at their website.'

Mills played for time by describing her plans over the break before broaching the topic of Rogerson's. 'Nina, about that forensic company I mentioned, Donna told me she'd heard they'd been "economical with the truth" in a case.'

'Sounds dodgy. Are you really doing work for them?'

'Not yet but they've been to see the lab.'

'If you have any more details of the case, I can see what I can find out.'

'Thanks, I'll ask Donna if I can speak to her friend.'

Mills rushed over to the Chemistry Department, where Donna was stuffing white coats into a laundry bag. 'I thought I'd get these sent off before I left,' she said, looking up.

'Great, yes, good.' Mills was composing what to say. She used an upbeat tone. 'It was interesting what you told me, you know, about Rogerson's. I'd like to talk to the guy you spoke to, if you can locate him.'

Donna reddened. 'I sent a text to my friend, she's given me his name, it's Piers. I was going to ring …'

'No need,' Mills said brightly. 'I can do it. What's the number?'

Chapter 8

Martin Butterfield was in the Microbiology Department's research lab hunched over a microscope when Mills found him. He jumped up when she called his name then hunted for his glasses, which were on his head. He blushed as he quickly positioned them back on his nose.

'Sorry for disturbing you but Simon said you'd made some progress.'

He nodded. 'Yes, it was a long shot but I tried using the...' He proceeded to describe in detail how he had selected the appropriate nutrient, quoting a reference in the scientific literature.

'I'm sure Simon will be fascinated,' she said, since he was offering to collect a copy of the paper from his office.

As he struggled out of his lab coat, she asked what would happen now. He looked surprised that she hadn't already guessed.

'This is where the tricky bit starts,' he said as she followed him along the corridor, his long curly hair bobbing up and down in time with his steps. 'I'm working through the common bacteria but not had any luck so far. If I draw a blank, I'll have to use more subtle techniques.' He mumbled about phenotypes and DNA. 'I may have to do genetic sequencing to identify the species.'

'But hadn't we decided it was either Streptococcus or Staphylococcus?' asked Mills.

As he shook his head, his hair waved round his face. 'No, definitely not, that's why I have to grow a better sample. It could take a week or several weeks. You can't hurry these things.'

'I guess with the holidays…'

'Oh I'll be here over the holidays. It's quieter with everyone off.'

Mills took the paper from him. 'Well, good luck then. I'll give this to Simon.'

She went straight to Simon's office, placing the paper on his desk where he would see it. There was no sign of him so she guessed he was probably in the lab. Now was an excellent opportunity to call the young man in Wakefield again. They'd said he was busy when she'd rung, so she'd left a message, but he hadn't responded yet.

'Piers? My name is Dr Sanderson. My technician gave me your number. She said you knew of a company that I'm interested in.' The poor lad sounded mystified so she backtracked. 'You spoke to Donna at the party last Friday. She used to be at Wakefield but now she works for me at the University of North Yorkshire.'

His response was a cautious, 'Yes?'

'She said you knew about Rogerson Forensics.'

'I've heard of them, yes.'

'You were involved in a prosecution case where they worked for the defence?'

'Yes.' He still sounded wary.

'Look, Piers, this is totally off the record. You told Donna that there was something dodgy about them.'

There was silence at the other end.

'Can you give me any information about the case? The defendant's name, for example.'

He answered hesitantly. 'I could find out, I suppose. Is it important?'

Mills considered her answer, hoping it sounded sufficiently casual. 'Not really, I was just interested, as we might consider working with them. Due diligence and all that.'

It seemed to do the trick. He said he would look up the file and send her a text with a contact name or number. She expressed her thanks, reassuring him that it was a purely informal enquiry, that she wouldn't be using the information in any official capacity. There were footsteps in the corridor so she terminated the call quickly and was stuffing her phone in her pocket just as Simon appeared.

'Hi,' she said. 'I dropped this paper in. Martin thought you'd be interested in how he's processing the Benson sample.'

He smiled. 'I'll have a look, although I can't guarantee I'll be able to make much more of it than you will.'

'I think he said he was going to use DNA to identify the bacteria.'

'Well that's definitely more in your department.'

'I only know about the DNA of people, not microbes.'

'Then it's our chance to learn.'

'I'd rather leave that to Martin, thank you.' Which gave her an idea. She was about to tell Simon when he stopped her.

'I know what you're going to say, Mills. You've just added another consultant to our list of experts, haven't you? Remember, he'll have to be trained up as an expert witness if he does any court work.'

Mills raised her eyebrows. It was a bone of contention that Simon still hadn't done his own training, claiming he was far too busy. Before she left, Simon asked if Martin had indicated how long it would take to identify the microbe. Mills warned him that it wasn't a sure thing yet and, even if he was successful, it could take weeks.

'Shame,' he said, 'Rachel was asking.'

'She called?'

'Actually she was here. I was just seeing her off.'

'You didn't say.'

He looked uncomfortable. 'She just turned up.'

'What did she want?'

'To get an update on progress. I told her there wouldn't be anything until after Christmas.'

'Well you can tell her it isn't Streptococcus or Staphylococcus, so her sister is off the hook.'

'Is that what Martin said?'

'He confirmed it's nothing so ordinary, that's why he's doing this other test to identify the microbe. It's in the paper I gave you.'

Mills didn't know why she was so irritated by Rachel Clark's visit. She certainly didn't want to have to speak to her again but was annoyed that Simon hadn't said she was coming. As she made her way back to her office, she wondered if Rachel realised the lengths Martin was going to with her mother's sample.

She ate a sandwich at her desk while she finished the last bit of marking, constantly checking her phone for a message from Piers. It finally came through just as she was packing up to go home. The defendant's surname was Headley, that was all he knew but he'd included the date of his own appearance as an expert witness in the Leeds Crown Court. The dealer was arrested with ten kilos of high purity cocaine in his possession. Piers hadn't provided any further information, so she was going to have to rely on what Nina could find out for her.

When she joined Simon in the car park, he asked if she'd finished her marking.

'Yes, all done.'

'So this could be the start of our holiday?' he said, turning to her with a smile.

Mills hesitated before answering. 'I thought we'd be at work tomorrow. I was going to drop the presents into Nina and Nige.'

She'd hoped to find out more about Mr Headley, the drug dealer. She planned to contact Nina with what information she had in advance, so they could discuss the case further. When Simon insisted there was no way he would be going back to the office again before Christmas, Mills said she would go alone to see her friends the following day. The rest of the journey was spent in silence, with the frosty atmosphere continuing during the evening.

Muriel popped round just as they'd finished eating to finalise when she would be looking after Harris. Mills chatted only briefly to her neighbour then felt guilty after she'd left, knowing she relied far too heavily on Muriel's goodwill. She wondered if she should have bought her a nicer present for allowing the lurcher to stay over Christmas, although the woollen throw was expensive and she knew Muriel would love it.

While Simon was busy on the phone to his parents, finalising arrangements for their visit, Mills sent a message to Nina, asking if she could find anything on the Headley drug case. She was busy wrapping toys for the children when Simon finally joined her.

'I hope Nina and Nige approve of our choices,' he remarked.

'We know Owen and Tomo like computer games,' she

replied. 'And it was Nina who told me Rosie is into knitting.'

'My Mum says hello, by the way.'

'That's nice.' Mills was concentrating on wrapping the parcel.

'She's really looking forward to meeting you, you know. She's panicking about food but I told her you'll eat anything.'

'Did you?'

'She asked if there was anything you particularly liked so I said chocolate. She makes a brilliant chocolate cake.'

'She shouldn't go to any trouble on my account.'

He stood watching her. 'You should ring your dad,' he said eventually before wandering away.

Next morning Mills left Simon with a list of instructions before saying goodbye to Harris, as it turned out there were loads of things to sort out. They'd run out of wrapping paper, Harris didn't have enough food to see him through the holiday season, and Simon announced he needed more socks. She instructed him to go shopping until he had everything on the list. She put the children's presents in the car then had to go back for the hamper they'd bought Donna.

Simon stopped her in the hall. 'We are going to have a really good Christmas, Mills, I promise,' he said, giving her a hug.

'I know, there's just so much to think about.' She didn't mention that she still dreaded meeting his family and was equally nervous of him meeting hers.

'I'm sorry to miss Nina and Nige but tell them I'm sorting out everything you've forgotten,' he said with a laugh.

'That is totally untrue and you know it, Simon Pringle!' she replied, kissing him on the cheek before dashing to the car.

The schools were off, the roads far emptier than usual, the Archaeology Department unusually quiet. The student term had finished the previous week so, although today was officially the last working day before the Christmas break, most of the staff had already gone. Mills went down to the lab to find Donna in the kitchen making coffee.

'Good timing,' she said, reaching into the cupboard for a second mug.

They chatted for a while, sorting out the last bits of work. They discussed their plans for the holiday, until finally, Mills thanked Donna for putting her in touch with Piers.

'Was he any help?' she asked.

Mills knew her technician hadn't warmed to their visitors from Rogerson's, so she shrugged, quickly changing the subject by producing Donna's Christmas present.

'Here's something to say thank you for all your hard work this year,' she said awkwardly, adding, 'It's from both of us.'

Her technician was suitably grateful, saying she would open it on Christmas Day. She expressed embarrassment that she'd not got anything for Mills or Simon. However, she did produce chocolate biscuits to have with their coffee while they chatted about work, or rather the lack of it. Mills tried to sound positive but knew that if things didn't improve, she would be having a very difficult conversation with Donna, who had left a secure job in Wakefield to join her. It was mid-morning by the time Mills left, suggesting Donna take the rest of the day off if she'd finished her work.

Back in the department Mills found herself with nothing important to do but scroll through her messages, hoping for a reply from Nina. The words Rogerson Forensics caught her eye but it wasn't a message from her friend. Her heart beat faster as she read the two short sentences from Damien Pawson. He had a sample of cocaine for her to analyse. It would be delivered by hand at the end of next week if she confirmed acceptance of the job. She sat for several minutes before replying. Despite her reservations, she said that Yardley Forensics would be delighted to do the work.

Chapter 9

The Featherstone home was filled with brightly coloured decorations. Mills had to dodge paper chains and bells hanging from the ceiling before squeezing past an oversized Christmas tree covered in sparkling baubles.

'The kids went overboard this year,' explained Nige as he cleared a space on the sofa by throwing toys onto the floor. 'Nina will be back soon. She's just fetching the boys from their friend's house.'

'In that case, I'll give these to you now.' Mills handed him a carrier bag of presents.

Nige took them upstairs then came back down with Rosie, who was carrying the sketch book Mills had given her for her birthday. She sat down beside her, turning the pages slowly to reveal beautiful pencil drawings of animals. They were still discussing her pictures of horses, when Tomos and Owen burst in, closely followed by their mother. The room was suddenly noisy and chaotic.

'Mills, come into the kitchen,' ordered Nina. 'We won't be able to hear ourselves speak in here.'

Rosie took her sketch book back upstairs, declaring she would come back later when her brothers had calmed down. Mills followed Nina out of the room and closed the door, leaving Nige in charge.

'The boys are totally manic at the moment,' Nina said. 'I think they've been on the fizzy drinks. Talking of which, would you like something?'

While Nina made a pot of tea, Mills answered her

questions about her plans for Christmas. Then they discussed the children's presents. Finally, as they sipped their tea, Mills asked Nina if she had any information on the Headley case.

'Hold on, I've got some notes in my bag,' she replied, disappearing back into the sitting room.

There was a pause while Nina could be heard reprimanding Nige for letting his sons jump on the furniture. When she returned, she was leafing through a notebook.

'OK. Headley was accused of handling large amounts of high-quality cocaine, carrying the heaviest sentence. His defence claimed the analysis carried out by the police forensic analyst was flawed.'

'Would that be the Wakefield lab?'

'Presumably.'

'They were saying that Wakefield made an error. How could they argue that?'

'With their own analysis, carried out by an independent laboratory, according to court records. However, their claim was rejected in the end. I assume the independent lab had made a mistake.'

'Hmm. Were there any repercussions, do you know?'

Nina shrugged. 'There's no mention of it.'

Mills made a note of the independent laboratory's name and location, not wanting to admit to her friend that she suspected the lab might have deliberately falsified the result to suit Rogerson's. She changed the subject to the other case that had been occupying Yardley Forensics: Mrs Benson's sudden death.

'Rachel Clark accused her stepsister of infecting her mother deliberately so Simon stupidly agreed to test a blood sample. Anyway, we've got a microbiologist working on it now who is sure it's not Staphylococcus so that should satisfy her.'

'Sounds like you're being kept busy then.'

'Not really. To be honest, I think we may have to let Donna go after Christmas.'

Her friend was about to respond when Nige announced that the boys were having a bath before their tea. Nina looked at the clock and Mills realised it was time to go. She went upstairs to say goodbye to Rosie, who gave her a hug and wished her a happy Christmas. The boys waved from their bedroom, where they were taking it in turns to leap from one bed to the other while Nige watched helplessly. Promising to get together before the New Year, Mills went back down to take leave of her friend.

'Have a good Christmas,' said Nina. She gave Mills a hug and thrust a bag at her, explaining it was just a little gift for them both. 'And about that forensic company – they may have influenced their lab to get the answer they wanted. It can happen, so you may want to think twice about working for them.'

'Yes, of course. Thanks.'

Mills left, wondering whether she had made a huge mistake in accepting Rogerson's work. She knew Simon would say she should have discussed it with him first. She couldn't tell him yet, wouldn't tell him until later, maybe after Christmas.

He'd promised to have a meal ready when she got back to the cottage and the smell of the curry hit her as soon as she opened the front door. Harris ran to greet her as she removed her coat, following her into the sitting room, where Simon was standing beside the Christmas tree with his hands on his hips.

'There!' he exclaimed as bright white lights flashed wildly. He fiddled with something at the back of the tree which slowed the flashing to a stop for a few seconds before starting again.

He stepped back, nodding approvingly. 'That's better.'

'I can see you've been busy,' Mills remarked.

He agreed. He'd bought the lights, the dog food, more wrapping paper and popped cards in to the neighbours. He had gone next door to give Muriel a bag of dogfood, as well as to mention that the lurcher was putting on a bit of weight. Their neighbour had promised she wouldn't overfeed him, but they both knew she would.

'Strict diet in the new year, Harris,' Mills told him.

The dog looked up then rolled onto his side with a soft moan. Simon disappeared into the kitchen, returning with a bottle of red wine.

'Here's to the holidays,' he said, handing her a glass. 'Now we can forget work for a few days.'

Mills clinked glasses with him before taking a large mouthful. It was easy for him to say. He hadn't agreed to work for a dodgy forensics company, at least he wasn't aware that he had yet.

'Tonight I need to get the washing on, unless you've done that as well?' Mills asked. 'Tomorrow we'll have to wrap Flora's present and pack, but I want to take Harris for a nice long walk as we won't be around for a while.'

'It's due to be below zero tomorrow,' Simon warned.

'Then we'll have to wrap ourselves up well, won't we?'

Simon's forecast had been partially correct. It had been cold but it was also raining; they returned to the cottage soaked to the skin. Mills tried to forget about Rogerson's as she busied herself ironing and packing, but her mood didn't improve. Eventually Simon demanded to know what he'd done to upset her.

'It's not you,' she explained. 'It's our last evening in the cottage and I'm going to miss Harris, that's all.'

To her relief, he accepted her explanation. He continued gathering the dog's toys into a bag while she went off to prepare their meal, reminding him to pack Harris's Christmas present too. It was a new ball with a loud squeak but she was certain that the dog would have silenced it by Boxing Day. Everything was packed, ready to go by the time they settled down eat. Neither of them spoke for a while.

'You know it's going to be fine,' Simon said finally. 'It'll be fun at your dad's and we can escape my parents by going for a walk if it gets too much.'

Mills smiled in agreement and carried on eating. She was thinking that perhaps she should admit now that she'd agreed to accept the cocaine sample from Rogerson's without consulting him first. That would get it over with before they left for London, but she knew a very heated discussion would follow her announcement, spoiling their Christmas break. She spent the evening watching television with Harris stretched across her lap, while Simon called his son in America. He returned looking depressed but Mills said nothing; knowing he would miss Arnie over the holiday, particularly as he usually spent Christmas with his son.

Next morning was dull and wet when they packed the car. Muriel came out as they were putting the last few things in the boot of the Mini. She followed them back into the cottage, where the dog was waiting to greet her.

'Simon has given you the low-calorie treats, hasn't he?' Mills asked pointedly. 'He should only have a few each day.'

'Don't you worry, pet.' She bent down to talk to the dog. 'We'll keep an eye on you, won't we, sweetheart?'

Mills looked across at Simon, who shrugged. They said their goodbyes on the step, watching Muriel being dragged out of the gate by Harris and into the cottage next door.

'He doesn't seem too upset,' Simon remarked.

'He thinks it's just for today, though.'

'He's perfectly happy with Muriel and it's only for a few days,' he answered sharply before disappearing upstairs, muttering something about Harris being only a dog.

Mills was poised to reply but kept quiet when she realised that this was about his son staying with his mother for the holiday. She'd offered to drive the first half of the journey so went outside to warm up the car. She sat waiting for a full ten minutes before Simon finally emerged, locking the front door after him, and shutting the gate firmly.

'I've turned everything off, and locked the windows and doors,' he announced, settling in the passenger seat.

It was time to leave. They passed the first hour listening to Simon's playlist until Mills, tired of his choice of music, turned it off, asking him to tell her about his parents. She knew they'd been married for nearly fifty years and had lived in the same place all that time, but she really wanted to know what they would think of her.

'You mustn't worry about them,' he said. 'They don't bite; in fact you'll probably get on well with Mum. She's into the local community, organising the lunch club and whist drives.'

'Would you call her quite mumsy then?'

Simon considered for a moment. 'No not at all. She can be very bossy with her church ladies when she's running the jumble sales.'

'So does she boss your father about?' asked Mills, thinking of Fiona.

'If she does, he disappears off for a round of golf with his cronies.'

He had painted a picture of a couple living an idyllic retirement in their Derbyshire village, surrounded by friends from the church, the golf club and WI. Mills felt she was going to be out of her comfort zone.

'What about Hugh?' Simon asked. 'Does he play golf?'

'Not that I know of unless Fiona has decided he should.'

'She's the boss?'

'Definitely. She's got Dad wound round her manicured finger. You'll see. He spends more time looking after Flora than she does, even though he's still working.'

'Does *she* have a job?'

'She's far too busy to work. She goes to the gym then meets up with the ladies that lunch. Then she has her hair and nails done, as well as fitting in some shopping time. Then she's so exhausted she must have a spa day. Do I sound bitchy?'

Simon laughed. 'You do. I don't suppose it's half as bad as you make out.'

'You'll be able to judge for yourself in a few more hours.'

The journey took far longer than they'd anticipated. It was Christmas Eve and everyone seemed to be heading for London. They crawled along the last leg of their journey through heavy traffic, failing at first to find the hidden entrance to the underground visitor parking bay that belonged to the apartment. Mills rang her father, who gave them directions, instructing them to come straight up when they arrived; he would help Simon with the bags later. So eventually they were taking the glass lift that rose from the basement into a spectacular view over London.

'Wow,' said Simon. 'This is the life!'

Chapter 10

A hubbub of voices greeted them as Mills pushed the apartment door open. She turned to look at Simon, who indicated for her to go in. Women in party clothes stood in groups clutching thin-stemmed glasses. Music was playing in the background as a girl dressed in black edged past them with a tray of some tiny, breaded nibbles. Mills was wondering how easily they could retreat so she could change out of her jeans, when her father appeared next to them.

'Did you have a good journey?' he asked, giving her a hug.

'What's going on?' she demanded.

Hugh looked over her shoulder. 'Hello Simon, how nice to finally meet you.' He offered him a hand.

Mills stood her ground. 'You didn't say you were having a party.'

Her father smiled sheepishly. 'It wasn't my idea. Fiona wanted to invite some friends from the book club… and the mum's group… and from her yoga class. Don't worry, they won't be here long. It was a bit spur of the moment. She didn't think many would turn up.'

There must have been around thirty people, mainly women, in the spacious lounge. Mills caught sight of Fiona in a silver sheath dress, deep in conversation on the other side of the room. Flora was seated on a sofa with two little girls, watching something on a tablet.

Mills felt scruffy and grubby. 'I've got to get changed,

Dad.'

He told her the spare room was ready, offering to go down with Simon to collect their luggage from the car. She retreated gratefully, shutting the bedroom door firmly before closing the curtains over the floor length window that covered the entire wall. She went into the bathroom, stripped off, standing under the hot shower for several minutes before using the expensive gels and moisturisers that Fiona had provided. When Simon arrived, she came out wrapped in a brand-new fluffy towel and sat on the edge of the bed.

'You'd better get changed quickly,' she told him.

'Your father says there's something to eat in the kitchen. Just needs a few minutes in the microwave.'

Mills pulled her best jeans and a clean shirt from the suitcase they shared and quickly applied her makeup. After running a comb through her hair, she ventured down to the kitchen, where two women were replenishing trays of food. They looked up when she entered.

'My father said there was some food for us?'

The older woman nodded, went to the refrigerator and filled two large bowls. Mills watched as she placed one in a built-in microwave before setting the timer. When she began heating the second bowl, Mills popped back to fetch Simon, who was now dressed in a clean shirt and chinos. When they sat down side by side at the central island to eat, the younger woman offered them the choice of red or white wine. Simon smiled at Mills, saying how nice it was that Fiona had thought to feed them. Mills asked him if he was being sarcastic.

'No, I'm serious. It's great. The apartment is amazing, and this food is wonderful,' he added.

'This chicken tagine?' she asked. 'It's a ready meal from that expensive organic farm shop, I saw the packets. She just heated them in the microwave.'

'Well, it's delicious.'

They had almost finished eating when Hugh arrived, looking flustered. Fiona was insisting they join her other guests.

'I did say you might want to rest after your long journey but she wouldn't take no for an answer.' He frowned. 'Everyone seems to have settled in for the evening. I wanted to get Flora into bed early tonight, she's so excited about Santa Claus coming, but she won't budge until her schoolfriends have gone home.'

'Right,' said Mills jumping up. 'Come on Simon, you're good with children. Let's go and entertain the youngsters.'

She took a deep breath before entering the room, which was hot and humid. She led Simon through the crowd, apologising as she squeezed between groups raising their voices to be heard above the din. The sofa was now occupied by two women, deep in conversation and there was no sign of Flora. Fiona was on her way over but was waylaid by a man in a flowery shirt.

'Has Flora gone to bed?' Mills called over to her.

'I said she could play in her room, now that her friends have gone home.'

They fought their way back out into the corridor. Mills found the bedroom with a large rabbit on the door, knocking gently before going in.

'Remember me?' she asked as Flora looked up anxiously.

She was rewarded with a hug before she was able to introduce Simon. The girl became shy until he asked her what she was watching on the television. She was soon telling him all about her favourite video.

'Have you come to put me to bed?' she asked. 'Only I can manage all by myself you know.'

'Do you want to go to bed now?' asked Mills.

'Yes, it's been a very tiring day and I'm supposed to be asleep when Father Christmas comes but I don't think he'll be here until after all the adults go home,' she said with a grin then yawned theatrically.

Mills concealed a smile, thinking how like her mother Flora was becoming, with her posh voice and her mannerisms.

'Can we stay here while you get yourself ready for bed, Flora?' she asked, hoping to avoid returning to the party.

'You can watch my video if you like.'

Mills didn't dare look at Simon, who thanked her and turned the TV back on.

When Hugh came in, he reported that one or two more people had left the party but there were still many remaining. Mills assured him they were happy to stay with his daughter, who was cleaning her teeth.

'I thought they were coming for a quick drink but Fi is arranging for a takeaway delivery. I'm afraid it might be a late night.'

'Will it seem rude if we keep out of the way, Dad? It's been a really tiring day and we don't know anyone.'

Flora came rushing out of the bathroom to give her father a hug. 'Mills and Simon are watching my video with me, aren't you?' she said, turning to them.

'Of course we are,' replied Mills. 'Shall we stay in here and watch Frozen?'

Hugh pulled a face as he left them to join the party again. 'Lucky you,' he called.

Flora climbed into bed while Mills and Simon sank onto the sofa. The child was soon fast asleep so they were able to change over to watch a comedy they'd missed. Mills woke up when Hugh came tiptoeing in with a large, decorated sack, putting his finger to his lips.

'Is she asleep?'

Mills looked over and nodded. She woke Simon, showing him the time on her watch. It was midnight, the apartment had fallen quiet. At last they could drag themselves off to bed.

Mills was woken by someone stroking her arm. As she surfaced, she could hear a soft voice calling her name. Flora wanted to show her what Father Christmas had brought her in the night. Simon was already awake.

'What time is it?' she asked.

'Six-thirty.'

'Seriously?'

'Yes,' Simon murmured. 'Apparently Daddy said it was too early to disturb Mummy because she has a tiny headache.'

'I'm not surprised. The way she was weaving about last night, Dad nearly had to carry her to bed.'

Mills left Simon playing a card game with Flora to go in search of coffee. She expected to find the debris of the party in the kitchen but there wasn't a glass or canape to be seen. Clearly the hired staff had tidied up before leaving. She searched the cupboards for a jar of coffee but found only beans so was examining the coffee machine when her father arrived.

'How's Fiona?' she asked.

He looked embarrassed. 'She's having a lie in.'

'What about lunch? I presume we're having lunch. Won't the turkey need to go in soon?'

He laughed. 'Don't be silly. It won't take more than an hour or so and we won't be eating until later.'

'So what are we having?'

He shook his head. 'I don't know, I didn't see it when it was delivered. Most of it came from Fortnum and Mason, although I think she had a Waitrose delivery as well.'

Hugh carried the coffees through to the lounge where Simon was sitting on the floor with Flora as she unwrapped more presents. The only decoration in the room was the Christmas tree. It brushed the ceiling and was covered in an elegant display of white and silver decorations that sparkled in the tiny white lights. Mills wondered what had happened to the gaudy baubles and trinkets that had dangled from the tree when she was a child.

In Fiona's absence they had a leisurely morning, eating bacon sandwiches while Flora opened even more presents. Hugh persuaded Mills not to give his daughter the karaoke set until Fiona had recovered from her hangover. When she finally appeared at midday, she announced briskly that they wouldn't be eating until at least three o'clock, so they should all go for a walk while she got on with the cooking.

It was a clear day but they were met with a sharp breeze as they emerged from the glass lift into Canary Wharf and Mills smiled down at Flora as the girl took her hand. Hugh led them to Cabot Square to see the art installations, where Flora ran ahead from one sculpture to the next, calling to them to keep up. But Simon stopped at each in turn, taking photographs and commenting on the artist.

'I can't believe you've got a Henry Moore just round the

corner!' he exclaimed.

He continued to rave excitedly about Canary Wharf as they were physically dragged from installation to installation by the little girl. Hugh wanted to show them more pieces further away but Mills pointed out it was time they went back because she was getting cold and Flora needed the loo.

Fiona was still busy in the kitchen when they arrived, insisting that everything was under control despite the beads of sweat on her brow and the hair flopping into her eyes. She shooed them away, telling Hugh to sort out some drinks, although Mills noticed that Fiona already had a glass of wine beside her on the work surface. Flora demanded a game of "Happy Families" and they sprawled on the floor because the table was already laid for lunch. Simon played one game before checking his watch then announcing that he was going online to see Arnie open his presents. Several glasses of wine later, Mills was feeling hungry and light-headed. The card game became increasingly boisterous with Hugh accusing her of cheating. Finally, at four-thirty, Fiona announced that dinner was served.

Chapter 11

To her surprise, Mills found herself wishing they didn't have to leave next morning. Flora had gone to bed exhausted at ten o'clock, falling asleep immediately. Her karaoke machine had been a great hit, despite Fiona's grimaces at being forced to join in. Mills was half-listening to Fiona quiz Simon about his work, while Hugh dozed. The topic had progressed to their joint venture in forensics and now he was explaining that work was thin on the ground although they had been approached by one company, adding that they probably wouldn't want to work for them. Mills kept her eyes closed until the subject changed to his time in the US, and his son. Mills decided to rescue him by changing the subject.

'You were saying how you really love Canary Wharf, weren't you Simon?'

'In that case you must visit us more often,' said Fiona. 'We've loved having you. Flora told me she wants you both to stay forever.'

Their laughter woke Hugh, who automatically asked if anyone wanted another drink. That was when Mills decided their visit had been too short, because she realised that she hadn't had a proper chat with her father, plus she would like to spend more time with Flora.

'I don't know why we didn't arrange to stay longer,' she commented as they left the city next morning.

'Because you didn't want to spend more than a day with "that domineering woman". At least I think that's what you called her. Of course Fiona is perfectly pleasant when she calms down, but I think she's stressed by your presence.'

'What d'you mean, *my presence?*'

'She probably feels a little uncomfortable with you because you're Hugh's daughter.'

'Did she say that to you?'

'Not in so many words, but you could tell she was trying to make it all perfect for you.'

'Not until she finally emerged from her hangover. And she still bosses Dad around, while spoiling Flora rotten.'

'I didn't see that, Mills. I think you're exaggerating and you can't be jealous of an eight-year-old.'

They were going to be in the car for three hours so Mills decided to ignore his criticism, remarking instead on how quiet the motorway was. She turned on her choice of music and dozed throughout the journey.

'So, this is where I grew up.'

Simon had stopped the car in the middle of a perfect Derbyshire village. It was the antithesis of Canary Wharf, resembling the Yorkshire Dales, complete with drystone walls and smoke drifting from the row of stone cottages beside the road. He turned the car down a narrow lane past more cottages interspersed between fields and woodland. Mills felt nervous as he finally slowed to manoeuvre through a wide entrance between stone walls. The house, which was bigger than the others, looked relatively modern even though it was built of stone. The front door opened as Simon parked in front of the big double garage, and a small women emerged, followed by a large golden retriever.

'She's called Bessie, the dog that is,' Simon said, as he climbed out to greet his mother.

He gave her a hug then bent to make a fuss of the dog while Mills stood quietly, waiting to be introduced.

'Hello.' Connie spoke quietly in a soft accent. She smiled but didn't attempt to kiss or hug Mills, much to her relief. 'You must be tired. Come in and have a cup of tea.'

She led the way, calling the dog to heel. When Simon grinned sheepishly at Mills, she understood that he was feeling exactly how she had when they first arrived in London. His mother led them into a spacious kitchen dominated by a large wooden table. Seated at one end was a white-haired man in an oversized knitted jumper. Simon introduced Mills to Ralph, who waved a hand then continued to peer at his phone.

'Who are they playing?' asked Simon.

'Man United.'

'Oh dear. Dad's a Newcastle supporter,' he explained.

Their bedroom was at the top of the stairs, spacious and comfortable with views across fields to hills in the distance. Mills noticed piles of old record albums and books in the corner, suggesting it was still viewed as Simon's room. She picked up a copy of "Private Eye" from 1999 to leaf through it.

'Are these yours?' she asked.

'Of course. Mum keeps threatening to throw them out but think what interesting reading they'll make. Perhaps we'll take them back with us.'

'No way,' objected Mills. 'You're not cluttering the cottage with your memorabilia.'

Connie called them down, saying tea was ready. They

were offered plates of scones with jam and cream, as well as chocolate cake. Simon looked meaningfully at Mills; his mother had remembered that she liked chocolate.

'Now it's stopped raining, Si, would you help your father mend the fence at the end of the garden?' Connie asked. 'Bessie keeps trying to get in to see the sheep. I know she won't hurt them but if they run away, she'll think they're playing and…'

'The farmer won't shoot her. It's nearly pitch dark out there,' interrupted her husband.

'Well I don't want to risk it. It won't take two minutes if Si gives you a hand. The security light will be on.'

Simon looked questioningly at Mills who nodded, indicating she was perfectly comfortable to be left alone with his mother. The men went off together, leaving her seated at the table while Connie cleared away the plates.

'I thought you might help me prepare the evening meal,' she called as she loaded the dishwasher. 'Just the veg and bits, that's if you don't mind?'

During the next hour, Mills peeled vegetables while she learnt about the couple's life in the village. It sounded idyllic to Mills. Connie was obviously an energetic member of the community, busy organising events, and entertaining friends. Ralph, on the other hand, was content to meet his pals in the pub or at the golf club, nodding off in front of the television in the evenings while his wife typed up minutes, made phone calls or disappeared off to WI meetings.

'So what about you?' Connie asked eventually. 'Your work must keep you both very busy.'

Mills explained the relationship between her research and the forensic business she ran jointly with Simon.

Connie said she couldn't imagine her son running a business of any sort. He apparently never had a head for finance.

'I look after that side,' explained Mills. 'In fact sometimes I have to make difficult decisions about who we work for.'

She might have even confided to Connie her concerns about Rogerson's if they hadn't been interrupted by the menfolk returning.

'It's freezing out there!' Simon called, pulling his jacket off.

Ralph appeared, asking, 'Is the pot still warm?'

'Don't be so silly,' his wife muttered. 'I'll put the kettle on again.'

They sat round the table chatting until Connie shooed her husband away to light the fire in the sitting room. Simon went to have a quick chat with his son online, leaving Mills in the kitchen. She found herself telling Connie all about her father having a young daughter, thinking she'd succeeded in sounding pleased with his decision to marry again. To her surprise, the woman expressed sympathy, saying that she must find her relationship with Fiona quite difficult. Then she asked Mills if she'd met Arnie yet?

'No, I haven't.'

'Not even on line?'

'No. It's not that Simon doesn't want me to, it's just that I'm not sure Arnie would want to meet *me*.'

'He's a nice boy.' Connie turned to her, wiping her hands on her apron. 'Very sensible for his age I always think.'

She was telling Mills how much Arnie had enjoyed the countryside when he last visited them, when her husband came in to fetch two bottles of beer.

'You'll want glasses for those, Ralph!' she called.

Later, after dinner, Simon said he'd like to show Mills the area, so if the weather was fine next day, they'd plan a walk before having a pub lunch. They pored over the local map, argued about which was the best pub in the area and finally settled on a four-mile walk along a disused railway line that would bring them out on the road, where Ralph and Connie could meet them to transport them to their favourite pub for lunch.

'I've had an email from Martin,' Simon announced suddenly.

He and Mills had been walking along the old railway line for about an hour, commenting on the scenery and chatting about their respective relatives. For a moment Mills couldn't place who he was talking about.

'You mean Martin the microbiologist?'

'Yes. I saw the message last night when I spoke to Arnie but I thought it could wait.'

Mills thought so too but Simon was keen to give her the news.

'He says he's isolated something unusual.'

'What is it?'

'I don't know, he doesn't know yet but he's doing more procedures to understand the structure. He sounded quite excited in the message; I'll show it to you when we get back.'

Mills had already expressed her views on wasting time just to satisfy Rachel Clark. She stopped, waiting for two cyclists to go past before asking, 'So would it be a bacterium or something else?'

'He says it's really interesting, like the sort of work he

was doing at Porton Down.'

They reached the road five minutes earlier than planned but the car was already waiting so soon they were seated in a cosy pub by a log fire enjoying remarkably good food. Ralph sat quietly while Connie orchestrated the conversation, it was the only way Mills could describe the way she manoeuvred talk round to Arnie, saying how she was sure he'd love to meet Mills. She was describing her own visits to the Yorkshire Dales as a child and how much she loved the area, when Mills found herself inviting the couple to visit them, while Simon bore a bemused expression.

It was getting dark when they finally left the pub. A light flurry of snow was blowing across the car park, covering the car in a fine layer of white.

'I hope it's not going to last,' declared Simon, 'or we'll be stuck.'

It occurred to Mills that she wouldn't have minded if they did have to stay but unfortunately there was no more snow overnight, so after breakfast they began packing the car to leave. The goodbyes took a long time because Connie kept pressing packages on them. There was a chocolate cake for Mills, and she'd made sausage rolls for Simon because they were his favourite. She ordered Ralph to hand over a half a dozen bottles of beer and while Simon took them to the car, Mills made a fuss of Bessie. When she stood up again, Connie surprised her by giving her a strong hug.

'It's been wonderful to finally meet you,' she said. Then she lowered her voice. 'To be honest I wasn't looking forward to your visit in case we didn't get on but you've been a delight.'

Mills felt herself going bright red. 'It's been so nice,' she mumbled.

She didn't add that it was because she hadn't been compared to Simon's ex, who hadn't been mentioned once during their visit. She wondered if, perhaps, Connie hadn't got on well with Dianne. In the car, she asked Simon casually if his mother had always been so welcoming to his girlfriends. He looked at her quizzically, asking if his mother had spoken to her about Arnie's mum.

Mills protested that she'd said nothing. 'Does that mean they didn't get on?' she asked.

His grip on the steering wheel tightened. 'Let's just say they weren't likeminded. Dianne would have got on much better with Fiona.'

Chapter 12

Harris had returned home a few pounds heavier. The Christmas tree was beginning to shed its needles and the holiday was definitely over. Mills wanted to spend a few days relaxing, maybe going for a good long hike, but Simon was keen to talk to Martin about what he'd discovered in Mrs Benson's blood sample, even though the university was technically closed until after New Year. Mills, not wanting him to come across a parcel from Rogerson's in Donna's absence, offered to keep him company.

The car park was empty, the campus deserted. Simon went off to find Martin, arranging to meet Mills later. Her footsteps echoed in the chilly corridor as she made her way through the Chemistry Department, turning on lights as she went. When she unlocked the door to the laboratory, she was struck by how quiet it was. Without the usual hum of the instrumentation and air conditioning, there was an eerie silence. She took the bag containing milk and biscuits through to the kitchen to make herself a coffee then stopped. There was a package on the table with a note to say that the receptionist had brought the parcel down for safe keeping, since the department wasn't manned over the holiday and it had been delivered by hand, "signed for". The large brown padded envelope was addressed to her in thick black pen so she guessed immediately that it was the sample from Rogerson Forensics. She hid it away in the desk drawer until she'd had the chance to explain it's presence to Simon.

Martin was in his office, hunched over his desk. Simon knocked on the open door, gently at first but then harder until finally the microbiologist looked up, removing his headphones. He apologised, offering Simon a seat while he searched his computer for something.

'Here,' he said. 'I've got some data I thought you'd be interested in.'

Simon tried to follow his description of the processes he'd been using but eventually admitted defeat. Martin frowned as if irritated by his lack of understanding.

He sighed. 'In simplistic terms I've been looking at the DNA of the species, which, under normal circumstances would tell me which group it belongs to.'

'So you've identified it?'

'No. As I said, normally I could unless it's a new type of bacterium.' He rubbed his chin.

'Are you saying it's impossible to identify?'

'Not exactly. I know that it's a form of botulinum toxin but I can't find a match for the DNA sequence in the database.'

Now Simon *was* confused. 'So she had food poisoning?'

Martin shook his head impatiently. 'It's not as simple as that. It's an unusual variant. Normally people can be treated for botulism with antibiotics.'

Simon stood up. 'Shame they didn't work in her case.' He was about to thank Martin for solving the mystery when he sat down again, realising that he wasn't finished.

'When I said it isn't in the database, I mean it hasn't been registered yet.'

'So what are you saying, Martin?'

He rubbed his chin again before answering. 'There are examples where a toxin was left out of the database because there was no known antidote for it, so therefore it was considered too dangerous to include, in case the information was used to make a biological weapon.'

Simon knew that Martin had worked at Porton Down, where presumably he had gained knowledge of such warfare.

'I'd like to spend more time looking at the possibilities,' he continued. 'If it's a new variant we need to know about it. It's quite exciting, isn't it?'

Simon thanked him and wandered back to the lab, trying to make sense of what he'd been told, pondering how best to express the outcome of the morning to Rachel Clark.

Mills had gone over to her office but when he called, she joined him in the lab, wanting to hear exactly what Martin had told him about Mrs Benson's sample.

'…so whatever it is, it's very rare,' he concluded.

Mills sounded horrified. 'But we know it's a form of botulism and he thinks it could be a biological weapon?'

'He didn't say that exactly,' argued Simon.

Mills typed on her phone while Simon finished eating his cake. 'There, it says here botulinum is used as a biological weapon.'

'It's also used for cosmetic and medical purposes,' he countered. 'Botox is short for botulinum toxin.'

Mills said she knew that, but she hadn't made the connection between Botox and food poisoning before. She was looking at the effects of the toxin on her phone. 'Her symptoms wouldn't have suggested botulism, would they? I mean she had organ failure not paralysis.'

'Maybe that's because it's a rare variant. So that's what I'm going to put on the report. By the way Mills, there's a parcel in the bottom desk drawer.'

Her heart was beating fast. 'Is there?' she asked casually.

'Donna must have shoved it away. It's addressed to you,' he continued. 'Are you going to open it?'

'It can wait until we're back at work properly. We're supposed to be on our holidays.'

'It might be a Christmas present. The address is handwritten.'

She ignored him and he knew better than to insist. They spent the next hour devising a suitably professional response to Rachel Clark's request for analysis of her mother's blood sample. She'd offered to pay the proper fee, so they discussed what to charge for their consultant microbiologist to do the work.

'He's not exactly given us a positive answer for her, has he?' Mills commented as she typed the letter.

'But he's done much more than the pathologist. Martin did DNA sequencing on the bacteria which is impressive, isn't it?'

'I guess so.'

'He wants to carry on investigating the variant, he seems pretty excited by it.'

'Hoping to get a paper out of it I expect.'

On the way home they discussed how Rachel might receive their report. Simon expected her to be delighted that they'd managed to identify the toxin as botulinum when the pathologist hadn't been able to isolate the toxin, but Mills feared they hadn't seen the last of Miss Clark. However, now all she could think of was the parcel in the desk drawer. Somehow, she was going to have to broach the subject with Simon.

*

Nina rang on Thursday to invite them to a New Year's Eve Party.

'Don't expect it to be exciting,' Nina confided. 'It's Nige's idea, so it's very last minute. There will be very few guests at this rate but, to be honest, that's fine by me. He says the kids can stay up so I'm expecting tantrums and tears as they get overtired. I've sent him out to buy snacks and nibbles, which means that we'll only be eating cheese and onion crisps, if he's got anything to do with it.'

Mills knew she was exaggerating, having attended one of Nina's last-minute parties before. 'I can bring something,' she offered.

'No, don't worry I'll do some of my mother's specials.' She recited a list of Indian dishes that went on until Mills stopped her.

'I thought you said there were only a few people coming.'

'Nige has invited around fifty…'

Mills envisaged their tiny sitting room, wondering how everyone would fit in.

'…but they won't all accept,' she concluded.

Mills confirmed they would love to come then lowered her voice. 'Nina, Rogerson Forensics have sent me a sample to analyse.'

'So you and Simon decided to work for them after all?'

'Not exactly. I agreed, Simon doesn't know yet.'

There was silence at the other end.

'Nina, are you still there?'

'Yes.'

'I'm going to tell him.'

'Of course.'

'Because he will have to do the analysis.'

'Exactly. Is that a problem?'

'You tell me.'

'Well, I was going to mention that I've done a bit more digging; to be honest I wouldn't rush to get involved if you don't have to.'

'What d'you mean?' Mills was about to ask Nina exactly what she'd heard about Rogerson's when Simon came back down from his chat with Arnie. 'So, thanks for the invitation, we'll look forward to seeing you on Friday,' she said as she put the phone down. 'That was Nina. They're having a party on New Year's Eve.'

Simon had received two missed calls from Rachel Clark when they returned from taking Harris for a long walk on New Year's Eve. It had been a crisp winter's day with a clear blue sky and a chilly wind. The lurcher had bounded across the open moorland above Gunnerside and they'd enjoyed a pub lunch before returning home to get ready for the party. Simon was unsure whether to call Rachel but Mills insisted. She somehow felt that the more moral high ground she could gain before telling him about the drug sample, the better.

She listened to his end of the conversation then demanded to know exactly what had been said.

'You heard me tell her that the exact toxin can't be identified but she'd read about the connection with botulinum in the report. She's looked it up on the internet to discover that it's associated with Botox. I told her it wasn't that strain but she latched on to it.'

'What's the relevance?'

'Her stepsister is a nurse.'

'I know. That's why she banged on about the MRSA.'

'She says that hospitals use Botox to treat patients for a

94

range of problems so assumes she has access to it. She's still thinking that her stepsister caused her mother's death.'

Mills told him to ignore her calls in future because the woman was obviously unhinged. She went up to change, although she wasn't going to dress up. Nina and Nige's parties were ones where you dressed casually to relax. Everyone there would be friendly and interesting, they always were. Someone would be playing guitar before too long and Nige would undoubtedly have the barbecue going outside, despite sub-zero temperatures. By the time she'd fed Harris, Simon was ready to leave. He was in such a hurry that he nearly forgot the box of ales for Nige.

They weren't quite the first to arrive, but Mills only saw one other couple in the sitting room as she made for the kitchen to seek out Nina, while Simon was handing over the beer to Nige.

'Quick, before you're too busy with your guests,' she began. 'You didn't finish telling me about Rogerson's. What is it you know?'

Nina gave her that look, the one which meant she shouldn't be asking her to divulge police information.

'Is it serious?' Mills asked.

'I'd be wary of them. They have history with the police. Nothing proven but they do keep some questionable company.'

'I suppose they *would* have criminal clients if they're working for defence lawyers.'

Nina grimaced. 'It's not that simple.' She turned to open the oven door, pulling out a tray of sausage rolls. 'As I said before, best to avoid that particular company.'

Mills bit her lip. 'But I've already agreed to help them.'

Nina sighed. She closed the oven door. 'OK, here's my

advice: keep records, email them with any queries and make sure they email you back with responses. Maintain everything in writing and when it's done, say you can't do any more.'

'Really?'

'Really. Have you told Simon yet?'

'No, he's not going to be happy when I do.'

Mills turned to leave, almost knocking a glass out of Simon's hand as she went through the door.

Simon caught her arm. 'I came to find you earlier but you and Nina were deep in conversation. Is everything all right?'

'Fine. Just catching up.'

He had such a quizzical expression, she suspected he'd overheard what they were talking about.

Chapter 13

'How are you feeling?'

While Simon was pulling back the curtains, Mills consulted the clock on her bedside table. It was nearly eleven o'clock.

'OK,' she replied, lifting her head then falling back on the pillow. Slowly she struggled to a sitting position.

She was far from OK. First there was the throbbing pain on one side of her forehead. Secondly, she had only vague recollections of the journey home after the party.

'You were totally out of it when we got back,' Simon informed her. 'Here, drink this.' He gave her a mug before handing her two paracetamols. 'Hopefully these will help.'

He left her to drink her tea while she recalled the previous evening. She'd convinced herself that Simon had overheard her conversation with Nina although he hadn't said anything. She'd spent the evening in a state of panic, drinking to calm herself, avoiding any serious discussion with him. To her shame, she remembered she'd stopped the car twice on the journey home because she felt so sick. She took the tablets before rolling over and going back to sleep.

Eventually, hours later, she knew she had to get up to face Simon. She lingered over her shower, washing and drying her hair, until finally she couldn't put it off any longer. She went downstairs quietly to be welcomed by Harris. Simon was in the kitchen, warming soup.

'I thought you wouldn't be able to face anything heavier,'

he told her.

They ate in silence until Simon said, 'So what was the problem last night?'

'What d'you mean?'

He laughed. 'It's just that I didn't have you down as a binge drinker.'

Mills sighed. She was sure he knew so she just wanted to get it over with. 'You heard me talking to Nina?'

He nodded. 'Is there something wrong? They seem such a perfect family.'

'No,' Mills replied, thinking quickly, realising that he may not have heard exactly what they were discussing. 'No, they're fine.'

'So what was it?'

She closed her eyes.

'Mills, tell me what's wrong.'

So she did. She told him about Rogerson asking her to do the analysis. How she'd agreed to the work without consulting him because she thought he might not agree. He listened without interrupting. Mills expected him to be angry but he just looked disappointed.

'I see,' he said.

He finished his soup without looking up then informed her he was taking Harris for a walk. It was obvious he wasn't inviting her to accompany them. She watched him leave, heading up the lane towards the open moors then sat on the sofa, wrapped in a woollen throw. There was a lump in her throat as she swore quietly to herself. She tried to pass the time by reading but her mind kept drifting until she found herself wandering back to the window. Simon still hadn't returned when it had begun to get dark so she switched on the outside light and lit the fire, wondering whether to begin preparing their meal. Without enthusiasm, she went into the kitchen to peel potatoes. They had begun to boil when she heard the front door open and Harris ran in, looking for his food bowl.

Simon came in to fetch a bottle of beer then disappeared into the sitting room without a word. Mills busied herself in the kitchen until dinner was ready but as soon as they were seated together at the kitchen table, she attempted to apologise. She began to explain why she felt it was important to have the income, when Simon stopped her.

'I understand that, I get it. I know you want your venture to succeed, but that's the point, isn't it? It is your venture, not ours. It's understandable; you were involved when it was Yardley Forensics, you brought it to the university so perhaps it should remain *your* business not ours.'

'Is that what you want?'

'Of course not.'

'Nor do I.'

'In that case, I think we need to change the way the business operates, so decisions are made by all relevant parties.'

Mills was puzzled. 'You mean me and you?'

'Well, I was thinking that it might help if there was a third party. It could keep us on an even keel.'

'What d'you mean?'

'I haven't got anyone specific in mind but it would be helpful if we could find someone with business experience.'

'But we can't afford to take anyone on.'

'No. We need someone who will invest in the business.'

'Like "Dragon's Den" you mean?'

They were both laughing now.

'But, Simon, we already have our own dragon: Brenda Yardley. She gave us all the equipment when she passed the business over to us. She's our investor, isn't she?'

'You're right. Maybe we should have asked her to join us.'

'We did, remember. She said she didn't want anything more to do with the lab.'

'But that was immediately after the fire. I wonder if she still feels the same. Perhaps we should ask her.'

Mills agreed to contact her to discuss it. She couldn't see how Brenda would fit into their decision-making process but she was just pleased that Simon was no longer upset with her. He now wanted to hear about the work he was expected to do for Rogerson's.

'That's what I was speaking to Nina about,' she confessed. 'She reminded me it was important to document everything in case there were any queries.'

'What sort of queries?' Simon asked anxiously.

'Just good practice,' she replied airily.

Brenda Yardley's Christmas card had included a change of address: she was now renting a flat in Whitby but her mobile number remained the same. Mills tried calling twice before leaving a message and when there was no response, she sent a text wishing her a happy new year, asking her if she was around for a chat. Brenda had always been rather disorganised, which was why she'd depended heavily on Mills to manage her lab in the past. But Brenda had a needle-sharp brain when needed so Simon was right to think of her as their sounding board.

Next morning Mills waited for Donna before opening the package from Rogerson's. There was no letter inside, just a compliments slip, asking for a purity analysis on the sample of cocaine, contained within.

'I suppose this is the sample but where's the chain of custody document?' Donna asked, peering inside the padded envelope, adding, 'There isn't one.'

Mills examined the plastic bag of white powder. There was no code number on it either, just the letters MOR'.

'Give them a call, ask whether they'd meant to include a chain of custody form. Explain that the results will not be any use in court without one.'

Her bad feeling about this work just got worse. Donna emerged from the office to report there was no-one answering but she'd left a message. Mills shrugged. It was par for the course, she told her.

They spent the morning on her tooth project, as they called it, since there was no other work, urgent or otherwise. Mills reminded herself that the project was actually very important because she needed research papers to prove her worth as a lecturer. Her department did not consider their forensic service as a significant contribution, particularly when it wasn't earning any money.

When the phone rang, Mills went to answer it, her heartbeat quickening when she recognised Damien Pawson's voice.

'Good morning, Dr Sanderson. I've just received your message. Don't worry about a chain of custody, it's not necessary on this occasion.'

Before Mills could protest, he continued by asking when the work would be completed. 'We should have the results to you by the end of the week,' she replied.

He didn't seem happy but accepted it would have to do.

She told Donna to proceed with the paperwork in preparation for the analysis, before going to find Simon. She needed to warn him that their technician would be bringing him the drug sample that morning, hoping he would agree to the deadline she'd set him.

She knocked gently on the open door before entering his office but he jumped visibly when he saw her.

'You looked miles away,' she said.

He laughed. 'Caught me. I was trying to work out how to reply to this message.'

'I don't suppose I can help?' she asked, hoping he would elaborate.

He looked at her sheepishly. 'It's from Rachel.'

'Oh, Miss Clark,' she commented, pointedly. 'What does she want now?'

'She's still concerned about the Botox angle. She wants to know if our microbiologist has any more information.'

She persuaded Simon to call Martin, who was more than happy to see them in his office because he had news. He'd been talking to a mate at Porton Down.

'I wonder what he's discovered this time,' said Mills as they walked across to the Microbiology Department,

'I don't care what it is, provided it rules out Rachel's sister as the source of the infection,' Simon replied.

Martin was seated at his desk behind a pile of papers. He peered round it when they arrived and Mills noticed that he'd begun to grow a beard. It was surprisingly red compared to his hair, which was a dark brown.

'Hi,' he said cheerily, rising from his chair. 'I'm glad you called because I was going to let you know what I found. It's been quite a puzzle but I think I'm getting there.'

'Simon said you've spoken to someone at Porton Down,'

prompted Mills.

'Yes, she's in the RIPL.... sorry, the Rare and Imported Pathogens Lab, a specialist centre for unusual viral and bacterial infections. When I told her about my findings, she suggested some further tests. I've managed a couple but the rest will have to be done by their Microbiology Services.'

It was Simon who asked him what he'd found.

Martin grinned. 'The sample I managed to isolate is definitely a new species. This is a very nasty bacterium.' He lowered his voice. 'I'm not even sure whether the lab is technically licensed to work with it.'

Simon looked concerned. 'Is anyone else involved, apart from you?'

Martin shook his head. 'No, I can't risk letting it out of my sight, in case… you know…'

They both nodded although Mills had no idea what he meant.

'So,' she began, looking across at Simon, 'does that mean this bug was not picked up in hospital?'

'Extremely unlikely,' replied Martin confidently.

'And is nothing to do with Botox?'

He looked puzzled. 'No.'

As far as Mills was concerned, their interest in the bug was over but Simon had started asking a series of technical questions. When they finally left for the cafeteria, Mills asked him what he was thinking.

'I was trying to understand more about where the bacterium came from. It appears to be a new strain. I wondered if it could be a random thing or man-made.'

'From where I was standing, his responses appeared rather cagey.'

'You're right, they were. I interpreted his answers to mean that it was incredibly unlikely for it to be a chance variant. That's when he became cagey, as you put it.'

'Is he really going to send it to Porton Down?'

'I suppose so. It sounded as though they were keen to have a look at it.'

'Well, at least you can assure your friend Rachel that her sister is in the clear.'

'I guess so.'

'I hope you're not going to tell her that Martin is still working on it?'

'Not unless she asks.'

Mills sighed, she rather hoped that they'd seen the last of Miss Rachel Clark.

Chapter 14

Mills finally spoke to Brenda the following day. She'd apparently only just returned from a mini cruise round the Isle of Skye. When Mills explained that they needed her expertise, Brenda guffawed, saying that she was retired and didn't want to start work again. It took all her persuasive powers for Mills to get her to meet them for a chat.

'Well, you'll have to come here. I'm not travelling all the way from Whitby.'

Mills agreed reluctantly, promising to get back to her with a day and time as soon as she'd discussed it with Simon.

'How are you two getting along?' Brenda asked. 'Personally, I thought you made an odd couple.'

Mills, accustomed to her bluntness, knew how to deal with it. 'Just because you fancy him yourself,' she replied with a laugh.

'If only I was a few years younger, Mills.'

'A few? You mean thirty!'

'Now then, young lady, don't be so cheeky. I'll have you know I've taken up cycling. It's electric but I still have to pedal, so it's no picnic at my age.'

At last Brenda was sounding more like her old self. They chatted for a while about Donna, who had been Brenda's technician down in Harrogate.

'Don't let her go, whatever you do, Mills. She's worth her weight in gold.'

This was what Mills wanted from her old boss: advice,

support, and good old-fashioned know-how. She was looking forward to having her on board if they could persuade her. So when Simon came to find her at the end of the day, Mills reported that they were going to have a day out at the seaside. He'd never visited Whitby so she told him about the connection with Dracula and where to find the best fish and chips. They agreed to go at the end of the week, once the deadline for Rogerson's sample was out of the way. When Mills rang Brenda back, she suggested they meet for lunch in a place of her choosing, knowing that she enjoyed nothing better than a pub meal.

Mills decided to wait until they were at home to ask Simon how the cocaine sample was going. But before that, she offered to walk Harris while he prepared sausage and mash. There was a sharp wind that became progressively stronger as she marched up the track, following the patch of light made by her headtorch. Harris pulled hard on his lead but she wasn't going to let him loose in the dark. She'd made that mistake more than once; he was well-trained but the temptation of a rabbit or deer was too much for him. Soon, when even the dog seemed to tire of being buffeted by the wind, they turned back to the warmth of the cottage.

Simon had opened a beer, so Mills joined him. While she watched him mash the potato, her curiosity got the better of her.

'So did you manage to have a look at that sample from Rogerson's?' she asked casually.

'Yes,' he replied, without turning round. 'Donna wondered if there's any point in doing it without a chain of custody.'

Mills tried to keep the frustration out of her voice. 'I expect it's useful additional information for their case, even if it's not admissible evidence.'

'I've started the prep, so I can test it tomorrow.'

'That's great.'

'Although it still beats me what use it will be.'

Mills kept quiet. There was no point in arguing. Clearly Donna had made her views known, despite Mills having spoken to Rogerson's about it within her hearing, confirming they were happy to go ahead. Simon carried their plates over to the table and they ate in silence for a few minutes.

'By the way,' she began, keen to change the subject, 'did you let Rachel Clark know the outcome of Martin's investigation?'

Simon waited until he'd finished his mouthful then put his fork down. 'Yes. I've sent her an email explaining that the infection is nothing like anything found in a hospital environment, therefore it could not have been introduced by her stepsister.'

'Introduced,' repeated Mills. 'I love your choice of word. So you didn't add "accidentally *or* deliberately", then?'

He laughed then his face changed into a frown. 'You know, I've been thinking a lot about what Martin said yesterday. It still leaves the question: where did this bug come from? He effectively admitted it wasn't random, which presumably means it was manufactured.'

'How?'

'Exactly. I guess that's why he's sending it to the experts at Porton Down.'

Simon didn't involve students in cocaine analysis and Donna wasn't fully trained, so it was down to him to do the work. It was a routine procedure which should have taken a couple of hours, but there was something odd about the sample. It was white, very white, which normally suggested it was of high purity. However, it was probably cut with something like lactose, quinine, paracetamol or similar. He just hoped there wasn't anything more sinister, like fentanyl. Initial tests clearly showed the presence of a surprising amount of powdered milk. Far more than one might expect in a street drug. Consequently, the purity of cocaine in the sample was exceptionally low. He had come across cocaine with purity anywhere between twenty and ninety percent but this sample contained only ten percent. Regular users of the drug would quickly register the unexpectedly low quality of their purchase.

He waited until coffee time before seeking out Patrick, a post-doctoral research student who knew more about class A drugs than was healthy in Simon's opinion. But now his knowledge could be useful. He found him in the spacious departmental kitchen.

'Hi, do you have a minute?' The young man looked up in surprise. 'It's nothing to worry about. I just wanted your opinion on a forensic sample I'm testing.'

'Sure,' he replied. 'Sorry, did you want a…?' He was pointing back at the kettle.

'No, it's fine. Perhaps we could sit over there?' He indicated a small table in the far corner. Once they were seated, he posed the question. 'Have you ever come across cocaine cut down to ten percent with lactose?'

Patrick scratched his hipster beard as he considered the question then shook his head. 'Nope, but I guess it happens.' He took a few sips from his mug. 'Must be pretty obvious that it's nearly all milk powder though.'

'That's what I wanted to check with you. I'd assumed

that a bulking agent would be milled with the cocaine back at the source of supply. The sample I've got looks lumpy, as though it's just been mixed roughly.'

Patrick shrugged. 'So probably comes from a self-employed street dealer, not an organized gang.'

It made little sense to Simon, who was more used to working with drugs cut with other opiates than bulked with inert fillers. He would have to test a few samples of the cocaine then send Rogerson's a report based on the range of results. He thanked Patrick and went back to the lab to start the analyses.

When Mills came to find him at lunchtime, he told her he was too busy to stop work, asking her to bring him something from the cafeteria. She returned with coffee and sandwiches which they consumed seated in the corridor outside the lab.

'So how's it going?' Mills asked.

Simon finished his mouthful. 'The sample's a bit heterogeneous so I'm doing it in triplicate.'

'OK,' she replied carefully. 'Is that a problem?'

'Not for me but it might be for our client, depending on what use he's making of the results. The drug has been diluted tenfold with lactose.'

'Lactose?'

'Milk powder. It's a common bulking agent because it's white, soluble, and cheap. Probably preferable to washing detergent or talcum powder.'

'Yuk.'

'Patrick reckons it must have been adulterated by what he called a "self-employed street dealer". Do you think that's whose brief Rogerson's is working for?'

'I guess so. They didn't provide any information.'

'I think it's important you let them know the poor state of the sample when you send them the report.'

'I was thinking I might deliver it personally,' said Mills. 'I'd like to find out a bit more about them. Besides, there will be what's left of the cocaine. I don't fancy sticking that in the post.'

Mills set off early, before Simon was even dressed. She promised herself she'd have a quick look round the shops after delivering the report, so decided to take the car. Nervous with the cocaine sample in her possession, she checked her bag several times to make sure the small, padded envelope was there before finally leaving the cottage.

She wasn't used to driving through such busy traffic and became increasingly stressed as she searched for a parking space in the unfamiliar streets. When she finally found an NCP car park close to her destination, she breathed a sigh of relief, sitting for several minutes after she'd turned off the engine. Calmer now, she gathered the report, checked the package was still at the bottom of her bag and made her way to the posh offices just round the corner, following the line of office workers entering the building. Some disappeared along the corridor on the ground floor, others took the stairs. Mills hovered by the board listing the companies, looking for Rogerson Forensics.

'Can I help you?' It was the same receptionist who had been on the desk when Mills first visited.

'I was looking to see where to find Rogerson Forensics,' Mills explained.

She waited while the woman scrolled through her computer monitor. 'No, not here I'm afraid. Have you got a meeting with them? I don't see the name on any of the bookings.'

'No, they're not expecting me. I just need to drop something off for them. If you tell me where their office is I can…'

'They don't have an office here,' the woman interrupted her. 'But they do use the meeting rooms occasionally. Do you want to leave something? I can keep it until they are next here.'

Mills, thinking of the contents of her parcel, said she really shouldn't bother her. Uncertain how to proceed, she sat down on the ornate carved bench that curved to fit the wall by the entrance. There was nothing left but to call Derek.

'Where are you now?' he asked when she explained how she'd come to Newcastle to deliver the report personally.

'Where we had our meeting.'

There was a long pause before he suggested she went for a coffee round the corner. 'It's easy to find. I'll get Damien to meet you there, although he could be a while.'

He rang off before she could ask how long exactly. She went over to the reception desk to ask where this coffee shop was located. The woman looked up from her phone and smiled. Apparently, there was only one place close by but it was really nice, she just had to turn right out of the door and keep walking. Mills buttoned up her coat before stepping back out into the cold.

Half an hour stretched to an hour. Mills was finishing her second flat white when Damien burst through the door, making straight for her table.

'Sorry, traffic was rubbish,' he said loudly, taking the seat opposite her before calling to the girl at the counter. 'A large americano, love!'

'Have you come far?' Mills asked, hoping to learn where he was based.

'Not too far. I was finishing something when Dad asked me to come over.'

Apparently, Damien was Derek's son, so a family business despite the different surnames. Mills wondered now if there were any more employees since Damien had come himself. Mills retrieved the A4 envelope containing the report from her bag.

'Here are the results. We've used the code we found on the bag: MOR.'

'Yeah, we use initials for anonymity.'

She expected him to look inside but he simply folded the envelope in half, shoving it inside the pocket of his waxed jacket before asking, 'What number did your guy get?'

'You mean the purity?' She lowered her voice. 'There's a range but the average is below ten percent.'

He nodded, as if it was anticipated.

She was rummaging for the package when the girl appeared with Damien's coffee. Mills froze with her hand in her bag until he'd paid her and she was back behind the counter. She looked around the café to check that no-one was watching before pushing the padded envelope across the table. It was not how she'd wanted to return it.

'That's what's left of the sample,' she whispered.

He peered at the package before stuffing it in his other pocket. She watched him sip his coffee slowly, waiting for him to mention their fees. When he got up to leave, she hurriedly asked whether he needed their bank details for the payment.

He slapped his forehead. 'Doh, I nearly forgot! Dad

asked me to give you this if the results were OK.'

He handed her a white envelope with Yardley Forensics scrawled in black on the front. It felt thick, presumably containing paperwork, but it was sealed so Mills didn't like to open it immediately. When she looked up, Damien was already out of his seat, turning to leave.

'Nice to see you, Dr Sanderson. I hope this is the start of a long business relationship.'

She grabbed her coat to follow him out but there was her bill to pay so by the time she emerged from the café he'd disappeared. She hurried back to the car before opening the envelope to see what paperwork they'd provided, but to her surprise it contained a wad of £20 notes.

Chapter 15

Mills counted the grubby notes gingerly. There were twenty-five twenties, a total of five hundred pounds; more than she planned to charge but not a great deal more. She quickly stuffed the money back in the envelope and, keen to get rid of it as soon as possible, she used her mobile to locate a branch of her bank in the city centre.

She approached the counter nervously and asked to pay the cash into the company account. She was seriously worried there could be questions about money laundering.

'Do you have any more of these?' The cashier asked Mills, causing her to blush.

'No,' she answered cautiously, her heart pounded.

'It's just that the paper notes will no longer be legal tender in September, so you have to change them for the plastic ones by then.'

Mills breathed out slowly, her hand was still shaking as she returned the empty envelope to her bag, hurrying to the exit. She needed the loo and another dose of caffeine, perhaps with something to eat this time. She found a quiet corner in a Costa, determined to relax, but her mind was still racing after coffee with a large brownie. Rogerson Forensics had just become even less professional in her eyes. When she read Simon's message asking how she'd got on, she replied that there was now five hundred pounds in the bank. But she omitted to mention that the money had been paid in used twenty-pound notes.

The walk back to the carpark in an icy wind along hard

pavements in her smart boots made her feet hurt and now she was getting a headache. She sank into the driver's seat, wanting only to get back to Swaledale. Once out of the city the traffic eventually thinned, the roads grew emptier and she could see hills in the distance. She played music quietly, refusing to think about anything until she was at home with a mug of tea.

Harris was next door when Mills got back, so she ended up having her tea with Muriel. Having refused the offer of more cake, she had to accept a cheese scone as something "more substantial". It was already dusk when she finally extracted the lurcher for a quick run before his dinner. It was bliss to change into her trainers to walk him up the track. The cold wind in the open countryside was exhilarating so she walked further than she meant to and it was almost pitch black when she turned back. If it hadn't been for the handy light on the dog's lead, she might not have been able to keep to the track until she could make out the row of lights from the cottages below her.

Simon was lighting the fire when they returned.

'So, how was your day?' he asked once they were sitting together on the sofa.

She didn't mention she'd met Damien in a café, she avoided the bit about the notes, just gave him the bare facts: that they'd paid up after she'd handed over the report with the sample.

'Did you give them a bill? How did they pay?'

'Bank transfer.' It wasn't a lie, after all she had transferred it to the bank.

Mills called Harris to come into the kitchen for his dinner, avoiding any further discussion, then disappeared upstairs to change. She sat on the bed, wondering if she could phone Nina without Simon eavesdropping on their conversation. Her friend might help her find the case relating to the cocaine labelled MOR. Maybe even discover whether their report could be used in court, something that could bring them into disrepute.

Once they were settled down in front of the television for the evening, she sent Nina a message, asking her to ring when she was free. Five minutes later her mobile rang.

Mills jumped up. 'I'll take this upstairs so I don't disturb you.'

'It's OK, I can turn it down,' Simon called, but she was already halfway up the stairs.

'I wasn't sure if you were home,' Mills began. Her friend continued to spend much of her time working with multiple agencies on domestic abuse so her hours were unpredictable.

'No, I've just got back from a parents' evening for the boys. It was a bit chaotic covering both of their teachers without Nige.'

'Oh yes, the field trip.'

'He called me to say the students were wet and cold, demanding to go home, but he managed to persuade them to stay by buying a round in the pub.'

'That must've hurt.'

'You know Nige!'

Mills asked how the boys were getting on at school then she went on to enquire about Rosie, until Nina interrupted her.

'I know you must be wanting to ask me something,' she said with a laugh. 'So why don't you just come out with it?'

Mills was suitably embarrassed. She sighed. 'You know me so well.'

'Is it about this sleazy company you're working for?'

'First you called them dodgy, now sleazy; is there something I should know?'

'Not at all. So what are you after?'

Mills told her about her visit to Newcastle, how she'd found herself handing over the package of cocaine in a coffee shop in return for an envelope of used notes.

Nina was laughing again. 'That could look rather incriminating on CCTV.'

'I was wondering how I can find out where the trial would be held.'

'Have you got a name for the defendant?'

'No.'

'That makes it difficult. Is there nothing on the paperwork they gave you?'

Mills snorted. 'What paperwork? They didn't even have a unique identifier on the sample, except for some initials.'

'Could that relate to the defendant?'

Mills responded slowly while she thought it through. 'I don't know but the MOR might be his initials I suppose.'

'You're assuming it's he?'

'It usually is, isn't it?'

Nina agreed. 'If you like I can do a trawl when I get time. It might be quicker for you to do one yourself, it's all online.'

'Great, I'll have a go and let you know how I get on.'

Much later that evening, Nina sent Mills a link to the court listings. It arrived too late to make a start and next day they were off to see Brenda, so it would have to wait.

The weather was unpromising as Mills and Simon set off for Whitby. The journey took nearly two hours and for the first hour was through driving rain. However, as they approached the coast, it finally began to brighten up. Mills was instructing Simon on how they should approach Brenda.

'We'll wait until *after* lunch before we ask her for help. She's always more amenable after a pint.'

'A pint?'

'Oh yes, probably more than one. We'll get her in a good mood first then let me do the talking. She trusts me.'

'Are you implying she doesn't trust me?'

'Not exactly… well, yes actually.'

'Charming.'

They were approaching Whitby so Mills pulled out her phone to give Simon directions. Brenda's flat was in a large old house overlooking the town and, while Simon parked outside, Mills rang her to say they'd arrived. They waited ten minutes before a familiar figure emerged with a wave.

'Couldn't find my keys,' she explained, as she settled into the front seat.

When they asked if she would like to suggest somewhere to eat, she directed them down to the harbour but then told them to carry on until they were on the other side of town, at an inn overlooking the sea. She explained that it wasn't her local but the food was good, and they would have a nice view. She was right on all counts.

Brenda proved Mills wrong by choosing a large glass of red, explaining that she couldn't eat as much as she used to so she'd reduced her liquid intake. Simon was looking puzzled as he read the menu.

'The chicken parmo sounds interesting,' he said.

Brenda roared with laughter. 'Have you not heard of parmo, young man? It's a Teesside delicacy, pet!'

Mills grinned. 'It's chicken in breadcrumbs with bechamel sauce, topped with grilled cheese.'

'Oh, in that case, I'll try it,' he replied.

She wasn't sure he'd like it but could see he was trying to ingratiate himself with Brenda.

When the food arrived, Mills could tell he was approaching the dish with caution but after a few mouthfuls he declared it delicious. She would ask him later if he was being entirely truthful. There was very little conversation while they concentrated on their meals but once it was over, Simon looked pointedly at Mills; talk about why they had really come couldn't be put off any longer.

'Brenda,' Mills began.

'Yes, pet?'

'The reason we've come to see you…'

'You said you need my expertise. Is it textiles?'

Brenda was a recognised authority on forensics involving all sorts of fabrics, including clothing.

'No, it's more related to business really.'

Mills knew, as she said it, that it would sound an odd request. Predictably Brenda responded with a laugh.

'You know me and business, pet. You had to keep *my* business in order in Harrogate.'

'Yes, but that's because you were too busy organising the work coming in.' It was not strictly true. Towards the end, before the fire destroyed the lab, Brenda had lost interest in the business side. 'Our problem is making the right connections to build up the work.' She looked across at Simon for support.

He leaned in with a smile. 'What Mills is saying, Brenda, is that you have a wealth of experience behind you that we'd like to tap into. You would be like a sleeping partner.'

'I told you before, I don't want to interfere with what you want to do.'

'I know,' said Mills. 'But that was after the fire when you'd had a dreadful time. I'm sure you felt you never wanted to see the lab again after that.' Brenda was nodding. 'But now you've moved to this lovely place, I bet you're looking to take on new challenges.'

Simon gave Mills a look that implied she was going a bit over the top.

It was Brenda who broke the silence. 'So, you two, what's really brought this on?'

Simon indicated that Mills should respond. 'OK, so it all started because of some work I got in from a forensic service company in Newcastle.'

'Rogerson Forensics,' added Simon. 'Have you heard of them?'

She shook her head. 'Defence work?'

'Yes,' he replied. 'Drug analysis.'

'Useful contacts then.'

'You would think so, but there's something about them.'

'Have they paid you?'

Mills jumped in. 'Yes, straight away.' She thought of those used notes. 'I suppose what Simon means is they aren't very professional.'

Brenda shrugged. 'Who else have you got on your books?'

They went through the companies, most of them were previous clients of Brenda's.

'And do they send much work?' she asked.

'No,' they responded in unison.

Simon went to the bar to fetch Brenda another drink.

Mills felt they were getting nowhere. Her old boss hadn't changed, she was unlikely to be much help to them.

Then, to her surprise Brenda asked, 'How is it working out with the two of you?'

'Fine.'

'I mean, running the business together. It must create some… tensions?'

Mills smiled. 'You could say so. That's why we need you on board, or should I say on *the* board. It's like our difference of opinion about how to find work. You could help us on that for one.' Simon was coming back. 'Please say you will.'

'If I do, I won't want paying.'

That was a relief because Mills hadn't even considered it. 'There'll be dividends.'

'Only if there are profits, pet.'

Simon was placing the glass down carefully while giving Mills a quizzical look.

'Does that mean you'll do it?' Mills asked.

'Let's get down to the nitty gritty first. How much of my very valuable time will this take?'

Chapter 16

'Well, *I* think it went well,' insisted Mills.

They were walking along the river Ure, heading for the pub at Cover Bridge. Mills had insisted they did their weekly shop on the way back from Whitby, to leave their Saturday free for once. They hadn't been out for a hike with Harris for ages because of the weather, but today the sky was clear and the chilly wind had dropped. She hoped the pub would have a roaring fire so they could enjoy a relaxing lunch, returning before dark.

'I'm not disagreeing, Mills. I just wondered why you felt it necessary to tell Brenda about Rachel Clark. It's not officially company business.'

'Yes, it is. She's paying for Martin's time, isn't she?'

'And as far as she's concerned the job is done. She doesn't know that he's treating it as a piece of research.'

'When will he hear back from Porton Down?'

'I don't know. I'll catch up with him on Monday but I still don't see why Brenda needs to be involved.'

Mills got the message, changing the subject back to their other customer. 'At least she didn't seem too worried about Rogerson's, did she?'

But Simon was distracted. 'Harris!'

The lurcher had run so far ahead that he was hardly visible. Mills took the hint, leaving further discussion until they were having lunch. She knew that a pint of Theakston's would put Simon in a good mood. It was early and the bar was quiet so they were able to chose a spot by the fire, settling Harris under the table. Initially they were preoccupied ordering drinks and choosing food, but once they had placed their orders, Mills tried again.

'But you do agree we're right to involve Brenda in our decision-making?'

He sighed. 'Yes Mills, I agree *our* idea was a good one but I'll wait to see how it pans out before judging its success.'

'OK.'

Mills knew when she was beaten. Instead they discussed their plans to redecorate the cottage now that Simon spent most of his time there. When he said he was thinking of renting out his place in Osmotherley, Mills thought it sounded very permanent and told him so.

'Is that a problem?' he asked.

'What will you do when Arnie visits?'

'There's a spare room in the cottage.'

There were so many questions she wanted to ask: would Arnie mind staying in her house, didn't he want time alone with his son, what if Arnie didn't like her? Instead she simply said, 'Fine, if you think he'd be happy to stay with us.'

'I'm sure he would be. You know how much he loved Harris.'

It was true. When they were first together, Mills had spent Christmas with her father and Fiona, so Simon had offered to look after her dog. Arnie, who was over from the States for the holidays, had grown fond of the lurcher. It was a big decision for Simon to move into the cottage, despite his place being bigger and closer to the university, but they both knew that Mills would never agree to leave her cottage in Swaledale.

Once the decision was made to rent out his house, Simon was keen to start the ball rolling. He insisted they went over to Osmotherley to decide what should remain if he let it out fully furnished. Mills queried whether someone renting a house might want to bring their own furniture.

'I've thought about that,' replied Simon, keeping his eyes on the road. 'I'll put it on with the university, they're always looking for accommodation for academic visitors, places that are handy for the campus to rent for one or two years.'

They hadn't been back to Osmotherley for over a month but nothing had changed. The garden was still a mess with dead foliage covering the flower beds, bare branches protruding from the hedge. Simon pushed the front door open, picking up a couple of circulars from the mat. It was cold inside and smelt of damp.

Mills shivered. 'You'd better put the heating on if we're staying long,' she said.

The lurcher ran round the ground floor excitedly, then stood by the back door. He was hoping to be allowed into the garden, which was adjacent to a field of sheep.

'No, you're staying indoors today, Harris. It's too cold and muddy out there,' said Mills.

While Simon fiddled with the boiler, she wandered into the sitting room. She'd never been particularly comfortable staying over in Osmotherley; it was part of Simon's previous existence, something she hadn't been part of. Was that why she had taken the irrational decision to stay in Mossy Bank rather than moving into this perfectly nice old house? No, she simply couldn't bear the thought of not being in her own cottage. It had been her grandmother's and she'd fallen in love with it the moment she'd seen it all those years ago.

'I don't suppose there's room for any more furniture in your place?' Simon was standing in the doorway.

'What do you think?' she replied. 'What did you have in mind?'

'Nothing really. There's a really useful desk in the small bedroom.'

'If it's let to someone visiting the university, they'll need it too.'

'I suppose so.'

Mills, sensing his lack of enthusiasm, suggested he did a tour of the house, noting down anything he needed to take with him, while she took Harris out. The lurcher loved the lane that ran alongside the house, pulling eagerly as soon as he realised where they were going. She was feeling rather emotional too, since this was the beginning of a more permanent future with Simon, and she wondered if they were moving too fast. She hadn't even met his son yet; he may have loved Harris but what if he hated *her*?

Simon made coffee when she arrived back. They sat side by side on the sofa sipping it black, having forgotten to bring milk.

'I'll go to see the Accommodation Office first thing tomorrow,' Simon said, putting his arm round Mills. 'Get it all sorted.'

'Don't you think we should tidy the place up first?' she asked, pointing out the layer of dust on the coffee table.

She offered to clean the kitchen if Simon would tackle the bathroom. Later, he'd finished dusting and vacuuming the rest of the house, but Mills was still working on the stove so he offered to go into Osmotherley to find them something to eat, returning with toasted sandwiches and proper coffees. By mid-afternoon Mills agreed the place was looking much better.

'What about the garden?' she asked, as they took a last look round.

'I'll see if the Accommodation Office can recommend a management company to deal with it all.'

'So, have you made a list of what you want to take?'

'No problem. My clothes are in those black sacks at the bottom of the stairs. The rest I've put in the loft.'

'Really?'

'Yes, the place is ready to move into as soon as they find a tenant.'

Mills couldn't believe that anyone could vacate their home quite so easily but Simon had only moved back to the UK a short time ago, so she supposed he hadn't accumulated as much stuff as she had over the past ten years. There were, however, several black sacks to force into the Mini so Mills insisted on driving because the only space left for Harris was on Simon's knee. They were too exhausted to think about cooking so they decided to stop in Reeth for a Sunday dinner, which formed a kind of celebration to mark Simon and Mills finally moving in together.

It was back to normal on Monday morning. Harris watched them rush through breakfast before Mills gave him a quick run up the lane.

'Muriel will be in later,' she called to him as she slammed the door.

'I'm going to be late for my first lecture of term,' Simon complained as they waited at the road works close to the university.

'You've plenty of time.'

'But I wanted to get in early so I'd be prepared.'

'Since when have you been so organised?'

It wasn't even nine o'clock when she dropped him off outside the Chemistry Department. Her own timetable began later in the week so she planned to spend the morning looking for MOR's court case. Clearly it was Nige's turn to drop the kids off at school because she had the office to herself. She flung her coat over a chair and turned on the computer.

An hour later she was still trawling through court lists when Nige appeared.

'Did you get back OK?' he asked.

'What?'

'From the party; you seemed a bit worse for wear,' he commented with a grin.

'Yes, sorry. It was a good party.'

'Everything all right?'

'Yes, why?'

'Nothing. Nina told me to ask you.'

'I'll call her.'

'Good.' He said he was off to the cafeteria.

Mills kept searching through the court lists until finally she came across a name that could be the initials MOR. Malcolm O'Reilly was due in court at Newcastle next month on a drugs charge. She couldn't access the details but at least she now had a name she could search for online. It didn't take long to find a piece in "The Chronicle" about him.

Malcolm O'Reilly, 38, had apparently been arrested as part of a police investigation into a nation-wide network dealing in class A drugs. The drug-ring was based in the North-East but had contacts across the country. He was in court on charges that could result in a sentence up to life imprisonment. Mills knew that sentencing would depend on the degree of involvement that Malcolm O'Reilly had in the importing and distribution of a Class A drug, also the value of the cocaine, which meant the purity. If the sample Simon had analysed was from him, then it was of very low purity, which would affect sentencing.

'Coffee?' Nige was offering her a paper cup. 'Flat white?'

'Thanks.'

'Busy?'

'Not really.' She closed the page, covering her written notes with her arm. 'Just some forensic stuff.'

Once he was back behind his desk, she continued searching for O'Reilly on the internet and soon found another reference to his case in a national newspaper. It was not his first offence, which led Mills to wonder if Rogerson's had worked on his behalf before. She waited until Nige had left for lunch before calling Nina's number.

'I know I shouldn't,' she began when her friend answered, 'but can I ask a favour?'

'Only if it's legal, Mills, you know that.'

'I've found the name of someone with initials MOR who's been arrested for drug dealing. Malcolm O'Reilly.'

'Doesn't ring any bells. Am I supposed to have heard of him?'

'No, I found him on the list for Newcastle.'

'Not one of ours then. So what can I do for you, Mills?'

'I want to be sure that the sample we analysed belonged to this guy, so I can check what happens to the results.'

'Because?'

'Because they mustn't use the data in court. It's not certified; Simon says the sample has been diluted down to

128

a suspiciously low value.'

'I guess all you can do is wait until the hearing. When is it?'

'The eighth of February.'

'Not long to wait then.'

'So I won't be able to find any details about the case before that?'

Mills heard Nina sigh theatrically. 'What was the name again? I've got a mate in Cleveland who might be able to help.'

Mills arranged to meet Simon in the cafeteria to hear about his visit to the Accommodation Office. He was already tucking into a Cornish pasty when she joined him at a table by the window.

'You're looking pleased with yourself,' she remarked. 'It went well then?'

'Very. They are always desperate for property at the beginning of the year, apparently. They've got several families on their books looking for somewhere immediately. One of them is even a new lecturer in my department.'

'So what do you have to do now?'

'Nothing,' he replied with a broad smile. 'I gave them the keys so they can take prospective tenants over to have a look. They'll deal with it all. There's a fee but it's quite reasonable. The only question they asked was how much and for how long. They suggested a market price that was higher than I thought it would be.'

'And how long?' Mills was curious.

'I said as long as they wanted.' He hesitated. 'That was right, wasn't it?'

Mills smiled. 'Of course.'

When lunch was over, as they walked back across campus, Mills asked if Simon had seen Martin again, guessing that he'd not had time. He admitted he'd completely forgotten about him.

'In that case, why don't we see if he's in his lair?' Mills suggested.

'His what?'

'Don't you think he's like a right boffin, the way he hides away in his lab with his deadly microbes?'

Simon laughed. 'Not really. He's just a bit introverted that's all.'

As anticipated, the microbiologist was in the lab, peering down a microscope, oblivious to them until Mills tapped him on the shoulder. His beard was getting longer, she noticed. Once she'd apologised for startling him, Simon asked if he'd heard from his friends in Microbiology Services at Porton Down.

Martin nodded slowly. 'I have to be careful what I say because it's rather sensitive you know.'

Mills asked what he meant.

He lowered his voice. 'Technically I shouldn't be working on anything so hazardous here. I've arranged to have it collected by the specialist team from Porton Down this week but please keep that to yourselves.'

They both agreed conspiratorially. Simon asked if his colleagues from Porton Down had any idea how the bacterium had originated.

'No, that's why it's all hush-hush for now. Hopefully they'll be able to make sense of it once they can see it for themselves. To be honest, I'll be relieved once it's out of this building and off campus.'

Chapter 17

The meeting with Martin had left Simon keen to have a better understanding of what Martin was telling him. That afternoon he began his own research, which lasted several days on and off between his academic commitments. The library and the internet provided him with the basic understanding he needed, so by the end of the week he was able to tell Mills that Martin was right to hand it over to Porton Down. She teased him for bringing home books on biological warfare to study, picking up a heavy tome that contained the proceedings of a conference held in the 1980s. She flicked through it absently but when she saw the words "University of North Yorkshire", she stopped. It was a scientific paper about bacterial agents and their toxins. She pointed it out to Simon, who studied it in silence for the next ten minutes.

'Interesting?' she asked eventually.

He mumbled something inaudible as she went to the kitchen to prepare their meal. When she returned to tell him their pizza was cooked, Simon was on his laptop busily typing and scrolling.

'Two seconds,' he said, holding up one hand. 'I just want to check this name.'

He eventually appeared after she'd called him three times.

'It'll be cold,' she warned.

'No problem.' He was shovelling salad onto his plate.

'So what was so interesting?' she asked.

'That American paper on pathogens. It was from 1983. I was checking the authors. They're all retired now of course, including one prof who came from our Biology Department. When I did a search, I found a postdoc who published a paper with him. Guess who that was?'

Mills shrugged.

'Robert Benson!'

'You mean Professor Benson? But he's ancient!'

'In his seventies I guess, but in 1983 he would have been only thirty.'

'So he was working with this prof in the Biology Department who co-authored the paper on toxins?'

'Looks like it.'

Simon finished off his half of the pizza before he spoke again. 'I wonder if that's what Benson had been working on in the States.'

He leapt up and left the room. Mills could hear him tapping on his keyboard. She washed up, gave Harris a chew and made coffee. When she handed a mug to Simon, she pointed out that she already knew Benson's doctorate was in drug discovery for the pharmaceutical industry.

'That's what's odd,' Simon said. 'Look at his list of publications; there are the pharma papers in the seventies, until 1975. There are papers from 1983 when he joined the university, but nothing for the eight years in-between. I've searched but his name doesn't appear in the literature.'

'You think he was working on biological weapons in the States?'

'I don't know but I guess we can find out.'

He finished eating quickly and went back to his laptop while Mills tidied the dishes away. When she joined him, he was hunched over the keyboard typing furiously. She peered over his shoulder. He was on the university website, scrolling through a list of scientific publications under the name of R. C. Benson.

'You see,' Simon said, pointing at the screen, 'nothing between 1975 and 1983, which suggests he was working on something confidential.'

'Perhaps he was developing commercially sensitive pharmaceuticals,' suggested Mills.

'No,' said Simon, clicking onto a different page of the website, 'because it says here that he was working for the US Department of Defense during that period.'

'Nige said there had been student demonstrations aimed at him when the Iraq war was on.'

'Why?'

'I don't know. Perhaps he continued to work for the US Department of Defense more recently.'

Simon hammered on his keyboard again but gave up in frustration when he failed to find sources of Benson's funding on the intranet.

'Tomorrow,' he said, 'I'm going to make a few enquiries in the Biology Department.'

Next morning Simon jumped out of the car, almost running to the Biology Department. He was determined to find out if Robert Benson had continued to work on biological pathogens in the UK. Mills wandered down to the lab, hoping there might be something to do. Donna, who was already in her white coat, looked up with a smile.

'I was just talking to Brenda on the phone. She sounds like her old self again.'

'Really? Did she want anything in particular?'

'I couldn't follow it all but she's going to bring someone

over next week. She said can you ring her?'

At last, thought Mills, picking up her phone.

When Brenda answered she sounded full of life. 'Mills, I've made a few calls, chased a few connections, and found a few new ones. I must admit it's been quite fun catching up with old mates. Well, the upshot is that I want to bring Harry Fraser down to meet you. You won't know him but we go back a long way. I didn't realise but he's set up his own business and… well, you'll see. He's a very useful contact.'

'What does he do?'

'Lots of work for defence lawyers but not like your dodgy customer. He's told me all about them.'

'What?'

'Harry can fill you in himself if he wants. How are you fixed for Thursday?'

Mills didn't have to consult her diary. Thursdays were free after a lecture first thing. 'Any time after ten-thirty.'

'No problem. He's coming from Leeds so he won't be with you before then. Let's call it eleven so I don't have to get up too early.'

'You'll come too?'

'Of course, I don't want to miss seeing Harry again after all this time.'

Mills immediately called Simon to give him the good news but he seemed distracted.

'Have you got your nose in biological warfare papers again?' she demanded.

He responded by telling her that Prof Benson had definitely continued to work for the US Government once he'd moved to the UK. 'In fact, I'm looking at his grant record right now.'

'Where did you find that?'

'In his departmental financial records'.

'But…'

'Don't ask. I just wanted to check. It's not difficult actually,' he admitted.

'Does it say what the work was about?'

'Not really. I think I'll see if he's around for a chat.'

'Shall I come?'

'No, best not Mills.'

Simon wandered along to Benson's office. The door was ajar but the room was empty. Resisting the temptation to poke around inside, he made his way to the departmental kitchen where a couple of research staff were making coffee.

'Have either of you seen Prof Benson this morning?' he asked.

The young man sniggered but the woman gave him a sympathetic smile. 'I think he's out the back.'

Behind the Biology Department was a small patch of land that consisted of ornamental shrubs and gravel, which was originally raked into patterns to emulate a Japanese Zen garden. Now weeds abounded and cigarette ends festooned the gravel. As predicted, Benson was sitting in the winter sunshine.

'Robert!' The old man quickly stubbed out his cigarette.

'Sorry to disturb you.' Simon joined him on the wooden bench.

The professor looked at him quizzically.

'Simon Pringle, you came to see me after your wife…'

'Yes, yes, of course. Pringle. That's right.'

To save his embarrassment, Simon muttered something about being out of context. They exchanged opinions on the weather for a while then Simon commented on how he'd worked in the States himself and understood that Benson had spent time there too. Soon they were discussing the very different research funding systems in America until Simon felt ready to ask the key question.

'So what were you doing in the States?' he asked casually.

Benson considered for a moment. 'My research was on drug development.'

'But I think you worked for the US Government as well?'

He turned to Simon with a puzzled look. 'How do you know that?'

'It's in the public domain, Robert.'

He raised his eyebrows. 'Is it? I didn't know.'

'Nothing is secret on the internet.' Simon watched for a reaction but was disappointed.

'It's getting cold,' Benson said, pushing himself up to a standing position with difficulty. 'I need to get back to work.'

With that he was gone, leaving Simon convinced he had touched a nerve. He returned to his office to check the names of the other authors on the paper that Benson had published on toxins. Two senior authors were long retired, but Simon assumed that those people whose names appeared after Benson's were possibly less important and therefore younger. It took all morning, with several false starts, but finally his search revealed that a co-author called Eric Stevens was now a professor at the University of Minnesota, publishing papers in epidemiology. Simon immediately emailed a scientist he knew in the Medical School over there, asking for an introduction. With luck Professor Stevens would be able to tell him what Robert Benson had been working on in those missing years.

Chapter 18

When Mills went to meet Brenda in reception, she could see that she had made quite an effort on her appearance, including a very fetching purple tweed jacket that took inches off her figure. She was even wearing lipstick.

'I do like your hair,' Mills commented, surveying her friend's new shorter style. 'It really suits you.'

She took her visitor down to the office, plying her with coffee while quizzing her on Harry Fraser's company.

'I looked at the website; the labs look amazing but it doesn't say much about the staff,' Mills complained.

'He has a highly experienced team but he's very fussy about who he takes on, which is why he has problems when they build up a backlog,' Brenda reported. 'I told him how skilled you and Donna are… and Simon, of course,' she added. 'Just act as if you know what you're doing when you show him round.'

Now Mills was feeling nervous. Donna was busy tidying up glassware in the lab so Mills called her in to chat with Brenda while she went up to Simon's office. As she left, she insisted Donna let her know the moment Harry Fraser arrived.

Upstairs, Simon didn't look up until she was standing right beside his desk.

'Sorry, I didn't see you,' he said, still staring at his screen.

'Something interesting?' she asked, slightly irritated. 'He'll be here soon. Brenda's already arrived.'

'Right, I'm just coming.' He was still reading his emails.

'It's from a mate in the States,' he explained.

As he followed her to the lab, he told her about his contact in Minnesota who'd connected him with a member of Benson's old research group. He was going to have a meeting online with someone called Professor Stevens who knew Robert Benson in the eighties.

'Why is it so important?' asked Mills, pushing open the lab entrance then stopping. 'Oh damn, he's arrived,' she said quietly.

Donna was making fresh coffee while Brenda was chatting with their visitor. When she caught sight of them, she struggled to her feet, calling, 'Come and meet Harry, I've been telling him all about you.'

Harry Fraser was much younger than Mills had expected. He was a tall, athletic-looking man with a thick well-groomed beard that was a shade darker than his fair hair. He was dressed in jeans, shirt and jacket but he looked so smart Mills guessed his clothes, like his leather brogues, were expensive. He had jumped up to shake their hands before relaxing back into his chair. Mills waved to Donna to join them and they squeezed round the table, with Simon perching on a stool.

Harry smiled across at them. 'So I guess I should tell you something about my company?' They nodded. 'Brenda has known me for a very long time,' he began.

'He was my student at one time,' she said proudly. 'Now look at him.'

He gave her a broad grin, raising his eyebrows across the table at Mills. 'Brenda was a great teacher. I learnt so much from her that has stood me in good stead in my business so far.'

Mills wondered if that was true, since her old boss was

not a good financial manager but perhaps he was referring to the forensic work. He was explaining how after working for Brenda he went into the police forensic service for a while before venturing out on his own. At one stage his company was a competitor that Mills had come across when she'd worked for Brenda.

'What made you eventually branch out on your own?' she plucked up the courage to ask.

'Ethics,' he replied. 'Sometimes you just have to go with your gut feeling. I wasn't entirely happy with the way some of the work was being managed.'

Brenda gave Mills a knowing look. 'Not every forensic service is as morally sound as it should be,' she declared enigmatically.

Harry went on to describe the work his company undertook for defence counsel, including the usual range of laboratory investigations that Mills was familiar with.

'I suppose the things I'm looking for are twofold,' he said, lacing his fingers and putting his elbows on the table. 'I need quick turnround on routine samples when we get too busy, such as examination of clothing, fluids and DNA. But I would also like to take advantage of your unique position here with an international expert in toxicology.' He looked across at Simon who responded with an appreciative nod.

'Excellent,' said Brenda. 'So that's settled then. I'm sure Mills can send you a price list in due course. Shall we have a quick look round before we head off for lunch?'

Mills looked at Donna and shrugged. She led them round the labs, explaining what the equipment was used for. When Simon took over in his domain, he spent some time alone with Harry discussing specialist analyses.

Mills was wondering whether to pop into the office to book somewhere for lunch when Brenda took her aside, whispering, 'I hope you don't mind but I'm whisking Harry away to a favourite pub of his not far away. It's a chance for me to find out what he really thinks of this place. I knew you wouldn't mind.'

They congregated back in the office, where Harry said how much he'd enjoyed the opportunity to see their facilities and promisd he'd keep in touch. Brenda said she'd give them a call the following week. Once they were gone, Simon expressed his annoyance at not being able to join them.

'Brenda wants to get his feedback,' Mills explained. 'He'll give her his honest opinion if we're not there.'

When Donna offered to fetch sandwiches, Simon gave her enough money to push the boat out.

'Bring back a decent selection… and some chips… and cake,' he said. 'I don't see why we should miss out.'

Mills laughed. 'I think Brenda has our interests at heart but she is also a bit taken with Harry, don't you think? Did you see how she'd smartened herself up since we last saw her?'

'Oh, I thought that was for my benefit,' Simon joked. He paused before changing the subject. 'After lunch I'm having a meeting with this guy Stevens in the States.'

'The one who worked with Benson years ago?'

'Yes, I hope he'll be able to tell me what secrets he was working on in the eighties.'

'I see. And why do you need to know?'

He shrugged. 'Just interested, that's all.'

Mills knew it was far more than a passing interest. Simon often mocked *her* for getting stuck into other people's business. He didn't usually have her natural curiosity so it was her turn to tease him.

'Do you think he'll turn out to be a spy, stealing secrets from the US army and selling them to the Russians?'

He grunted.

'Actually,' she continued, 'that's not such a daft idea if he really was working on pathogens.'

'I didn't say he was, Mills.'

'But the books…'

'That was background information for Martin's investigation, nothing to do with Prof Benson. That's *you* getting carried away, Mills.'

Simon was usually the grounded one in their relationship. He wondered if Mills had infected him with her obsessive nature, which often led her into trouble. He knew it was unwise to mention the possibility that Benson had been working on pathogens forty years ago. Instead he asked what she thought of Harry Fraser and they talked around how good it would be if he sent some work their way.

Donna returned laden with the best that the cafeteria could offer. Mills put the kettle on while they shared out the treats and there was a celebratory feel to their meal as they discussed the visit.

'Brenda was looking really well,' Donna said, adding that she missed her old boss. 'She's such a great character.'

'She's doing a grand job for us, using old contacts to drum up trade,' agreed Mills.

As soon as they'd finished eating, Simon went off to take his transatlantic call. He put his list of questions in front of him before clicking the app to start the meeting. As the university professor came into view, Simon was struck by how old he looked. Of course, he'd been a student in the eighties, which meant he would be over sixty now. They greeted each other politely before Simon introduced himself, explaining that he was interested in finding out more about Professor Robert Benson's career when he was in the States. The other man wore a puzzled frown as he enquired, in a distinctive sing-song Minnesotan accent, whether his old colleague was still alive.

'Yes, indeed,' replied Simon. 'In fact he is still seen in his department occasionally.'

'So why don't you ask him?'

Simon stumbled over his reply. 'It's… well, you see…' Then he thought of something. 'It's for a testimonial, I don't want him to find out.'

Stevens smiled. 'I understand. But that makes it tricky because what I can tell is not really for general discussion. Robert wouldn't thank me for breaking that particular code.'

Simon feigned surprise. 'Really, is it official secret stuff?'

'Well, yes, I guess. We were working for this guy who did a lot of stuff with the United Nations around the time of the Iraq-Iran war.'

'That would be in the eighties?'

'Yah,' he replied in the Minnesotan way.

'Can I assume that this guy working for the UN was interested in biological warfare, chemical weapons, and so on?'

'Yah, he was making trips to Iraq to check them out.'

'And you guys were researching those kinds of things?'

'You could say that.'

'And it was for the US Department of Defense?'

He nodded, almost imperceptibly.

Simon looked down at his list of questions while Stevens sat quietly waiting.

'Sorry, just one more: do you know if Robert has continued to work on the same topic since leaving the States?'

The Minnesotan shook his head slowly then shrugged. 'I wouldn't know, sorry. We lost touch decades ago. To be truthful we were never friends, he was older and more senior than me. But if you see him, tell him Hairy Stevens says hi. I used to have long hair in those days,' he explained. 'Now look at me!' He ran his hands over his bald pate chuckling.

Simon laughed before thanking him for his help, assuring him he'd pass the message on, knowing that he wouldn't. Eventually they finished saying goodbye and Simon ended the call, leaning back in his chair. So Benson's work had been associated with biological weapons in some capacity when he was abroad, but what about when he arrived in the UK?

Chapter 19

Rachel Clark was seated in the departure lounge with an hour to kill before her flight to Japan would be boarding. She had wanted to stay longer but work was getting increasingly insistent that she was needed back in the office. Anyway, she wasn't sure she could tolerate another evening with Janine, who was popping round regularly to check on her father. Rachel resented the implication that she couldn't look after him, a row had ensued when she challenged her, sending Dad into a rage when he heard them exchanging insults. It occurred to her that he was not coping with her mother's death as well as it had first appeared. She'd noticed there were times when he mislaid things, forgot mealtimes and on occasions confused her with Janine. He became quite overwrought when he thought his wallet had been stolen until Rachel found it in a kitchen drawer. She supposed that it was a sign he was ageing. When she spoke to her stepsister about her concerns, she was told to stop fussing because she would soon be across the other side of the world, while Janine would be picking up the pieces. The final straw was when she discovered her stepsister going through Mum's things, insisting that Dad would want to keep her jewellery, clothes, and other bits and pieces. Rachel wasn't particularly interested in taking anything valuable but had hoped to retain something personal of her mother's.

There was a phone call Rachel needed to make before she left the country. She wanted to speak to Professor

Pringle one last time, to urge him to continue to investigate her mother's death. He'd neither replied to her last voicemail nor responded to her email. She listened to his office number ringing unanswered until it switched to the recorded message. After the beep, she simply explained that she was flying back to Japan but would keep in touch.

Simon was seated at his desk, listening guiltily to her message as she was recording it. He didn't pick up because there was no news to pass on to her. He'd felt bad that he'd been ignoring her messages but what could he tell her? Sorry Rachel, but the bug that killed your mother has been sent to Porton Down because they suspect it's some sort of man-made bacterium, too lethal to be listed in any database? He didn't think so.

His musing was interrupted by a cheery greeting. It was Pawel, a biology lecturer who had joined the university at the same time as Simon, so they'd attended the same Faculty induction courses and training sessions together.

'Someone said you were looking for me?' Pawel said. 'How can I help? I hope it's not teaching because my schedule is completely full.'

'No, no, nothing to do with work really.'

'I'm intrigued,' he replied, moving a chair closer to the desk.

Simon had noticed that Robert Benson was loosely attached to the research group that the lecturer was also a part of. It was a long shot but he thought Pawel might know something of Benson's interests both past and, more importantly, current. He'd thought about how to broach the subject, deciding to use the same approach that he'd used on the guy in Minnesota.

'Actually it's a bit delicate, Pawel. You see, I've been

asked to write a piece about Robert Benson.'

Pawel looked at him. 'Like an obituary? I know they prepare them well in advance, that's how they have them ready when someone pops their clogs, isn't it?'

Simon nodded. It didn't matter what he thought provided he kept it to himself. 'Well, it's kind of hush-hush.'

'Of course, I understand. It's not something I'd want to know about myself, not that...'

'No, of course not,' Simon interrupted. 'So I was specifically wondering about his work for the US Government because there are no publications for that period.'

Pawel shook his head. 'I don't know anything about the work he did abroad.'

'What about in this country? I assume he continued to keep that connection; it must have been lucrative. I wondered if there might be some information about the grants he gained.'

'I don't know but I'll try to find out.'

Simon panicked. 'I don't think you should...'

'Don't worry, I'll be very discreet. I can ask Deborah to have a look in the files.'

'Deborah?' Deborah in the Faculty Finance Office?'

'Yes, she's my fiancée, didn't you know?'

Deborah was a very quiet young woman who Simon knew by sight but they'd not exchanged more than a few words.

'Well congratulations,' Simon said. 'If you're sure it won't get back to Robert?'

'You have my word, and if you're going to the party tomorrow, I can introduce you to her properly.'

Simon didn't know of any party.

'Yes, you do!' Pawel insisted. 'The Prof's Christmas party, postponed because he was ill, don't you remember?'

He did remember. He'd been disappointed when his old Head of Department, now Head of Faculty, announced the traditional party wasn't going ahead, because the last time it was held was the first time he and Mills had gone as a couple. She was visibly relieved when he told her it wasn't happening, because of the dreaded karaoke, which was the highlight of the party. Staff were expected to participate and although their duet had been a triumph, Mills still insisted that she would never repeat the performance.

Mills, who was determined to set aside Fridays for her personal research, told Donna they would review the historical data on her tooth project. Her technician had run the calculus samples with Simon's help so now it was time to analyse the results.

'By the way,' began Donna. 'We've finally received some modern teeth. Not a large number but they've sent the details of the patients with their typical diets and I've checked they lived all their lives in the Dales. Two of the group are vegetarians so I thought that would be useful if the point of the project is to compare meat eating in the seventeenth century with the present day.'

Mills examined the newly arrived samples before asking Donna to start their preparation. She was pleased to see there were sufficient samples for the modern part of the study. At last it looked as though the project might have a successful conclusion by the deadline in March. She went back to the spreadsheets to begin performing a statistical evaluation on them, hoping to show that Dales folk in the seventeenth century ate less meat. However, only the final results would tell her if her hypothesis was true.

Mills was still poring over the data, papers strewn all over the table in the office, when Simon came to find her.

'Time to go home,' he announced, 'or we'll miss the chip van!'

Mills stretched her back and yawned. 'Already?'

'How's it going? Did Donna do a good job?'

'Looks like it. I'm beginning to see a pattern, I think.' She gathered up the papers and grabbed her bag.

'You're not bringing them with you?' Simon asked.

'Yes, of course. I thought you could help me with some of the interpretation. I'm not as familiar with the methodology as you are.'

'I thought we'd have a clear weekend,' he began carefully. 'It's the Head's party tomorrow and I thought you might want to go shopping.'

'What party? It's the first I've heard.'

'You remember, it was postponed before Christmas.'

Mills didn't answer. They walked in silence to the car. Simon wasn't sure if he'd fooled her into thinking he'd told her about the new date, or whether she was silently planning how to get out of it. Whichever, he was determined to go, to make contact with Deborah from Finance, who held the key to Prof Benson's grant record.

He continued his effort to convince her once they were on the way home. 'And we don't do enough stuff together, do we?'

'We're together all the time now you've moved in.'

'But that's not doing stuff.'

'I don't mind doing stuff, as you call it, but just not that karaoke party.'

148

He was right then, it was the karaoke that was putting Mills off. 'What if I promise we won't do karaoke?'

'Can you do that?'

'Of course.'

'Really?'

'I promise we won't do karaoke.' He didn't know how but he would think of something, even though it was expected, particularly of the senior staff.

To his relief, Mills appeared to have accepted they would be attending the party because she began worrying about what to wear as soon as they were home. He offered to take Harris down to meet the chip van while she perused her wardrobe, at once appearing supportive while avoiding the trauma of clothes strewn across the room with questions about suitability.

Simon continued to tread carefully until Saturday evening, offering to drive, so Mills could drink at the party. She had selected the red dress she'd bought at Christmas that he'd told her, truthfully, she looked stunning in. He noticed that she was wearing the gold earrings he'd bought her for their anniversary. It was already dark as they pulled the door closed gently, leaving Harris with a handful of treats and a promise to be back soon. Simon commented he was looking forward to a night out and Mills agreed, albeit reluctantly.

In fact Mills was surprised to find she recognised most of the people at the party. She supposed it was because the lab was in the Chemistry Department so she came across most of academic staff in the corridor from time to time. Those she didn't recognise came over to greet Simon, telling her they'd seen her around. It was very different to the previous party, where she was definitely a figure of speculation as Simon's new girlfriend. The Head made much of their relationship, with his wife suggesting Mills might wish to join the "wives club".

'You don't have to be married to an academic,' she giggled. 'We accept partners.'

Mills looked to Simon for help but he shrugged, so she simply muttered something inaudible about being very busy. She pulled him away to the bar, demanding a gin and tonic, muttering something about "living in the dark ages". Simon scanned the crowd for Pawel but there was no sign, so once their glasses were filled, they set off in search of food. They headed for a table in the conservatory and, to Simon's relief, his friend was seated there with Deborah from Finance.

'Oh look,' said Simon to Mills. 'There's Pawel with his fiancée.'

'Who?'

Without replying he made a beeline for them to introduce Mills.

'We've met before,' said Deborah. 'You're Mills Sanderson with the forensics lab.'

'Yes.' She looked at Simon before sitting down. 'How are the wedding plans going?' she asked. 'It must be quite soon.'

'April.'

Simon gave Pawel a quizzical look. He nodded in return. They sat listening to girl talk: dresses, bouquets, hen nights and honeymoons. Eventually, Pawel jumped into a lull in the conversation.

'Deborah found out some interesting information that will help the obituary,' he said.

His fiancée smiled. 'Yes,' she said. 'You wanted to know if he worked on US projects while in post here? I have a printout of the grants he received from the US Department of Defense up until 2005, if that helps. I'm afraid they don't give the research titles.'

Simon took the sheet of information, folded it neatly and put it in his pocket without looking at it. 'That's very helpful, thank you Deborah.'

'So what is it for?' she asked.

'Yes, Simon,' said Mills. 'Do tell.'

He hoped he didn't look as red as he felt. 'I can't really discuss the details... but it involves... a possible honour... from the United States.' He was pleased with his idea because it would never be traceable if it didn't materialise. Fortunately, at that moment, they were interrupted by the Head and his wife, who were being perfect hosts by passing round the forms for the karaoke.

'What's this?' asked Deborah, who had clearly not attended one of the Head's parties before. Pawel explained. 'You are kidding!' she exclaimed. 'I'd rather die than make an exhibition of myself. I work in the Finance Department; I'd never live it down.'

Mills was smiling. 'Don't worry, you don't have to do it.'

Pawel gave her an astonished look. 'Really? How do you reckon on that? I've only attended three of these but I've never escaped.'

Mills looked at Simon, who shrugged. 'You said we wouldn't have to,' she said.

'We don't. Just don't fill in the paper.'

Pawel shook his head. 'No, they'll be back to collect them. We have to do it.'

Mills asked to borrow his pen and filled in their piece of

151

paper, folding it carefully. Simon breathed a sigh of relief. Meanwhile there was dancing in the huge room cleared of furniture except, bizarrely, for a decorated Christmas tree. Mills had consumed several glasses of wine by the time the karaoke began, so Simon hoped it would go smoothly, assuming they would repeat their previous performance which had gone down extremely well. They were entertained by a series of solo and double acts, even three women covering a hit by "All Saints". He was shocked how hard Mills gripped his arm when it was announced that the next act was Simon Pringle and Mills Sanderson. The Head read from the form completed by Mills, that they were going to perform the "Ladies Excuse Me".

She was trying to pull him towards the door. 'You said we wouldn't have to do it again!' she yelled above the roar from the room.

The crowd had obviously enjoyed their previous performance because there were shouts of "New York" which turned into a chant. Feet were stamping, hands clapping. Simon knew that Mills had given in to the inevitable as her grip loosened and she shoved him towards the stage.

Chapter 20

Mills went straight to bed when they arrived home after the party, leaving Simon to take Harris out and settle him in his basket. They'd hardly spoken since leaving the stage after their performance, which had been so enthusiastically received Simon wanted to stay to see if they'd won first prize. Mills, insisting they had to get back for the dog, thanked the Head and his wife politely. Simon anticipated a telling-off about the karaoke as soon as they were in the car, but she had a different axe to grind.

'Since when are you writing an obituary for Prof Benson?' she asked.

'You know I'm not.'

'So what was your friend talking about? And what did Deborah give you?'

'I was just curious. She found me some details of his funding from the States.'

'Why?'

'Because I asked her to.'

'No, I mean why on earth do you want to know?'

It wasn't the time to start an argument so he looked straight ahead, driving quickly along the empty lanes. Mills soon fell asleep, unsurprising since she'd consumed quite a few glasses of wine during the evening. When he woke her, she stumbled out of the car and into the cottage.

To his surprise, next morning Mills was out with Harris even before he came downstairs. He made a cooked breakfast and they chatted as if the friction of the previous evening hadn't occurred. Eventually he risked mentioning that he was sorry that she'd had to perform in the karaoke; it had been a total misunderstanding with the Head.

'That's OK,' Mills replied, helping herself to marmalade. 'I quite enjoyed it really. Brought back memories.'

Simon waited.

'Actually that wasn't what I was annoyed about,' she continued.

Simon took a deep breath. 'I know, it was the obituary thing.'

'Yes. What *was* that all about?'

He explained his preoccupation with toxins, which sounded like the sort of obsessive thinking that Mills exhibited. *He* was supposed to be the sensible, objective member of the partnership.

Mills looked amused at his admission. 'Do you seriously think there's a connection between the bug that Martin's investigating and Prof Benson's research interests?' she asked with a laugh.

He shrugged it off, changing the subject by suggesting a walk. It was part of his plan for them to spend more time together, doing things that couples did on their weekends. Mills argued that she'd brought her tooth data home to work on, but he told her she could do that later when it was dark, pointing out that the sky was blue and the sun was already creeping up from behind the opposite side of the dale. Mills agreed reluctantly but only on condition that they went over to Dentdale. It was a walk she had only done once before, in the summer, starting at the isolated Dent station. She remembered walking up to Arten Gill viaduct and over the tops where the air was full of the song of skylarks.

'You'd better wrap up well though,' she instructed Simon. 'It'll be freezing if there's a wind.'

She was right, an icy wind greeted them when they climbed out of the Mini. They donned woolly hats, scarves, and gloves before putting Harris on his long lead. Mills had packed Simon's rucksack with sandwiches and a thermos, and he complained about its weight when he lifted it onto his back. He hadn't travelled on the Settle-Carlisle line so they stepped onto the platform to take a a look. When he asked if there were any trains running, Mills indicated three passengers standing on the opposite platform, which suggested one was due soon.

'So will it be a steam train?' he asked.

Mills laughed. 'If it was a steam train there would be a lot more people around, I'm sure. Sorry to disappoint you but it will be a diesel.'

He insisted on waiting to see it arrive while Mills jumped up and down to keep warm. When the two-carriage train arrived, Harris barked furiously; it wasn't something he was used to seeing.

'Please can we go now?' Mills insisted, as the train disappeared leaving an empty platform on the other side of the tracks.

It was more sheltered as they made their way downhill to Cowgill and along the road past "The Sportsman Inn". It was firmly shut, proving Mills right in loading Simon's rucksack, despite his protestations. They joined a track that rose steadily until they reached the eleven-arch viaduct. Simon admired the feat of engineering, stating that it was presumably constructed by the same navvies who built the Ribblehead viaduct. Mills agreed, pointing out that the dark limestone quarried locally had been used in the construction. Simon teased her about her lecture on industrial archaeology before they continued up the track to find a suitable spot for their picnic. There was no sound of skylarks on the tops this time but Mills thought she heard the cry of a solitary curlew. Simon wanted to stop for something to eat but Mills thought they should wait until they found a wall to shelter behind.

Harris was having a great time ferreting about. The cold didn't seem to worry him as he hunted for rabbits in the undergrowth. His biscuits were quickly consumed when they finally found a spot out of the wind, then he waited patiently for the bits of cheese sandwich and apple that came his way. As soon as they'd drunk their hot tea, Mills started to pack up, ready to move on. But Simon wanted to ask her a question. He'd been waiting for the right moment but he never seemed to have her full attention. Now was his best chance.

'Mills, you know I want to spend time with Arnie this summer, and you said we could have him stay with us in the cottage, but I've been thinking… it might be best for you to meet him properly on his own turf, so to speak.'

'You mean go to the States?' They'd talked about his son's visit before, and she thought they'd agreed he would join them in Mossy Bank. She wondered if Arnie's mother, Dianne, had raised objections.

'It will be fun,' Simon continued. 'I can show you the sights; we can take Arnie on camping trips. You'll really enjoy it.'

'Have you discussed it with Dianne?'

'She's cool with the idea.'

'Really?'

He rambled on about the various places of interest they

could visit, as if it was decided, even suggesting the most suitable date for flying out. Mills was too busy imagining how she would feel. Where would they stay? Surely not in the family home. The more she thought about it, the more she was convinced his ex-wife had put the idea in his head.

'Was this Dianne's idea?' she asked innocently.

Simon nodded with a smile. 'I think it's really thoughtful of her to offer. I was surprised at first, especially when she offered us the house.'

'So where will *she* be?' she demanded.

He looked puzzled, replying that he hadn't discussed any of the details yet. Mills made it clear she was not going to accept an invitation to be the house guest of his ex. Simon looked harassed, mumbling something about sorting out the logistics, while he pulled the rucksack onto his back.

They communicated little during the rest of the walk and dinner was a subdued affair, partly because they were both tired after battling across the moors in strong winds, but mainly due to the unsatisfactory conclusion to their discussion about the proposed trip. Simon went upstairs for his usual Sunday evening online chat with Arnie and, Mills suspected, to catch up with the boy's mother to sort out their summer plans. Mills suppressed the temptation to sneak up the stairs to listen but instead settled down with the data from her tooth project.

Simon found her an hour later, fast asleep on the sofa. His conversation with Dianne had been difficult. She was adamant that Arnie would not be travelling to England in the summer because he needed to prepare for his transition to private school. It was something they'd talked about for several years, although Simon had done his best to discourage the idea. Dianne was ambitious for their son;

she wanted him to go to an ivy league university to study law like her brother. Simon didn't believe his son was sufficiently focussed academically to succeed but she said that was exactly why Arnie needed a private education. It would be expensive, despite Dianne's parents chipping in, so the rent from Simon's cottage in Osmotherley was going to become increasingly important in future, although he hadn't mentioned any of this to Mills yet. She was snoring softly. When he pushed a few strands of hair back from her face, her eyes opened.

'How's Arnie?' she asked, struggling to sit up.

'He says he's looking forward to seeing you but it's got to be stateside because he's starting this posh private school so there's loads of preparatory work to do in the holidays.'

'Really? Is that what he said?' Or was it what Dianne had told him to say? 'If that's what he wants, I suppose there's no further discussion,' she added, lying down again.

Simon was looking pleased. 'Does that mean you'll come?'

'I'll have to think about it. There's Harris to consider.'

Simon knew better than to push Mills into making an instant decision. He settled down next to her, turned on the television and absently stroked the lurcher's back while thinking about plans for the summer. They could afford to wait a few weeks or even months while Mills came round to the idea.

Nina had left a message for Mills to call her at work on Monday morning before ten. It turned out that her friend had some interesting news.

'You asked me about Malcolm O'Reilly, Mills.'

'Yes?'

'I've got some information about the case from a contact in Cleveland. Have you got a pen? Because I'm not putting this in writing.'

'OK.'

'He's on a drugs charge, but you knew that. What's more important is the amount and the quality. It's big, it's kilos and it's high-grade. He's likely to get ten years for it.'

'Do you know the purity?'

'No, he just said very high-grade.'

'Interesting because when we measured…'

'Mills, you know I can't get involved. I'm just telling you what he said, and you didn't hear it from me, all right?'

'Yes, Nina. Thanks.'

Mills put the phone down and digested the information. The police had not seized the low-grade material that Rogerson's had sent her. She'd wanted to ask Nina where they'd had the sample tested. She needed the name of her contact in the Cleveland force but knew she couldn't press her friend further. She gathered up her pile of folders and wandered slowly through the lab, where Donna was preparing chemical reagents.

'I'm going to finish working on the historical tooth data today,' she told her technician. 'How's the prep for the modern teeth coming along?'

'They'll be done by the end of the week,' she promised before continuing her work.

Mills thanked her but was at the door before she asked, 'Did the Cleveland Police send drugs to Wakefield for testing when you were there?' she asked casually.

'Yes,' Donna replied without turning round.

Mills walked back to the Archaeology Department,

where Nige was humming to himself.

'You sound cheerful,' she commented, dropping the files onto her desk with a thud.

'Heard my grant application was approved. It means I'll be able to go to Italy on that field trip this summer.'

'What does Nina think about that?' she asked, knowing her friend had problems juggling work in the school holidays, even when Nige was around.

'I've only just heard so she doesn't know yet.' He looked across at her. 'How are you fixed for some child-minding in August?' he asked jokingly.

How was she fixed? Mills shrugged. 'No idea what's happening in the summer, Nige.'

Her mind was elsewhere. If the cocaine they'd tested for Rogerson's had also gone to Wakefield police forensics lab, maybe Donna could find out exactly how high-grade their sample had been. If she walked quickly, the technician would be on her coffee break.

'Donna!' she called as she entered the lab.

'In here.' She was seated in the office with a coffee mug in front of her. 'Want one?' she asked.

Mills said she would make it, busying herself with the kettle while she planned how to broach her request. When she finally sat down, she began by hinting at what Nina had told her.

'I've heard something interesting about that sample from Rogerson's: the police have charged it as high-grade although we reported it as very low.'

Donna put her mug down, looking concerned. 'Do you think we misreported?'

'No, I don't believe we made an error but I'm sure the other forensics lab wouldn't have either.'

160

'Not if it went to Wakefield, that's for sure.' Donna had often spoke about how impressed she'd been when she worked there. Now was the chance for Mills to ask for the favour.

'I really want to get to the bottom of this. Do you think you could make a few discreet enquiries of your old colleagues to find out what results they got?'

Donna's expression was somewhere between confusion and distaste. It was a few seconds before she replied frostily, 'No, I'm sorry but I can't. It wouldn't be ethical, would it?'

Mills felt herself reddening. Her technician was right, of course, she should never have put her in that position. She apologised, took her mug to the sink, pouring the coffee away before she left.

Chapter 21

Simon was already waiting in the car at the end of the day. 'I expected to see you in the lab this afternoon,' he commented as Mills climbed in beside him.

'I'm working on the teeth data,' she replied, without admitting that she'd been avoiding Donna.

'We're going to work on your modern material on Wednesday.'

'Donna told me. That's great.'

'I've also heard from Martin; he came to see me this afternoon.'

'What did he want?'

'He asked me to sign an NDA.'

'A what?'

'A non-disclosure agreement.'

'Why?'

'Apparently Porton Down want to ensure I don't talk about the sample he sent them. I don't know anything about it anyway but he said it's routine procedure. He was a bit twitchy because they told him he wasn't licensed to handle that sort of material.'

'So what happens now?'

'Nothing yet apparently. But when they've finished investigating the toxin, they'll get back to him. He'll be able to tell me what they say, now I've signed their NDA.'

'Thank goodness it's not our problem anymore.'

Simon remembered Rachel's last phone message but decided to say nothing since Mills had already begun telling him about the results of her data analysis.

'...so it looks as if the fatty acids in the calculus are related to the occupation of the owner of the teeth.'

'Good, I'm glad I could be of help.'

Mills was aware that without the use of his expertise in the analytical techniques, she wouldn't have been able to attempt the study.

'I'll put your name on any papers I publish,' she offered.

He laughed. 'You definitely don't need to do that, but you should acknowledge Donna's hard work.'

Reminded of her faux pas in asking her technician to seek information from Wakefield, Mills confessed to Simon that she'd messed up. 'I feel really bad about asking her now,' she admitted, 'but at the time I was thinking about protecting our good name.'

Simon agreed that she hadn't done anything illegal but suggested she sought further information from the people at Rogerson's. 'After all, isn't the prosecution required to provide the analysis of the cocaine sample under disclosure?'

'Gosh, I think you're right! Should I ask them for it?'

Simon considered for a moment. 'I think it would be very sensible to get the prosecution's results. That way we can be sure there's no funny business.'

As soon as they were home, Mills sent a message to Rogerson's asking to see the police test results. She thought about providing a reason for her request but decided she would wait for their reaction. If they asked her why she wanted it, she could say it was routine for comparison purposes.

Her inbox contained an email from Brenda asking her to ring as soon as she got the message. She answered straightaway.

'Listen, Mills. I got some interesting information from Harry about your friends at Rogerson Forensics. Have you met, Derek MacDonald?'

'Yes, he seems to be the boss.'

'He is. I've made a few enquiries. There's another man called Damien Pawson.' She was obviously reading from notes. 'Do you want me to spell it?'

'No, I've met him.'

'Well he's some relation of the boss. I contacted an ex-CID guy from way back who knows about him. He has a past,' she said knowingly.

'A past? What d'you mean, Brenda?'

'His name has been associated with a company run by a man called Rodriguez. He had what they call a PONZI scheme together.'

She began to explain what she meant but Mills interrupted her. 'I know, it's a scam which gives returns for investors with money from later investors.'

'You're better informed than I was before this, pet,' Brenda admitted. 'Anyway, nothing was ever proved but MacDonald has got a mark against him as far as the police are concerned.'

This wasn't what Mills wanted to hear. 'Are you sure it's Derek MacDonald? He might have confused him with someone else.'

'No, he was definitely talking about MacDonald at Rogerson Forensics. And Damien Pawson, his son I think he said.'

'So has *he* got a record as well?' Mills asked irritably.

'No, neither of them have a record per se. Damien was found in possession of drugs but for his own use.'

'You mean it's all assumption?'

'I mean, Mills, it all adds up to a very dodgy forensic service.'

Mills agreed it sounded suspect, but she wasn't going to admit that to her old boss. When she came off the phone, Simon asked what Brenda had wanted and Mills explained, adding that she was stirring trouble by dragging up the past.

'Don't be silly, Mills. She's looking out for us, isn't she? She doesn't want us to be tripped up by association with these people.'

Mills knew he was right but told him that she'd wait to hear back from Damien. Simon was on his laptop, asking Mills for Derek and Damien's surnames. When she gave them, he asked why the company was called Rogerson.

'I don't know,' she replied touchily.

'I do,' he announced a few minutes later. 'The third company director is an Alan Rogerson. I wonder where he fits in?'

Mills sighed. Simon was trying to find problems where there may not be any. She went into the kitchen to prepare their meal, hoping their discussion was over. When Simon joined her half an hour later, he reported that he could find nothing on Alan Rogerson, then changed the subject to whether she'd thought any more about the trip to the States. She hadn't and told him so. He leaned across to take her hand, replying that, at the moment, it seemed as if everything they tried to discuss resulted in a stony silence. Mills nodded sadly.

'Then let's not talk about anything important this evening,' he suggested. 'We'll only speak if it's about something trivial.'

Mills smiled in agreement. It solves the problem for this evening, she thought, but what about tomorrow and the next day? It was all her fault. If only she'd not agreed to do work for Rogerson Forensics.

Mills was lecturing all morning but as soon as she was free, she took a sandwich and coffee back to her office. She wanted to find out more about the mysterious Mr Rogerson, who was so significant to the company that it was named after him. All three directors were listed under the same address in Newcastle, which appeared to be their registered office, belonging to a global investment company, but Companies House showed that Alan Rogerson was the major shareholder. She wasted the morning searching the internet without finding anyone of that name associated with forensics.

It was getting late, Simon would be seeking her out to leave in half an hour, but before that, she quickly made some calls. The first was to Nina who, as usual, expressed exasperation at her friend for yet another inappropriate request for police information but eventually agreed to see what she could find out about Alan Rogerson.

Mills began her call to Brenda by asking what Harry Fraser had said to her about his visit to the lab.

'He said he was surprised how well organised the lab is, considering.'

'Considering what?'

'That it's set up in a university, run by academics.'

'Charming.'

'No, listen Mills. He was very impressed with what you've done and with the expertise you have.'

'You mean Simon's, I suppose.'

'No, both of you... and Donna of course. No, he says he can see himself making use of your facilities so will be sending samples over very soon.'

At last, thought Mills. 'That is good news, thanks. And can I ask you for another favour?'

'Go on.'

Mills explained who Alan Rogerson was, asking if she could make discreet enquiries about his background. Brenda was delighted to help, saying it would give her something to do because she was bored with being stuck in during the bad weather.

Finally, Mills called the lab, hoping her technician was still around. She was about to give up when Donna answered, sounding out of breath.

'Sorry,' Mills said. 'Were you about to go home.'

'I was just locking up.'

'I'll be quick then. It's about Mr Alan Rogerson of Rogerson Forensics. I wondered if any of your mates in Wakefield know him.' She went on to explain why she was making enquiries.

'I can ask.'

'Would you? That's great.' Mills was startled by Simon appearing at the door, so quickly changed tack. 'Good luck with the analyses on my teeth. Bye.' She put the phone down. 'That was Donna,' she said, unsure why she felt it necessary to hide the true reason for her call.

Simon shrugged. 'Obviously.'

'I was just checking everything was on for tomorrow.'

'Yes, we were just discussing it in the lab. I thought you'd be there.'

'Ah, I've been rather busy,' she said. Then thinking of her conversation with Brenda, added, 'I've got some good news. Harry Fraser was very impressed with your great expertise and will be sending some work for us soon.'

'That's welcome news because I've just had a quick look at our account which is running very low.'

'I thought finances was my job.'

Simon held up a hand. 'I know but I wanted to recharge for the items I'd used for analysing the cocaine sample. I'll leave it until we've got some more income.'

'Is it that bad? I haven't done the accounts for this month yet.'

'There's a few hundred pounds in addition to Donna's salary but if we don't get money from somewhere soon, we're going to be in the red. Let's hope we don't have to rely on any more work from Rogerson's to keep us afloat,' he added.

Mills wondered whether if push came to shove, was it better to go bust than undertake work for a disreputable outfit? The atmosphere on the way home was subdued. She realised their pact to not discuss anything controversial was resulting in an absence of anything but the most trivial conversations. That evening she avoided further discussion by working on her research report, while Harris snored in front of the fire.

She didn't know that while Simon looked busy marking year-one practical reports, he was really pondering the sheet that Pawel's fiancée had handed him at the party. It listed a series of grants received by Prof Benson over the years since he'd come back to the UK. They made very interesting reading, particularly now that Simon had read up on biological warfare. Benson's research at the university had clearly been funded by the US Department of Defense for many years. The titles of the projects were innocent enough but the purpose behind them was clear, once one knew what he'd been associated with in his younger days in the States. He had been working on biological weapons throughout his career. No wonder students had been protesting outside the university during the Gulf war. It was time to confront Professor Robert Benson.

Chapter 22

Simon planned to have a casual chat with Robert Benson over a cup of coffee, purporting to be fascinated by the work he'd been undertaking over the years on biological weapons. But when he wandered up to the professor's office at coffee time, the door was locked. He went to see the departmental administrator, who told him that the old man had finally decided to retire. She giggled, saying it was about time because he must be getting on for eighty.

'I don't suppose you can give me his address?' Simon asked innocently.

'Did Pawel say you were preparing an obituary for him?' she asked, tapping on her keyboard.

Simon nodded as a printer on the opposite end of the office burst into life. He watched her walk across, returning with a sheet of paper.

'It's in Darlington,' she commented, handing him the address and telephone number. 'Let me know if you need any help with the obituary,' she offered before sitting back down at her desk.

'Thanks,' he replied. 'I want to talk to him about the interesting work he's been doing.'

'Nice old gentleman, shame about his wife. I reckon that's why he's not coming into the department. It affects people more than you realise, losing someone after so long. Actually,' she began, as she opened her desk drawer, 'I've still got the sympathy card that some of his colleagues signed. Could you take it with you if you're going to see him?'

'Sure. I thought I might go this afternoon.'

He went back to his office, pleased that he now had an excuse to call him.

'Professor Benson? It's Simon Pringle from the Chemistry Department.'

It took a few attempts before the old man understood. Once he realised who was calling, he seemed uninterested.

Simon persisted. 'I've got a card from your colleagues. I thought I could drop it in. Will you be at home?'

The old man confirmed that he would be in all day. Simon was about to suggest early afternoon when he remembered he was supposed to be helping Donna in the lab.

'I'll be passing between five and six this evening, if that's all right?'

Benson responded that it didn't matter when he arrived, before finishing the call abruptly. Simon knew he would have to come clean with the reason for his interest in Prof Benson if they were taking a detour into Darlington on the way home. He grabbed a couple of coffees before making his way back to the lab, looking for Mills.

'She said she had departmental work to do,' explained Donna, as Simon gave her the spare drink. 'By the way, there's a letter for you. It looks important.'

She handed him a thick brown envelope. He ripped it open, unfolding several sheets of paperwork before scanning the contents.

'It's a request to attend court, I think,' he said.

Donna came over. 'From Rogerson's? I thought they said it wouldn't be necessary.'

Simon handed the papers to her. 'I don't understand. It's not from them.'

She surveyed the front page, turned to the next sheet, then handed them back to him. 'That's odd, the prosecution want you to give evidence. Why would they do that when we sent the report to the defence?'

'Is it unusual?' Simon asked, sensing her concern.

'I've not heard of it before, but I've only ever done work for the police so always appeared for the prosecution.'

Simon had never been an expert witness before, he'd had no training and wasn't sure he'd be any good at it. He did know he wouldn't want to do so on behalf of Rogerson's and said so.

'But you're being called for the prosecution,' Donna reminded him. 'Anyway, the role of an expert witness is to assist the court, not for one side or the other.'

'I can tell you know the ropes.'

'Oh yes, I did a two-day training course when I was at Wakefield.'

Mills had an early lecture followed by a tutorial but spent what was left of the morning in unsuccessful attempts to contact Brenda and Nina about the mysterious Mr Rogerson. She rang Simon to catch up with him over lunch, only to find he was too busy to meet her in the cafeteria.

'Can you fetch a sandwich for Donna as well, please Mills?' he asked. 'We're in the middle of your teeth, so to speak,' he added with a laugh.

His joke hid the concern he was feeling about his impending court appearance. Donna had been relating stories about times she'd been cross-examined by defence lawyers; sometimes they were very aggressive.

'Of course, I was always acting as an expert witness for the prosecution,' she said, as they washed their hands before going to the office for lunch.

'Why were you required to appear?'

'Because I'd done the forensic analyses. The defence like to try to pick holes in your results.'

Which didn't make Simon feel any better.

Mills was waiting for them with their food. 'Cheese for you, Simon, and chicken salad, that's right, isn't it?' she asked, passing it to Donna.

Simon unwrapped his sandwich slowly, wondering how to break the news to Mills. But Donna was already telling her.

'Simon has got to give evidence in the Rogerson case,' she said, biting into her sandwich.

Mills frowned. 'They didn't say they needed us to appear. I told them about the lack of chain of custody and we warned them about the dilution with lactose. Why on earth are they asking us to act as expert witnesses?'

'They're not,' explained Simon quietly, trying to cool the situation down in front of their technician. 'The request is from the prosecution.'

'What? They want you to stand up in court to defend our analyses when the samples have obviously been tampered with? They'll destroy you. No, they'll destroy *us*!'

Donna looked across at Simon anxiously. 'I'll go and put the next set of calculus samples on,' she said before retreating.

Mills looked close to tears, so Simon refrained from pointing out that it was he who had been against working for Rogerson's from the beginning. Instead he made them both a cup of tea before suggesting they talk through what needed to be done before the court date, which was set for the eighth of February.

'But that's…'

'Less than three weeks, I know. I need to get trained up in how to handle myself in court. Donna did a course; can you find one for me?'

Mills was biting her lip. 'But that still won't prepare you for what they'll do to you.'

'It's a start. From what Donna has been telling me, all I need to do is tell the truth. If they ask about a chain of custody, I'll tell them there wasn't one. I did the analytical work in the correct manner. I can't help that their sample was suspect.'

Mills went quiet. Simon waited. Finally she told him what she would do. 'I'll contact Rogerson's to ask for whatever they've disclosed to the prosecution. They may not have handed them anything since you weren't called by them but…' She paused. 'I suspect they're using our report in the case, which is how prosecuting counsel got your details. By the way, is the defendant a Malcolm O'Reilly?'

Simon reviewed the letter then looked up in surprise. 'Yes, it is.'

Fortunately he didn't ask Mills how she knew but went back into the lab to join Donna while Mills rang Derek MacDonald. He answered almost immediately. When she explained that Simon was required in court, there was silence at the other end, so she persisted by asking why their analytical report had been submitted as evidence without discussing it with them. Again he didn't respond.

'Perhaps it would be best to put me in touch with your defendant's solicitor,' she suggested frostily.

He agreed enthusiastically, giving her the name and number of a firm in Liverpool. 'Ask for Mr James,' he told her before putting the phone down with a thud.

Mills discovered that Mr James was a very busy man but the receptionist said he would return her call when he was back in the office. When asked what it concerned, Mills answered as professionally as she could.

'I wish to speak with him as a matter of urgency. It concerns the O'Reilly case. The prosecution has called our forensic analyst to give evidence.'

Her officious message appeared to work because within half an hour she received a call back from his number.

'Dr Sanderson?' he asked in a strong Liverpudlian accent. 'How can I help you?'

Mills explained how her laboratory had received a sample from Rogerson's for forensic analysis. That it was not a viable sample because there was no accompanying chain of custody.

'Is that a problem?'

Mills tried to retain her composure. 'Yes, it most certainly is. Anyone could have tampered with it or switched it for a completely different sample. As it is, the cocaine had been roughly diluted with lactose, as you've probably already seen in the report.'

'Look, actually I've not had a chance to examine the report in detail. There is a difference of opinion regarding the forensic evidence, which forms part of the case, but we just submit the information.'

'Rogerson's agreed we wouldn't be offering to appear as expert witnesses in the case. Derek must've told you.'

He ignored her question. 'Why don't I have a look at the report again. I'm sure there's been a mistake somewhere along the line. I'm sorry, I've got to go now, there's a call on the other line.'

Mills put the phone down quietly. She should have guessed. No self-respecting lawyer would work with Rogerson's so why did she expect Mr James to be any better? She rang her old boss to see if she had any advice for her.

'Have you ever been in this situation, Brenda?' she asked after explaining what had happened.

'No, pet, not exactly. I've been cross-examined by the prosecution when appearing for the defence, sometimes that comes to the same thing. The important thing to remember is that you're not working for one side or t'other…'

Mills finished it for her, '…you're working on behalf of the court.'

'Exactly. So if the defence hasn't done its job properly then it's for you to say so.'

'Really?' Mills thought about this. 'But what if Simon is asked about chain of custody?'

'He answers truthfully of course. He'll be under oath.'

'But won't that reflect badly on us? After all, why would we accept such a sample in the first place?'

'You tell me, Mills.' Her tone was serious.

'Because Derek MacDonald assured me it didn't matter.'

'So did you put that in the report?'

'We stated that there was no traceability, of course.'

'Well then, you're covered. It sounds as if Simon will need to be prepared for a rough ride but it should be fine, if he's honest.'

'He needs to do a training course in the next couple of weeks.'

'No problem, there are witness familiarisation courses online these days. Donna will know where to find them, I'm sure.'

Mills was about to finish their call when Brenda remembered something. 'Harry rang. He's sending a courier over this week with DNA samples for Donna. You can be certain they will be accompanied by all the correct documentation, including a chain of custody for you to sign.'

'Thank you, Brenda, that's great news.'

'Thought you'd be pleased.'

Mills was so busy relaying the events of the afternoon to Simon that she didn't notice which way they'd turned out of campus. It was only after a few minutes that she demanded to know why they were going in the wrong direction.

'Prof Benson has finally drifted away from the department but his colleagues have signed a sympathy card. I said I'd drop it in.'

'Why you? You hardly knew him. He wasn't even in your department.'

'I don't think many people *knew* him and I've probably had more to do with him recently than the others.'

Benson's address was in a row of detached Victorian houses on the edge of town. They were set back from the road, so it was difficult to read the house names until Simon slowed the car to a crawl. Most of the houses appeared to be divided into flats, rather smart ones judging by the cars in the paved front gardens. But when they finally reached the one with the name "Arcadia" etched into the stone gatepost, the contrast was obvious. The front garden was overgrown and the wooden double gates, which were propped open, looked as if they'd collapse if moved. Brambles pulled at their clothes as they walked up the brick path. There was no response when Simon rang the bell, so he resorted to knocking on the ornate stained-glass window in the front door.

'Is he expecting you?' Mills asked after they'd stood under the porch light for several minutes.

Simon knocked again. 'I rang him earlier. Come on, he might be in the garden.'

Mills sighed. It was cold and dark so it seemed very unlikely that he would be outside. She followed Simon gingerly as he took a path leading round to the back of the house. Her foot slipped on something slimy and she grabbed his coat to steady herself. The rectangle of light illuminating the back garden came from what appeared to be the kitchen. Inside someone was seated at the table reading a newspaper.

'There he is,' said Simon, tapping on the window.

The old man peered in their direction with a startled expression.

Simon waved. 'Professor Benson, it's me, Simon Pringle.'

He rose from his chair and came over to struggle with the back door, finally forcing it open, It was hardly warmer inside than out. The professor was wearing a thick sweater with a woollen scarf wound round his neck. Simon introduced Mills, explaining that they were just passing on their way home. Benson resumed his seat, inviting them to join him in a glass of wine, which Simon immediately accepted, congratulating him on an excellent choice of Malbec. Mills refused, since she would now be driving them home, but there was no offer of an alternative cup of tea or coffee. Because Simon was already chatting with Benson, she asked the professor if she might look at his beautiful Victorian house.

He waved a hand dismissively, saying that it was far from beautiful but she'd find the sitting room through the hallway. He was right, the house had not been maintained well and she suspected it was a long time since it had seen a lick of paint. The sitting room, which was sizeable, was filled with big old furniture, uncomfortable-looking chairs, and a threadbare sofa. It was dominated by a large ornate fireplace, spoiled by the insertion of a modern gas fire. She shouldn't criticise, she decided, because the couple had been getting on in years, his wife was unwell and it would be difficult to keep up a place this size. As she wandered back towards the kitchen, she could see that Simon was deep in conversation with the professor, who was opening another bottle of wine. She decided to explore upstairs.

The wide wooden staircase curved round onto the central landing. There were six doors, three on each side. The bathroom door was open, revealing a suite in avocado green. Next to it was the professor's bedroom. The only other door that was ajar led to a smaller room. It was a study lined with bookshelves, a heavy desk at the window and cupboards on the end wall. Mills studied the book titles as she wandered round the room; they were mainly scientific monographs. There were piles of journals on the floor with titles including words like pathogens, disease and toxins. A glass-fronted bookcase contained bound journals and on the top shelf, she spotted a single tiny glass vial with a rubber septum like medics use for injections. Curious, she tried the cupboard door but it was locked.

She was tiptoeing back down the stairs when Simon appeared in the hall, calling her name.

'What are you doing?' he asked in a whisper.

'Just looking round,' she replied. 'He said it was all right.'

He ushered her back into the kitchen saying, 'Thank you, Robert, for the wine and the chat. It's very interesting to talk to you.'

'You must come again,' the old man replied cheerily. 'I don't get any visitors except for my daughter, Janine.'

Mills insisted on driving home, pointing out that while he was knocking back the wine, she had been touring the house.

'Really?' Simon asked.

'For your information, his study is packed with books and journals on toxins.'

'Interesting.'

'And there's a vial of liquid in his cupboard.'

'I wonder what that is?'

'I couldn't see because the cupboard was locked.'

Simon was quiet for a while, so Mills asked what he'd discussed while she was snooping about.

'This and that. I wanted to find out when he gave up research on biological warfare. He was non-committal at first but he was beginning to open up a bit when he suddenly changed the subject. I'm sure if I saw him again…'

'Simon, are you thinking he is somehow related to the mysterious bacterium that Martin sent off to Porton Down?'

Chapter 23

Mills had insisted that Simon contact Martin first thing in the morning to find out what progress he'd made. She'd told him she'd be in the Archaeology Department catching up on her academic commitments, including a first-year practical and third year tutorial, so there would be no time to talk before lunch.

He knew she would expect an answer by then, so was outside Martin's office when the microbiologist arrived for work just after nine. The poor guy looked nervous when he came down the corridor, asking anxiously if there was something wrong.

'No, everything's cool,' replied Simon, realising how silly he sounded. It was a habit he'd picked up from Arnie and he resolved to break it immediately.

'We... I was wondering if you've heard back from Porton Down yet?'

'Yes, didn't I message you? They're happy it's not a problem, it says so in their report.'

'You've got a report?' Simon was irritated that he hadn't told him sooner.

'It only arrived yesterday. I'll give you a copy,' he added, unlocking the door to his office. 'It's a bit of a disappointment. They weren't too worried about it.'

'Why?'

Simon could see the Porton Down header on the sheet of paper he picked up from his desk. 'It's to do with its mode of transmission. They conclude it won't spread among the population because it can't self-replicate in the field. The route of infection is entirely through ingestion. If it was made in sufficiently large quantities, it could be dispersed to infect a whole population, but you saw how difficult it was to culture. Their conclusion is that it's a toxin with no future as a weapon, although they didn't say the last bit in so many words,' he added with a grin.

'So you're saying that even if it was the cause of... our woman's death, it isn't a threat to anyone else?' He carefully avoided naming Mrs Benson.

'Not unless they're infected in the same way.' Martin looked anxiously across his desk. 'How *did* she ingest it?'

Simon shrugged. He didn't really want to share his half-baked conjecture with him at this stage. He made an excuse about a teaching duty and left, after asking Martin to email him a copy of the report. Mills found him in his office several hours later, deep in thought.

'You look busy,' she said sarcastically.

'What?' He looked at her for a second before leaning back with a yawn. 'Yes, sorry, I was thinking.'

'Well, I've had a busy morning too but I've been able to have a quick look through the results Donna gave me.'

'The teeth *I* helped her with?' he asked pointedly.

'Yes, thank you, Simon, for your assistance. So, they're looking really good. It's brilliant having a vegan and a big meat-eater in the modern group. It demonstrates the hypothesis perfectly.'

Simon did his best to respond enthusiastically but Mills wasn't fooled. She approached the new topic diplomatically. 'Did you get a chance to speak to Martin?'

'Yes.'

'And?'

He replied by passing her the letter from Porton Down.

'Am I allowed to read this if I haven't signed the Official Secrets Act?' she asked, half-joking.

'You are, Mills, because there's nothing secret about it, as they explain.'

She stood reading the contents then placed the letter back on his desk. 'So where did the bug come from?' she asked.

'Who knows?' he replied with a sigh. 'C'mon, it's time for lunch.' He was putting on his jacket as he headed for the door.

'Hang on a minute, Simon. Martin should be able to help. Why don't we ask him?'

'Because he asked me the same question. All they know is that she "ingested" it somehow, it isn't contagious and unlikely to affect anyone else. I quote, "it is a toxin without a future". So shall we eat?' He omitted the bit about "as a weapon" because he didn't want to share that thought with Mills, not yet.

Immediately after lunch, Mills went to find Donna. She was busy copying the serial numbers from plastic bags into their registration file. When Mills enquired where they were from, Donna explained that they'd arrived by special courier from Harry Fraser's lab, as Brenda had promised. There was nothing too challenging: fingerprint and DNA on items from a particularly violent robbery. It was routine work for Donna. When the technician had completed the formalities, she took the samples through to the secure storeroom in the lab. When she returned, Mills had a question for her.

'Brenda said you'd know of an online witness course we

can put Simon onto.'

Donna pulled a face. 'It's a while since I did one of those,' she admitted. 'Let's have a look.' Mills waited while she searched the internet until she found what she was looking for. 'This is the place. I did one of their courses a few years ago. It was two days with quite a bit on role playing but there were eight of us on the course and we all had a turn to be cross-examined.'

They read through the details on the screen together.

'It obviously takes less time if there's only one person being trained,' observed Mills.

'And it says here that it's best to do the course three weeks before the trial, to allow time to reflect on what's been learnt,' Donna added.

'I reckon we could run through some role-playing with him as well,' suggested Mills. 'We'll have to consider how damaging Simon's evidence will be to us.'

Mills made enquiries online and when Simon came into the lab at the end of the day, she told him he was booked for a one-to-one with the training company on the following Tuesday.

'Meanwhile, Donna has set aside Monday morning to give you the benefit of her experience and don't say you're busy because I've checked your calendar.'

Donna was within earshot so Simon's response was suitably positive but once they were in the car, he complained that he could have organised the training himself.

'I'm sorry, Simon, but it's too important to be left to the last minute.' Before he could object, she continued, 'Donna has done loads of cases and I've been in the Crown Court before. Believe me, it's no fun and this time it's worse than usual so we need you to be up to speed and well-prepared. Don't take this the wrong way, but you've got no experience of what appearing as an expert witness involves, have you?'

'I hear what you're saying, Mills, but give me some credit. I want us to survive this as much as you do.'

She apologised for becoming overbearing.

He patted her knee. 'I'm used to it,' he muttered with a sigh.

'So you're OK with this court appearance thing?'

'If it helps the business. But for what it's worth, I don't think we should take any more work from Rogerson's in future.'

At last, that was something they could agree on. Mills told him that Donna was now working on Harry Fraser's samples, from a legitimate forensic service thanks to Brenda's help. She had Simon to thank for that indirectly, since he had suggested going to her old boss for advice. At last they were back on an even keel. As they drove home on Friday evening, Mills told Simon they would have to spend the weekend tidying the cottage because it had become a tip since he'd moved in. It was true that the place seemed to have shrunk now that the spare room was full of Simon's personal belongings from Osmotherley. Her cottage had a tiny attic where he could store things like Arnie's roller blades and Simon's cricket bat until the summer.

Next morning, the lurcher left pawprints in the thin layer of snow that had fallen overnight. Icy winds whipped across the moor, making her eyes water as Mills turned round at the top of the track. She thought about the porridge that Simon had promised to have ready by the time they returned and jogged quickly back down to the cottage.

'It's icy on the road but we've got stuff in the freezer so we don't need to go out today,' she explained, adding that they would have the whole day to make the place habitable again.

It was a bone of contention that Mills was basically a tidy person. She liked "a place for everything and everything in its place". Simon wasn't particularly messy but he didn't appear to mind a clutter, as she called it. When he'd first moved in, she'd allocated sections of the bookcase, drawers and cupboards to him but he'd laughed, saying he didn't want to take over half her house. Consequently his belongings were all over the place. During the day she moved his books and clothes around, pointing out their new locations. Simon, exasperated, asked whether she planned to label the drawers and cupboards with his name.

'Where's that device you use to print out labels in the lab?' he asked, half-smiling. 'Shall I fetch it?'

Mills reluctantly admitted she might have been going over the top and offered to make lunch.

The wind had dropped on Sunday but it had snowed overnight once again, lying deep where it had drifted against the stone walls. Mills suggested walking to Gunnerside for lunch because there was something she wanted to discuss with Simon and it was always easier over a Sunday roast. The pub was crowded but they found a corner where Harris could settle under the table as usual. Simon placed their order and fetched their drinks, while Mills rehearsed how she would broach the subject.

'Come on then, out with it!' he said, placing a glass in

front of her before sitting down with his pint.

'What?'

'What is it that's worrying you? You've been quiet for the whole walk. What's on your mind?'

Mills hesitated before launching into her speech. 'I've been thinking about how Professor Benson's wife's death could be related to what you've found out about his background.' She waited.

'OK, and…?'

'I'm thinking it could be more than a coincidence.'

Simon was spluttering with laughter.

'What?' Mills asked.

He put his pint down to wipe his mouth. 'Is that all? I thought you were going to announce that you wouldn't come to the States with me this summer.'

That discussion was for another day, thought Mills. 'No, I wondered if you've thought about the possibility of there being a connection.'

Simon put his fork down. 'I did, but it seems so implausible. People get nasty bugs all the time, don't they?'

'But you said it was a particularly nasty bug, a strange one that hadn't been seen before.'

Simon agreed but he couldn't see how the old professor could have anything to do with it.

'Did you ask him about it when we visited him?' Mills asked.

'Of course not. I was just getting him to talk about his early research.'

'What did he tell you?'

'Very little.'

'Cagey then.'

'No, Mills. He'd just forgotten about it. It was a long time ago.'

'But you said he was still working for the Americans until a few years ago.'

'I started to ask him, but that was when he said he was getting tired, so I called you.'

'If you ask me, he'd drunk too much wine by then.'

Simon grinned. 'Probably.'

'But he enjoyed your visit so perhaps we should go again.'

'You think?'

'Maybe find out a bit more about your old friend Robert Benson.'

Simon knew she wouldn't leave it alone. She was like a dog with a bone once she got her teeth into something. Which reminded him that his lunch was getting cold.

'OK Mills, but can we get on with our meal in peace now please?'

'Certainly, although we *could* drop in to see him on Wednesday, after work.' She was already planning what she would do next time they visited the Victorian house with the evocative name, "Arcadia".

Chapter 24

More snow had fallen overnight. Despite their best efforts there was no possibility of getting down the lane, onto the road leading out of the dale. Simon was already in conversation with his technician, sorting out the practical session he would miss in the afternoon. Mills had no face-to-face commitments but there was plenty to occupy her on her laptop. When she called the lab to say they wouldn't be coming in, Donna reminded her that she'd offered to talk Simon through the role of witness, in preparation for the trial. Mills found him lighting the fire and offered to brew coffee before they settled down to work.

'Have you remembered that Donna is doing training with you this morning?' she called to him. His response was muffled. 'She's sending you an invitation to do it online, at ten as you agreed. You've got an hour to get ready.'

'What d'you mean?'

'To prepare yourself. She's going to go through your testimony. Have you read the report thoroughly?'

He appeared in the doorway. '*I* wrote the report so I should know the details.'

'Just saying. I don't want her giving you a hard time.'

He laughed. 'I don't think that's going to happen. I've had to show her how to use the equipment I used, remember?'

She bit her tongue. Donna had a sharp analytical brain so Mills was sure she would have scrutinised the report,

189

highlighting all the places where the prosecution might attack it. When the allotted time arrived, Mills offered to move into the kitchen so Simon could have some privacy. She hoped the session wouldn't last any longer than the planned hour because it wasn't the warmest part of the cottage. She heard Simon greet Donna when he logged on, asking about the weather. It seemed there was no sign of snow on or around the campus. Mills tried to concentrate but could hear their conversation, particularly when Simon's voice increased in volume as he became muddled and irritated.

'…with a methodology that I've been using for years with standards that are recognised internationally. What do you mean? I…'

She could hear Donna suggesting that perhaps he wasn't used to routinely analysing street drugs. That as an academic he was more used to working with pure materials. This time he retaliated that he'd run projects in the States involving crack cocaine. Now Donna was going through the findings in the report, one at a time. When she reached the part about the dilution of the drug with lactose, Simon spent far too long explaining what heterogeneity meant. Mills could sense that Donna was waiting to the very end before introducing the item that would blow the case out of the water.

'Can you tell me why there is nothing in the report about chain of custody?' Donna was asking.

'Isn't there?'

Mills cringed while Donna explained the importance of that particular missing link between the crime and the forensics.

'Without the chain of custody you can't prove the sample

was the one found on the defendant,' she was explaining patiently. Simon asked Donna how he should respond. 'You'll be under oath, just tell the truth.'

As soon as Mills heard Simon finishing the call, she went into the sitting room to warm herself up again by the fire, asking how the interrogation had gone.

'Nightmare, Mills. It was a car crash. You're going to have to help me sort this out.'

'Of course. So let's start with the last issue. Remember we put in our report that there was no chain of custody.'

'So why did they submit the forensics as evidence?'

'Exactly. We don't understand why so you can say that. If necessary, tell them you know it doesn't make sense. I'm going to contact the defendant's solicitor again, to see if the lawyer has read our report yet. Whether he has or not, I'll ask him to withdraw the evidence and explain why. It's not too late, Simon. In fact, if you heat up some soup, I'll ring him now.'

It didn't go as she'd anticipated. Propelled by the disastrous responses Simon had given to Donna, Mills was determined to get their forensic report removed from the case. She began her conversation with Mr James assertively, explaining that the sample was not received in a suitable manner to be used as forensic evidence. Her analyst could not defend the findings and it would be laughed out of court.

'I hear what you're saying, my dear, I am sympathetic but it's not that simple.'

Ignoring his patronising tone, she continued to list reasons why the evidence would not help his case but he simply offered to discuss it with their barrister and get back to her. Mills thanked him politely, certain that any lawyer worth their salt would understand how problematic the evidence was.

'It sounds promising,' she told Simon when she joined him in the kitchen.

Mills had teaching commitments the following day. The snow hadn't thawed completely but when Simon returned from walking Harris, he reported that the main road was clear. When Mills popped next door to warn Muriel that they would be leaving Harris as usual, her neighbour insisted on giving them flapjack "in case you get stuck on the way", warning that the forecast was looking bad. Once they left the dale, however, all signs of snow evaporated and once again Simon questioned whether it was sensible to continue living in Mossy Bank during the winter. Mills said nothing because they'd had this conversation several times in the past and he knew she wouldn't leave the cottage, even for a few months.

As soon as they reached campus, Simon rushed off to prepare for his online witness training course. Mills spent the morning teaching before returning to her office, where Nige greeted her in his usual cheery manner.

'Where were you yesterday?' he asked.

When she responded that she was snowed in, he raised his eyebrows and snorted in disbelief. 'By the way, Nina said to ring her.'

Did that mean she had some information on the mysterious Mr Rogerson, Mills wondered. She waited until Nige disappeared before making the call.

'Dr Sanderson.' Her friend responded in her "official" voice, so Mills knew she was not alone in the office.

'Detective Sergeant Featherstone.'

'You asked me to make some enquiries?'

'Mr Rogerson?'

'Exactly. It seems that there is previous form, principally for financial irregularities but also there are possible links to organised crime.'

'A criminal record?'

'No. But I'd like you to keep me informed if you find anything that we should know about so I can update the relevant people.'

'Understood. And thanks Nina, we're trying to distance ourselves from the company to be honest.'

'That's probably very wise, Dr Sanderson,' she replied before ending the call.

Mills considered her options while she wandered over to the Chemistry Department to find Simon. Not that she intended to share Nina's news with him, her main focus was to extract him from his court appearance.

'So how did the course go this morning?' she asked him when she found him in the lab.

'Brilliant,' he replied, pressing a few buttons on the instrument in front of him before removing his lab coat. 'They said I would make a very good expert witness.'

Mills laughed, thinking he was joking.

'No, seriously. They said I had gravitas which would instil confidence in the jury. There's another session of role play this afternoon.'

'OK, so let's get some lunch so you can tell me what you covered.'

As Simon described the course in detail, Mills understood why he'd performed so well. Professional courses work with role play, using relevant examples, because legally they are not allowed to rehearse witnesses for their own court appearances. The evidence that Simon was given to work with had nothing to do with his own area of expertise, so didn't carry the flaws of their forensic evidence. Mills was unsure whether to point this out to him or not, because the course had clearly restored his confidence. She decided to congratulate him before changing the subject.

'I've started writing my paper on the teeth,' she began. 'The European Meeting on Forensic Archaeology is being held in Germany in August. I thought I'd put an abstract in.'

'When is it exactly?' he asked without looking up.

'Twenty-fifth and twenty-sixth, in Dresden. We could make a trip of it.'

Mills guessed why there was no response: he was probably thinking about the plans to visit his son. She'd checked when the US schools closed for the summer and it seemed as though he would be off from June to September, leaving plenty of time, even if she did decide to go with him. His silence made her wonder if he'd already arranged dates with Dianne. She waited until they'd finished eating before asking whether the conference dates were a problem.

'Can we discuss it later?' he asked, looking at his watch. 'I've got to get back for the other half of my course.'

Mills returned to her office to complete the abstract for the conference, submitting it before heading to the lab to tell Donna. Her technician had just finished examining fingerprints on the burglary items from Harry Robson.

'Bit like old times,' Mills commented. 'By the way, thanks for putting Simon straight yesterday.'

'I'm sure he'll find today's course really useful,' she

replied. 'He told me it was going well.'

Mills explained that she hoped to avoid O'Reilly's defence from using their forensic evidence in the case altogether.

'I tried to find out about Mr Rogerson, Mills. But no-one in the Wakefield lab had heard of him.'

Mills confided that he might have criminal connections, which was a good reason for avoiding any further connection with Rogerson Forensic Laboratories.

Simon had been keen to tell Mills about his witness training, spending most of the previous evening describing the course in detail. Although she was already familiar with the process, she'd encouraged him to explain it all again, for his benefit rather than hers. She was pleased to see him so enthusiastic about that aspect of their forensic service, hoping he would be able to make use of his newly gained knowledge eventually, because she was certain he wouldn't need it in the O'Reilly case, once the defence barrister saw reason.

Mills had suggested they visit Professor Benson after work the following day, but this time they should take a bottle of wine plus some cheesy snacks. Simon agreed. He was keen to chat with the old man again, hoping to delve into his more recent research interests. Mills had a different idea, which she kept to herself.

They found "Arcadia" a little more easily than on their first visit but the evening seemed darker as they struggled up the path to the front door. Simon had tried calling ahead but there had been no answer so they were relieved to see a light on in the hall. They knocked loudly for several minutes until a shadow appeared and door opened slowly.

This time Benson recognised Simon, inviting him in like an old friend. He gave Mills a puzzled look before ushering them down the hall into the kitchen. Delighted by the bottle of wine, he immediately fetched two glasses, ignoring Mills, which suited her fine as she drifted quietly into the hall and up the stairs to the study. There, she went straight to the glass-fronted cupboard to try the handle but, of course, it was still locked. Looking round, she made for the desk, quietly opening each drawer in turn to examine its contents. In the bottom drawer on the right was a tobacco tin containing several small keys. She took them over to the cupboard, trying each in turn until there was a satisfying click.

She turned the glass vial in her hand but there was no label, nothing to indicate what it contained. She placed it carefully in the small plastic box she'd brought specifically for the purpose, returning it to her coat pocket. She thought there was little risk that the old man would notice it was gone. She listened for any sound from downstairs as she locked the cupboard, before replacing the key in the tin and back into the drawer. She flicked through the letters and papers on his desk, without finding anything interesting, and was about to check his filing cabinet when she heard the front door opening.

'It's only me!' a woman's voice called.

Mills crept out of the study towards the bathroom as she heard footsteps retreating down the hall. She flushed the toilet before descending the stairs, ready with her excuses. Expecting to find Rachel Clark in the kitchen, she was surprised to meet a plump woman wearing a nurse's uniform.

Chapter 25

'This is my partner, Mills.' Simon looked uncomfortable as he explained who she was.

'I was just visiting the…' Mills pointed at the ceiling.

The nurse was smiling as she raised a chubby hand in greeting. 'I'm Janine. I usually pop in after my shift when I can. Mondays and Wednesdays, not on a Friday, but two or three times a week, don't I Dad?'

Her father was nodding without enthusiasm. Mills assumed this was his biological daughter, who Rachel thought was responsible for her mother's death. The woman deposited a large casserole dish on the table before telling them how she needed to keep an eye on him now that he was living alone, speaking as if he wasn't there. She commented that it was nice for him to have some company, adding that he had to be careful not to overindulge with his heart being what it was, indicating the empty wine bottle.

Mills told her they were fascinated by the work her father had been doing over the years.

Janine shrugged. 'We're very proud of his work. I don't understand what it's about but I know he's won awards over the years. But that's all over now you've decided to retire, isn't it Dad?'

She directed the last remark at her father, who responded grumpily that he'd given up driving so it was difficult to get to the university. She beamed at them as if to say, "what can you do with him?" and Mills smiled back in sisterly accord. She liked the warm, down-to-earth woman, who was so unlike her stepsister. When Janine told her father she'd heat up his dinner, Mills indicated to Simon that it was time to leave.

'Do come again,' insisted the nurse when she saw them to the door. 'The university was his life. I don't know how he'll manage without that focus.'

On the way home, Mills asked Simon what they'd talked about when they were alone.

'I asked him if he'd worked on any interesting projects funded by the US recently.'

'That was a bit direct.'

'He's rather… I don't know… all over the place. I don't think he's coping well with his wife's death. He was more coherent when he came to see me before Christmas.'

'Maybe he's on medication for depression; that might make him disoriented.'

'Possibly. Anyway he was telling me about a project called Medusa.'

'Like the gorgon?' asked Mills who was interested in Greek mythology.

'Possibly. Anyway, this was an American project that he worked on over here, but I don't know what it refers to.'

'Medusa turned people to stone. It was a curse.'

'Really?'

At home, Mills waited until Simon was busy upstairs before transferring the plastic box into the bag that she carried to work each day. She would tell Simon about it, of course, but she'd have to find the right moment. He could be difficult about her actions sometimes, if he thought they weren't entirely "above board". He announced he had a Zoom call and, when he re-appeared, he was anxious to discuss their potential visit to the States again.

'How about three weeks starting in the last week of July?' he suggested.

He'd obviously just been discussing dates with Arnie's mother.

'I haven't said I'd go yet.'

'It won't interfere with your conference.'

'I don't even know if they'll accept my abstract. If they don't, I won't get the funds to go anyway.'

He looked exasperated. 'When will you hear? Because I've just got Dianne to alter her plans so we can use the cabin on the lake for some of the time.' He sat down and put his arm round her shoulder. 'Look, it'll be fun. You'll love it, I promise. What's not to like?'

Mills wouldn't admit how strongly she feared his son would dislike her. She remembered the intense feelings of animosity she'd had for Fiona at first. It had taken years for her to learn to accept her father's wife.

Desperate for anything to turn the focus away from her relationship with his son, Mills decided to admit what she had in her bag. 'There's something I want to tell you,' she began.

He leaned in, sympathetically. 'What is it, love?'

'It's about that vial.'

His faced straightened as he moved his arm from her shoulder. 'What vial?'

'I told you about it, the one in Prof Benson's study. Well I brought it out with me. I thought we could ask Martin to have a look at it.'

It took a moment for Simon to absorb what she'd just told him. 'No, Mills, you can't do that. We'll have to take it back. He'll know you've taken it. What is it? Mills, are you mad?' His voice was growing louder.

'I knew you'd go nuts, that's why I wasn't going to tell you.'

'I'm glad you have, so we can do the right thing. I'll return it and explain it was a mistake.'

Mills laughed. 'You can't do that!'

'I can and I will!'

'Then I won't go to America with you,' Mills shouted as she left the room.

Simon was no fool. He knew further discussion was pointless until Mills calmed down. And he'd already guessed the reason for her outburst: she couldn't accept that Arnie was excited to meet her. He knew she had reservations about the trip, having seen how she was around Fiona. Given the rest of the evening to think about it, Simon decided to turn the threat around. When he went up to bed, he told her that he would let her test the vial, but only if she promised to accompany him to the States.

At breakfast Simon asked, in a light-hearted way, whether Mills had decided to accept the terms of his truce.

'I know it's a big ask for you to come all the way across the Atlantic to meet my family but it would mean a lot, you know that don't you?' She nodded. 'And you know that I feel really uncomfortable with you taking stuff from someone's house without their permission?'

Mills spooned the last drops of milk from her cereal bowl. 'All right, you win,' she said grudgingly, hoping she sounded convincing. 'I'll *think* about it.'

Simon was delighted. He talked non-stop in the car about the places they could visit, including the cabin on the lake belonging to his ex-wife's parents, where they could fish and swim with Arnie.

'Won't he get bored on his own with us?' she asked.

'No, I've promised we'll bring his dog. By the way, Muriel says she's fine with the dates.'

'But three weeks…'

'Harris will love it. He's spoiled rotten when he's next door and she said her grandchildren were visiting for the last week so he won't be bored either!'

As soon as they reached the campus, they went together to find Martin. His lab was empty but a student said he was expected back in a few minutes so, while they waited, Simon asked to see the vial. Mills extracted the plastic box from her bag, opening it on the bench.

'It's very small,' he remarked, examining it closely.

'Hopefully Martin will only need a tiny amount to culture.'

'So what are you expecting him to find?'

Mills shrugged. 'I don't know. Maybe a match to the other bug.'

'The one that killed Mrs Benson.' It was a statement not a question. He'd put two and two together already but really didn't want it to make four. 'So that's what you're asking Martin to look for, nothing else?'

'Well, if he finds anything interesting…' She stopped as Martin burst through the door carrying a pile of notebooks.

'Oh, hello. Did you want me?'

'Yes.' They both answered at once.

Simon indicated that he would let Mills speak.

'Martin, I've got a sample here.'

He was staring at the tiny vial. 'So I see.'

'It's not work, more of a favour really…'

'She means we can't pay you for it,' interrupted Simon.

'OK,' he said slowly, putting the notebooks down on a bench.

Mills handed him the tiny bottle. 'I'd like to know if it contains anything related to the sample you cultured for us. I know there's only a little there but I'd like to keep as much as possible, so could you take just a tiny amount please?'

He held it up to the light, before asking, 'Where did it come from?'

'We can't divulge that,' Simon interjected quickly before Mills could respond.

Martin removed his glasses to rub them on his jumper, before replacing to scrutinise the sample again.

'There is a relatively simple set of experiments I can do, now I know what we're looking for,' he said. 'But you'll have to wait until next week before I can give you an answer.'

'That's brilliant! I thought it might take longer. Although is there any chance I could have the vial back before that?' she begged.

'Of course, I'll have taken what I need by tomorrow.'

Mills was able to collect the vial from Martin on the following afternoon. She checked to see there was plenty of liquid left before packing it carefully into the plastic box. She found Simon with Donna tidying up the lab, a job they were all supposed to help with on a Friday afternoon.

'Have you got it?' Simon asked conspiratorially when Donna went to empty the bins.

Mills nodded. 'In my bag. Shall we put it back this evening?'

'What if his daughter's there.'

'She won't be, will she? Didn't you hear her say that she doesn't go on Fridays?'

'If you're sure. I'll certainly be glad when it's back in its rightful place.'

They went off early, leaving Donna to finish the cleaning. The car park was already almost empty, with most members of staff anxious to get home before the snow forecast for the weekend. While Simon drove, Mills messaged Muriel to say they'd be back a little late.

'What excuse are we going to use for going back so soon?' he asked. 'He'll think it odd we keep turning up.'

'Well, Janine won't be dropping in with a meal for him so we could ask if he wants us to fetch fish and chips, as it's Friday.'

'Really? Is that the best we can do?'

'Chances are he'll say no.'

'Let's hope so.'

When they arrived at the house, it was in darkness but a light went on in the hall when they knocked. The professor looked as if he'd just woken up as he shuffled down to the kitchen. He didn't seem to notice Mills going straight upstairs using only the light from the hall.

'How are you, Robert?' Simon asked, taking a chair at the table.

The old man shook his head. 'What did you come for?' he asked.

'We wondered how you were, whether you fancied fish and chips if we fetched some?'

Benson was looking up at the ceiling anxiously. Simon could hear Mills walking around above them. 'She's just popped up to the bathroom,' he explained.

'Janine wanted to know what she was doing in my study.'

'She isn't in your study. She went to the bathroom.'

He looked annoyed. 'Janine saw her through the window when she was parking the car last week. She asked why she was in there.'

Simon tried to think of an excuse but simply said, 'I don't know. Perhaps she got lost.'

He hoped Mills would appear quickly to break the uneasy silence that had descended on the room.

Despite working in semi-darkness, it took just a few minutes for Mills to open the cupboard, replace the vial and lock up again. As a precaution, she flushed the toilet before going downstairs to join the others.

'Here she is!' announced Simon cheerily. 'I told Robert you needed the bathroom.'

Mills blushed. 'Did you ask him if he wanted us to get…?'

'No. No, he doesn't.'

'Can't take the fat in fish and chips these days,' Prof Benson declared grumpily. 'Bit of cheese and a glass of wine does me.'

Mills noticed the half-empty bottle on the table. She looked at Simon, who nodded and rose to his feet.

'In that case, Robert, we'll leave you in peace. There's a chance of snow again tonight so we'd better be going.'

The old man muttered something about seeing them out but remained seated, so they left unceremoniously. As soon as they were at the gate, Simon checked with Mills that she'd put the vial back in precisely the same position so Benson wouldn't notice.

'Simon, you can see how he is. He wouldn't have registered if I'd left it on his desk.'

'By the way, his daughter spotted you last time we were there. He was asking me why you were in his study.'

'Not to worry, he's probably already forgotten about it.'

'I agree he's not as bright as he was. His wife's death has clearly affected him really badly, poor guy.'

'Hmm.'

'What does that mean?'

'Nothing.'

'You think he's suffering from something else?'

'Yes, a guilty conscience. I'm sure that vial has something to do with her death.'

'Ridiculous.'

'So why are you delving into his past research? Admit it, Simon, you think there's a connection too.'

Chapter 26

Mills woke early on Saturday morning to the sound of gentle whining. She pulled on a sweater and shoved her feet into her fluffy slippers before venturing downstairs. It was just past seven, according to the kitchen clock.

'What's up Harris?' she asked, switching on the light before unlocking the back door.

As soon as it was open, the lurcher bounded outside into a deep layer of snow. After shaking himself, he cavorted round the tiny garden, throwing snow in all directions. Mills watched from the doorway as she waited for the kettle to boil. When the tea was made, she enticed him in with a treat then grabbed him in a towel to remove the worst of the snow from his paws. Twenty minutes later she had showered and dressed, ready to take him for his early morning walk, leaving Simon fast asleep.

In her opinion, Swaledale in winter was perfect. The dale was at peace with itself: sheep fed on forage collected in the summer and cows warm in their barns, smoke rising from cottages and pubs served good home cooked fare in front of roaring fires. Harris' footprints were the first to deface the smooth white surface of the track up the fell. He raced ahead, pushing his nose into the pristine snow.

'Slow down!' she called, as she did her best to keep up with him.

Soon he found rabbit tracks and was off in pursuit. Mills wandered along, knowing there were no sheep on this side of the fell, so there was little danger of losing him completely. Despite the snow, there was no wind to spoil her walk, so Mills was feeling relaxed as she strode across the moor. She told herself that it was the weekend so she should forget the worries of the week and enjoy Simon's company.

'I've got an idea,' she told him at breakfast. 'Why don't we walk to the "Punch Bowl" for lunch?'

He looked at her for a second before asking, 'At Low Row?'

'Yes. It's not too far. There's no point in trying to drive there until they clear the road.'

Eventually he was persuaded and they set off in plenty of time to arrive for lunch. As they walked, Simon raised the question of their trip to the States now that Mills had agreed to consider going. He could check availability of flights, assuring her that she wouldn't have to worry about a thing. Meanwhile she was thinking she would need a completely new wardrobe if she was going to meet Simon's ex-wife.

'You should join us on my next call with Arnie,' he suggested without looking at her. 'What d'you think?' he asked when she hadn't replied.

'He may not want me butting in on your Zoom time,' she replied.

'He'd like it. He's very mature for a twelve-year-old and genuinely pleased that you might be coming over to see him.'

'If you're sure.'

They knocked the snow off their boots and pulled the excess from the lurcher's paws before venturing into the pub. They removed their jackets, scarves and woolly hats before heading to the bar, ordering their drinks and food at the same time. There was quite a crowd for a Saturday but they found a table within sight of the fire, where Harris settled quietly at their feet, knowing that if he waited patiently, he would finally be rewarded.

'This is nice,' Mills said, looking round.

Simon sipped his pint. 'Makes a change from shopping.'

They sat in silence while Mills tried to think of something to say that didn't involve their work or Simon's family.

'Have you thought any more about joining the quoits team this year?' she asked eventually.

When he'd heard that the pub was looking for new members to play quoits, Simon had asked what was involved. When she'd explained, he'd said that throwing a metal ring over a small post sounded easy. If that was the case, Mills had retorted, perhaps he should apply.

'I wonder if I'd be better at it than darts,' he pondered.

Mills laughed. Having witnessed his poor efforts, she commented that he couldn't be any worse.

They lingered over their meal, ordering coffee, enjoying the opportunity to relax. When they finally settled the bill and struggled into their outdoor clothes, it was nearly three o'clock. The sun was rapidly disappearing behind the hill, so there was a freezing chill in the air when they reached the cottage in the dusk.

That evening, huddled together in front of the fire, Simon tried once more to persuade Mills that she would enjoy their first trip abroad together. He described where Arnie was growing up with his mother, details of the house and yard, which he reminded her was how they described the garden. Mills explained that she had been to America once before, to a conference in Washington, so it wouldn't be a completely new experience. Simon showed her a view of the beach house owned by his ex-wife's parents.

Mills could see a stretch of blue water behind it. 'It's bigger than this cottage or even your place in Osmotherley,' she commented.

He explained that Dianne's father had made his money "in oil".

'The beach house has five bedrooms, three bathrooms, and a large games room. It has its own jetty, except they call it a dock, with a small dinghy. We could spend a couple of weeks there if you like, swimming and having barbecues on the beach. I know Arnie would love it.'

She admitted that it sounded idyllic, adding that she was sure it could be a great holiday, *if she decided to go.*

Mills was determined to get to campus after the weekend despite the poor road conditions. It was an anxious time, with just a week to go before the start of O' Reilly's trial, with still no word from the solicitor. When Simon returned from walking the dog, he announced that the snow was still thick in the lane. Mills argued that it would be clear once they reached the road to Reeth. In the end she persuaded him it would be passable in the Mini, although he insisted on fetching a shovel, blankets and a flask of coffee in case they got stuck.

Mills was glad she'd let Simon drive as they slipped and slithered their way down the lane to the road. It had obviously been cleared at some stage over the weekend but still had a thin covering of snow, making progress slow. They didn't see another vehicle until they reached Reeth, where the road was suddenly clear, despite the surrounding fields lying under a thick layer of white that glistened in the headlights. Gradually as they approached campus, all signs of snowfall disappeared.

Mills hoped to catch the elusive Mr James in his office first thing on a Monday morning. The receptionist picked up straight away, said she would put her through then left her hanging on for what seemed like several minutes. Just as she was about to give up, a man's voice asked what she wanted.

'Mr James?' There was a grunt at the other end. 'I'm calling to see if you've read our forensic report yet?'

He cleared his throat. 'Well, yes and no. It's not my area of expertise so I passed it on to the barrister. She's rather busy on another case at present.'

'So where does that leave Professor Pringle? Is he required in court next week or not?'

Another nervous cough. 'You'll have to take that up with her.'

'How do I…'

The phone went dead before Mills could get the barrister's contact details. She swore as she replaced the receiver, just as Nige came into the office.

'You sound in a good mood, Mills,' he commented, swinging his rucksack off his shoulder.

She described the concerns she had about Simon having to appear in court.

'Nina complains whenever she must appear. She's never a hundred percent happy with what she has to present. You should talk to her.'

'She's already warned me about Rogerson Forensics and about Rogerson himself. Why would the lawyers be any different?'

She thought about it while Nige unpacked his rucksack, piling books, files, and a lunch box on his desk. Perhaps there was a way to discover the name of the barrister defending O'Reilly.

'Is Nina at work today?' she asked Nige.

'Always.'

Mills sent a text, hoping her friend would respond quickly to her simple request, then went over to the lab, where Donna was finishing off the forensic work for Harry Fraser. The fingerprint results had already been dispatched; now the DNA samples were complete so Mills spent the rest of the morning checking Donna's report before it was sent off.

'Let's hope Mr Fraser is happy with our work,' Donna said as she pressed the send button on her computer.

'You've done a great job, with a very fast turnround. I'm sure he'll be delighted.'

'Hopefully he'll send us some more work, otherwise I'll be twiddling my thumbs.'

Mills agreed. There was no way to hide the fact they had nothing else for her to work on.

On the way home she told Simon what a good job Donna had done on Harry Fraser's samples.

'I'll call him tomorrow to let him know we can take on more work,' she suggested. 'And I could call Brenda to see if she can find us any more contacts like him.'

Mills waited until after dinner, when they'd washed up the dishes and settled in front of the fire, before asking Simon if he'd had a good day, hoping there was news about Prof Benson's vial.

'I called Martin this morning,' he said, 'but he's struggling to culture anything.'

'He did say it was difficult when he did the original sample.'

'But he thought he knew how to do it successfully now.'

When he, in turn, asked her if she'd had a good day, she replied that there was good news and bad news. He asked for the bad news first.

'O'Reilly's solicitor says we need to speak to the barrister but rang off without telling me how to make contact. If we don't persuade him to withdraw our report, you'll have to appear for the prosecution.'

'And is there any good news?'

'I asked Nina to help me find out who is acting as O'Reilly's defence. She's given me the name of the chambers and the barrister.'

'Did you get his contact details?'

'*Her* details. I found her online. Quite young, only qualified for a few years. I imagine she's unaware of exactly what she's got into. I've got the number of her clerk so I'll call in the morning.'

'Please do whatever it takes to get me out of appearing next week,' he begged.

She could tell he was deeply anxious about the impact his performance could have on not only his reputation but that of their forensic business. She tried to reassure him that she'd do her best but they both knew it all depended on the defence lawyer now.

Chapter 27

When Simon checked his inbox on Thursday morning, he found a message from Rachel Clark. He assumed she wanted to know why he hadn't returned her calls. But the message was even more worrying: *My stepsister has been in touch accusing me of asking you to snoop round our father's house. I'm sure it's all a misunderstanding but he is apparently distressed by your visits, which I'm sure are perfectly easy to explain. Of course, if you have discovered anything that you can share, I'd be very grateful. With kind regards Rachel Clark.*

Simon sat with his eyes closed. No, he wouldn't be sharing the fact that Mills had taken the vial from the house. Prof Benson was certainly worried by their intrusion, which could mean he had something to hide, of course. Eventually Simon decided he'd wait for the results of the tests on the vial before responding. He immediately contacted Martin, who said he was free later that afternoon.

When Simon met Mills for lunch, he told her they could see Martin at four. She said she hoped he'd discovered something interesting but Simon was more circumspect, warning her that there might have been nothing to find.

'Don't be so negative,' she complained.

'You're a fine one to talk. You've been going round with a long face all week.'

That was true for several reasons. She hadn't been able to get hold of O'Reilly's barrister, despite leaving messages with her clerk. Although Harry Fraser was pleased with their work, he still hadn't sent any more samples, and Brenda was too busy to talk about new leads because she was about to go on a coach trip to Scotland. Now, to top it all, Simon was suggesting Martin would have nothing for them. She was lecturing for the next two hours, so she picked up her tray, telling Simon she'd meet him in the Microbiology Department.

It was a relief to be doing something constructive with her time that afternoon. The first-year students were an enthusiastic bunch, so she'd divided them into groups to undertake mini-projects on the site she'd planned for their field work that summer. The time was taken up answering questions about the history of the area, the excavation itself and how they should write up their reports. She described the field work using photographs of the site from the previous year, depicting students at work dressed in shorts and T-shirts. Mills tried to explain that it would be fun although she understood that the students might find that hard to imagine as they sat shivering in the lecture theatre, in artificial light.

At the end of the session she ran from the lecture theatre directly to the Microbiology Department. Simon was already in conversation with Martin, so she asked outright whether the news was good or bad.

'Depends on what you call good,' the microbiologist replied. 'It's been quite an odd one really but I think I understand what's been happening.'

Mills looked at Simon questioningly but he just raised his eyebrows and nodded towards Martin. 'Listen,' he told her, 'it's really interesting.'

'Should I go through it all again, Simon?' he asked.

'I think you better had. I'm not sure I can explain it to

Mills as well as you can.'

Martin coughed nervously. 'I cultured a sample from the vial in the same way as before, because that's what you asked me to do. However, at first it produced nothing. Then I looked for the same markers I'd seen in the original sample, the one that went to Porton Down. And that's when it got interesting.' He was waiting for Mills to react.

She looked at Simon but he wasn't giving anything away. 'So what did you find?' she asked.

The microbiologist grinned. 'What is fascinating is that it contains two species with components very similar to your original sample.'

Mills cut him short. 'So are they the toxins that killed...' She stopped, realising that they hadn't shared Mrs Benson's identity with him.

Simon touched her arm. 'Martin believes these two species are not lethal but somehow when they're combined in the body, they may have formed a more deadly combination.'

Mills turned to Martin. 'Have you tried combining them?'

Her question appeared to startle him, rendering him speechless for a couple of seconds. 'No, no I haven't and I don't think I should.' Another pause before he asked, 'What exactly is the purpose of this work?'

Mills looked at Simon for help but he stared back at her. 'I, er, we... that is... we just wanted to understand where the killer bug had come from.'

'So where did you find this sample?'

Her face felt hot. 'I'd rather not say.'

Martin shrugged. 'Well I've done what you asked. I'll destroy the cultures and send you a brief note of the results.'

Mills felt they had lost the microbiologist's trust, he was frowning, the atmosphere had changed. Simon began thanking him awkwardly for his help but Martin ignored him as he fiddled with the papers on his desk. They left, closing the door gently behind them. Neither spoke until they were outside the building when Simon commented how difficult that had been.

'I couldn't tell him where we'd found the vial, could I?' Mills reasoned.

'Where *you* found it.'

The lampposts on the walkway shone dimly in the failing light as Mills picked her way along the paving stones avoiding the lines.

'Martin *has* proved there's a connection, hasn't he?' It was a genuine question because she thought she might have misunderstood.

'It's true that Mrs Benson was infected with the same microbes that Martin identified in the sample from the vial, but that doesn't prove how she died.'

They stood outside the Chemistry Department for a few minutes while Simon pointed out that the link between Mrs Benson's death and the contents of the vial was, at best, tenuous. He'd been asked for help by Rachel Clark but, so far, he hadn't given her any indication of how her mother had died. It would be irresponsible to tell her that he thought she'd been murdered by her husband. He explained this patiently to Mills before they returned to their respective offices without further discussion.

Simon spent the next hour formulating a response to Rachel's message. Robert Benson was responsible for the material in the vial, which could have resulted in his wife's death, if she'd been exposed to it. But how or why that had happened might never be known. So in the end he sent a simple response saying that he didn't know why her stepsister thought they'd been snooping; they had simply dropped in to see how Robert was enjoying his retirement. However, under the circumstances they wouldn't bother him again.

Back in the office, Mills quickly scrolled through her messages, but there was still nothing from the barrister. She checked her watch before trying the clerk's phone number again, to be told that she was out and would be in court for the whole of the following day.

Then, before she signed out, she spotted a message from the organisers of the archaeology conference. At last a piece of good news: they were inviting her to present her talk on the first day. Mills calculated she would be back from the first-year field trip with five days to spare before she would need to leave for Germany. It was going to be a busy summer.

When she told Simon her news on the way home, he sounded pleased for her but after she suggested he accompanied her to Germany, he said it was better if he didn't because of the cost.

'But my expenses will be paid for, so it's only the air fare and food for you.'

'I've been looking at flights to the US for the two of us, it's going to be an expensive trip.'

'I haven't said I'll come yet.'

'But you must. You'll be busy when you're at the conference so I'd just be in the way. Anyway, Harris will be happier if I stay at home.'

'You do realise that I'll be working in the field for a week between the US trip and Germany?'

'It sounds as if Harris and I will be having plenty of me-time then.'

It was only later in the evening that Simon felt ready to divulge that he'd heard back from Rachel Clark.

'What does she want now?' she asked.

'Janine has told her that you were snooping round Robert's study.'

Mills looked suitably shamefaced. 'What did you say?'

'I lied. I told her that Janine was mistaken but we wouldn't visit Benson again if it upset him.'

'Shame, I'd like to work out whether he's as confused as he appears most of the time. It could be a very clever act.'

'Really? You think he's pretending to be an absent-minded professor when he's really a wife-murdering psychopath?' Simon was looking at her in disbelief.

'I didn't say that.'

'You don't have to. I know you have your suspicions, but I believe there is probably an innocent explanation…'

'…after Martin's proved the vial contains the bacteria that killed her?'

'It doesn't make him a murderer though. It could have been an accident, couldn't it?'

'I think we should talk to the police.'

'By which you mean your friend Nina, I assume?'

'She'll know whether there's a case to answer.'

Simon shook his head with exasperation. It was typical of her, rushing to accuse the poor old man of an outrageous crime. There was probably a perfectly rational explanation.

'If there is, what is it?' asked Mills.

Simon thought for a moment. 'Robert worked on some

nasty bacteria for the US in the past. He's kept an example of his work locked in a cupboard at home. His wife, who is dying of cancer, decides it is a way of ending her life.'

'So she finds the key, opens the cupboard, locates a syringe to self-administer the contents of the vial to end it all, really? She wasn't even terminally ill, was she?'

'We don't know if she was or not, she may have been hiding it from her family.'

'Perhaps we should find out. Meanwhile, I'm going to ask Nina.'

Chapter 28

Mills suggested that, as it was Friday, they could take fish and chips round to Nina's that evening. She checked with Nige as soon as he was in the office.

'Sounds good to me. I'll get some beers in,' he replied. 'Though I'd better let the wife know.'

He called her immediately. If Nina suspected there was an ulterior motive for their visit, she didn't tell her husband. He gave Mills their order after explaining where to find the best local fish and chip shop.

'It will be good to catch up with you both,' he said. 'We'll all be in by six.'

Mills tried to contact the barrister again without success. This time the clerk said her current case had finished early so she'd taken the rest of the day off. Mills repeated her request for the woman to call her, without any real hope of a response at this late stage.

She turned her attention to finalising the following week's lectures until she was surprised to see Nige leaving because it was already after five. She was packing her bag when Simon appeared.

'Did you see my message about going to Nina's?' she asked.

'What about Harris?' he snapped.

'Muriel will give him his tea and settle him down in the cottage. It's all sorted.'

He was strangely subdued on the short drive to the chip shop, leaving Mills to fetch the order. When she returned with the food, she asked him what was wrong, assuming it was the stress of the court appearance, following a practice run with their technician.

'How did it go with Donna? Was it helpful to talk through it?' she asked.

'Yes, I guess so.' He paused as he concentrated on pulling out into the traffic. 'When we were discussing Rogerson's, she mentioned they had criminal connections. I said we didn't know that but she said *you* told her. Is that true?'

'I didn't want to worry you, not with the court thing hanging over us.'

'Well thanks a bunch!'

As soon as they parked outside the house, Mills went straight to the front door with the bag of food. Simon appeared beside her just as Rosie flung the door open to usher them inside. There was a flurry of activity as the children helped their mother with plates and cutlery, while Nige appeared with bottles of beer. The adults took their seats at the table, while the children sat in a row on the sofa with their food on their laps.

'This is nice,' began Nina. 'It seems ages since we've seen you properly. What have you been up to?'

'Don't ask,' said Simon without looking up.

Mills didn't want him discussing Rogerson's with Nina. It would only serve to reinforce the fact she'd not told him of her qualms about them.

'Simon is having to give evidence in court next Tuesday,' she remarked. 'It's his first time.'

Nina looked across at Mills. 'Is this the case you told me about?' she asked with a knowing look.

'Yes. I'm sure it will be fine though.'

Then Simon asked Nina to tell him about her own court appearances. Mills relaxed as her friend tactfully provided a series of anecdotes about times when things had gone wrong, but in an amusing way. As soon as they'd finished eating, Tomos and Owen wanted to show Simon their latest video game, so they disappeared upstairs with Nige, leaving "the girls" to tidy up. Soon Rosie had drifted away, leaving Mills free to express her concerns about Professor Benson. Her friend listened attentively until she had finished then asked a series of pertinent questions.

'Let me get this straight, Mills. How do you know he keeps poison in his house?'

She had to admit that she'd "sampled" his vial. Her friend looked appalled. She closed her eyes, opening them again slowly.

'So are you accusing him of deliberately storing a dangerous poison in his house that ultimately killed his wife?'

'Sort of, it's more of a bug than a poison.'

'That's beside the point. I have dangerous things in my house: bleach, medicines… all sorts of stuff that are hazardous to health but you're not suggesting he killed his wife, are you?'

'I don't know,' she answered sheepishly. 'I thought they might initiate a review of the original investigation.'

'Was there an original investigation?'

'Yes, they questioned him about his wife's death. In case he'd helped her commit suicide.'

'And had he?'

'Apparently not. Her daughter said she wasn't terminally ill and was recovering from her cancer.' She went on to explain that Rachel had asked for their help to establish the reason for her mother's death.

'I suppose I can at least say that you were working on behalf of the daughter. I'll see if I can trace who dealt with the original case,' Nina conceded. 'But I can't promise anything. Please don't *you* do anything, Mills, or you really will get yourself into trouble. You have your professional integrity to protect. Talking of which, Simon seems rather jittery about giving evidence next week.'

'He is, particularly now he knows how dodgy Rogerson's company is.'

'He'll be fine as long as he sticks to the truth.'

'That's what we keep telling him.'

Simon seemed in better spirits on the way home. Mills wasn't sure if it was due to the beer, or time spent with Nige and the boys, but he stretched out in the passenger seat chatting cheerily throughout the journey home. She hoped it meant he felt more confident about his forthcoming performance at the Crown Court in Newcastle.

Mills spent Sunday worrying about the online call that evening. Simon had insisted she join him on his five o'clock chat with Arnie. Despite her protestations, he was adamant she should meet his son face-to-face before their visit in August.

'But what will we talk about?' she groaned. 'I don't know any boys of his age.'

'You get on all right with Rosie Featherstone, don't you?'

'That's different, she's a girl.'

'And what do you discuss with *her*?'

'I don't know, books she's read, what she's been doing at school.'

'There you are then.'

In her view, American books and school were alien to her, but Simon told her his son was a Harry Potter fan and had read everything by Roald Dahl.

'And he'll be delighted to explain the American school system to you,' he added.

He suggested a quick snack before a brisk walk up on the moor until it was time for their call. They wrapped up well, and even tried putting a coat on Harris despite his protestations. Mills gave up eventually, declaring it had been a serious waste of money. It was a grey afternoon with a fierce wind that seemed to come straight at them whichever direction they were walking in. It was hard work to make progress but the lurcher appeared to be enjoying the exercise. They walked steadily uphill until they reached the point where they could look down on Muker and up to Keld in the distance, and then on until they joined the "Coast to Coast" route. Eventually, when the sun had disappeared behind the hills, Simon suggested they turn back, anxious not to be late for his son.

There was just time for a quick mug of tea before Simon set up his laptop. They arranged themselves on the sofa with Harris between them. It seemed odd that the lurcher needed no introduction when Mills did.

'Hi son!' Simon called as a skinny blond lad in a Manchester United football shirt materialised on the screen. 'I see you got the kit.'

The boy nodded. Simon looked at Mills expectantly.

'Hi Arnie. I'm Mills. How are you?' She immediately felt silly for asking.

'I'm very well thank you. How are you?' he replied in a broad American accent.

Simon burst out laughing. 'Wow, you've learnt some manners at last!'

He discussed premier league football with his son for a while then asked about school.

'Mills wants to know what you do in class these days,' he prompted.

Arnie was happy to explain which subjects he liked and those he disliked. When his father mentioned that Mills was an expert in archaeology and forensics, he was full of questions about things he'd seen on the "Discovery Channel". The hour and a half they spent online went quickly but Arnie had to go for his lunch. Mills knew their calls usually finished with Dianne joining the call to discuss stuff related to their son, but thankfully she didn't appear, so Simon closed the call after a subdued goodbye.

'There, that wasn't so bad, was it?' Simon asked, giving Mills a hug.

She agreed his son was a lovely polite, intelligent boy, mature for his years, although she'd had little idea of what to expect, if she was honest. Admittedly, she felt more relaxed about possibly meeting him in the flesh now. However, she stated that she would not muscle in on their family time every week, but make an intermittent appearance. It was all that he wished for, he assured her.

Simon shut himself away in his office on Monday morning, contemplating that he was less than twenty-four hours away from his court appearance. It wasn't a thought he wanted to dwell on but he felt it was important to be properly prepared mentally. He was therefore slightly annoyed by a tentative knock on his door. Tempted to ignore it, he called for whoever it was to enter. He repeated the invitation twice more as the door was opened gingerly by Pawel.

'Sorry, I couldn't hear you,' he said, shutting the door behind him. 'Am I disturbing you?'

'No, do sit down.'

The young man continued to hover by the door. 'I just wondered if you'd seen the notice about Prof Benson's leaving do. I assumed you'd be involved but when they said you weren't, I thought you should know.'

'When is it?' asked Simon, thinking about his court appearance.

'Wednesday lunchtime. I thought you might be giving a speech as you've been asked to do his obituary?'

Simon was put on the spot. The tale that he'd spun to get Pawel's fiancée to release confidential information had come back to bite him. He mumbled that he wasn't sure he could make it because of his appearance as an expert witness. Pawel was impressed, wanting to know more, but Simon said that unfortunately he wasn't allowed to discuss it. The young man checked his watch before rushing off to his next lecturing assignment, leaving Simon feeling uneasy.

That evening he shared his discomfort with Mills, explaining that he was almost pleased he had an excuse to miss Prof Benson's lunch. She agreed that it was best avoided, immediately changing the subject to ask what time he wanted to leave for Newcastle next morning. She'd offered to drive him there but he'd requested a lift to the station, preferring to take the train, in case they got stuck in traffic. Mills had wanted to go to court with him but Simon had been adamant he didn't want an audience for his performance.

They sat quietly in front of the television, avoiding further discussion of how the next day might pan out. Mills was thinking about Prof Benson's leaving do and how she might get an invitation to attend, since she was not part of his department. She felt that their work for Rachel Clark was a good enough reason so she would say she was there to represent the forensic team. There was no need to bother Simon with her decision, she thought, because he had more important things on his mind.

Chapter 29

Mills waited anxiously at Darlington for the train to arrive. It was ten minutes late when she checked her phone to see if Simon had messaged her yet; she'd not heard from him since she'd dropped him off in the morning. Unable to settle to anything properly all day, apart from a two-hour lecturing slot in the morning, she had wandered aimlessly between the lab and her office waiting for news. Even Nige had noticed how distracted she was, asking if she was unwell. When she explained where Simon was, he understood immediately.

'It's no big deal,' he reassured her. 'Nina's in court all the time, I don't let it worry me.'

'I don't suppose you do, Nige, but she's got years of experience. This is Simon's first time so I have good reason to be nervous.'

When people began to appear from the station, she got out of the car to look for Simon. When he finally emerged with the last trickle of passengers, Mills observed how smart he looked in his long black coat. He was wearing his only decent suit with the tie she'd picked out for him; he rarely had to dress so formally.

'Well, that was a waste of the day,' he commented before she could ask.

He settled into the passenger seat, clutching his briefcase on his knees. Mills waited until she reached the road out of the town before asking him to elaborate.

'They didn't need me,' he said.

'Oh that's a relief.' Mills suddenly felt as if a weight had been lifted.

'Not today, but I'm on the stand tomorrow. It was so boring. I thought I'd at least be able to sit in on the case, but I wasn't allowed into the courtroom.'

Mills hid her disappointment. 'You'll only be able to observe after you've given evidence,' she explained.

'I'm not sure I'll stay once it's over.'

'I could have picked you up earlier.'

'I didn't know I wasn't needed until this afternoon.'

He'd apparently been impressed by the striking building of the Law Courts on its quayside location, so had spent the time exploring after he'd sampled the café bar on the corner. He admitted that he'd be setting off with less trepidation the following day.

'I'll catch the earlier train so I have time for a decent coffee at the café first,' he declared.

'So that means you won't be able to attend Prof Benson's leaving bash.'

'No, thank goodness. Pawel thought I was going to give a speech.'

'So who should I send your apologies to?'

I don't know. Presumably it's being organised by the departmental administrator but you don't need to do anything, I'll send my apologies.'

'OK.' Despite that, Mills was going to call in next day to say how much she would like to give Robert her best wishes personally. Simon didn't need to know.

It was a tense drive to Darlington next morning. They set off late because Harris had to be persuaded from his bed earlier than usual. Simon was taking the bends faster than

Mills liked but she kept quiet, not wishing to make matters worse. Their parting was somewhat formal, as she took the car keys from him and wished him luck. She watched him disappear into the station, tempted to wait to see if the train was on time but deciding it wouldn't help to know one way or the other.

Simon found the railway carriage oppressively hot; the windows were steamed over and people were coughing loudly. But an advantage of taking the earlier train was that there were empty seats. He wondered briefly if he should go over the report again but decided that it was too late if he couldn't remember the finer details of his analysis by now. Thankfully the journey was over quickly, so he hardly had time to fret about it. Jumping up to retrieve his briefcase, he was the first to head for the door, pushing through the crowds on the platform, walking with determination to the café where he knew he could get a good strong coffee with a fresh Danish pastry.

Once inside the Law Courts building, it was the same process as the day before as he settled into the witness waiting room. People came in, sat for a while, then disappeared. No-one spoke so he couldn't guess if they were involved in his case. Eventually, after an hour, during which he was becoming increasingly edgy, he was ushered into the courtroom, which was laid out exactly as Donna had described. Taking the oath was precisely as he'd practised online with the professional trainer. So far so good. Then the prosecution lawyer began his questioning, asking him first to explain the forensic work he had done on the cocaine found in O'Reilly's flat when he was arrested.

Simon had gone through this in his head so many times

he feared it sounded over-rehearsed. He looked across at the jury, as he'd been trained to do when giving evidence, and their faces were all turned towards him. As he explained how he tested the sample, the young woman in the front row seemed to be taking notes, a man next to her kept nodding, as if agreeing with him. Mills had warned him to just answer the question but he'd been asked to describe the process, was he getting too technical?. He suddenly stopped to ask the barrister if he was providing too much detail. The judge interjected, politely suggesting that the prosecution get to the point.

'In that case, Professor Pringle,' the barrister continued, 'perhaps you could tell us about what you found.'

'The results? Well, basically the cocaine was mixed with a large amount of lactose.'

'And that, I understand, is a common way to dilute the drug?'

'Yes, it is.' He remembered to look at the jury when he replied.

'Can you explain why your analysis is at odds with those from the police forensic laboratory? The same cocaine that you analysed.'

Simon hesitated while he thought about how to respond. He felt himself getting hot as he answered, 'I'm not aware of the results obtained by the police forensic laboratory.'

'Well let me tell you, Professor Pringle.' He indicated that the jury had already been informed of the data, emphasising that it had come from an accredited laboratory. 'The sample recovered by the police was found to be of a very high quality, which proves that Mr O'Reilly is not someone selling cocaine on the street but higher up in drug dealing circles. Would you agree that would be the case, since you are an expert in illegal drugs, Professor?'

'I would.' He wanted to say more but remembered Donna's advice: *less is more.*

Then the barrister started to dig in, starting with the question that Mills had anticipated.

'So how can you know the origin of the sample you were given, when apparently you had no evidence of chain of custody?'

Simon had his response ready. 'We informed Rogerson Forensics that there was no chain of custody form associated with the sample, but we were told that it was not necessary. We therefore assumed the results of the analysis would not be used as evidence and did not require our usual rigorous standards of control.'

'Who told you that?'

'Rogerson Forensics.'

The barrister laughed. Turning to the jury, he said, 'I think we have already formed a view on the value of forensic evidence from that particular company.'

He indicated that he had finished and the defence lawyer shook her head when the judge asked if she wished to cross-examine. So Simon was told he could stand down without further questions. It wasn't a satisfactory end to his first appearance as an expert witness. He was puzzling over his interrogator's final comment, which suggested there had been additional forensic evidence given in court that had also been trashed by the prosecution.

It was a relief to step out onto the front steps of the building, where a blast of cold air seemed to come straight from the river. He pulled his coat tight as he rang Mills, dreading her scrutiny of his performance. When it went to voicemail, he told her he'd wait in Newcastle until he was sure she'd be at Darlington to meet him. It was a good excuse to grab something to eat at the café down the road. It was obviously popular with city workers but he was able to find a free corner and ordered a panini with a large cup of coffee. He was preoccupied sending Mills a text when he was aware of a man pulling a chair up to his table.

'Mind if I sit here?' he asked in a local accent.

Simon didn't have time to respond before he was shown a warrant card.

'Stuart Caldicott, Detective Sergeant.' He removed his trench-coat, hanging it over the chairback. 'I was in court when you were examined by our man.'

'Did you follow me here?' Simon asked, still smarting from his treatment by the prosecution.

Avoiding the question, the DS seated himself at the table. Simon guessed he was around fifty, his hair was greying and he was overweight, but his raincoat looked expensive and his suit was smart. The waitress was placing Simon's coffee on the table so the detective ordered himself an americano. When she'd gone, he apologised to Simon for disturbing him.

'I'm also sorry you had to go through that grilling this morning. It was an unusual situation that you found yourself in, being called by the prosecution when you were working for the other side.'

Simon sipped his coffee while he compiled his response. 'So was it your case?'

'Not exactly.' He broke off as the waitress arrived with his coffee. 'I've been leading a review of eight recent cases where evidence was handled by that outfit. You know they work almost exclusively with drug cases? Some of their dealings have proved particularly interesting.'

Simon listened, waiting to hear where the conversation was leading.

'This latest case follows the same pattern as the rest, except this is the first time Yardley Forensics has been involved.'

'It's the first case we've had from Rogerson's, and it will definitely be the last.'

'I got that impression this morning. The Yardley Forensics that I'm familiar with had a good reputation. There's a woman who runs it?'

'Dr Sanderson?'

'No, the name was Yardley.'

'Brenda, Dr Brenda Yardley. She retired and we, I mean Dr Sanderson and I, have taken it over.'

'I see.'

Simon felt that DS Caldicott really didn't see at all. He decided to ask about the prosecutor's comment that had puzzled him.

'What did the barrister mean when he said that the jury had already formed a view on the evidence from Rogerson's?'

The DS laughed. 'Oh you wouldn't have been in court when that was discussed. Just another piece of falsified evidence.'

Simon tried to remain calm. 'We didn't falsify evidence,' he said through clenched teeth.

If the waitress hadn't appeared with his panini, he would have got up and left.

'I'm sorry, mate.' The DS paused for a few seconds before continuing. 'What I meant was that we've got our eyes on Rogerson Forensics. There's plenty of circumstantial evidence but we just need something conclusive to tie a bow on it. What I'm telling you is in the strictest confidence, it mustn't go any further at this stage, understood?'

Simon nodded, wondering what was coming next.

'Do you think they will be sending you any more work?'

'After this morning? I doubt it. And anyway, my business partner won't countenance it without all the proper documentation.'

'OK, we'll deal with that when it comes along but I need you to do one more job for Rogerson's. We're planning to send them our own sample so we can follow it through as a test case. Up to now it's hearsay but this will be the final definitive evidence.'

'I'd have to discuss it with my colleague.'

'Maybe later but not until it's all arranged. So you're in?'

He hesitated. 'I suppose so.' What else could he say?

They exchanged contact details before the detective struggled into his coat, leaving Simon to ponder what exactly he'd just agreed to.

Chapter 30

The centre of the seminar room in the Biology Department had been cleared by pushing the tables and chairs against the walls. Mills spotted Professor Benson as soon as she entered. He was surrounded by three elderly men in suits who looked past retirement age themselves. In fact the room was divided into two distinct groups: around a dozen dons from Benson's generation had come to wish him on his way, and half a dozen young lecturers and researchers, who had probably only turned up for the free lunch and booze. Mills recognised none of them except the departmental administrator who had given her permission to attend the gathering. She was filling Professor Benson's glass with red wine before coming over to offer some to Mills.

'Thanks, but I'm driving over to pick Simon up this afternoon,' she explained. 'But thank you for inviting me.'

'To be honest I'm glad you're here to boost the numbers,' she replied.

Simon had already left a message to say he was ready to leave Newcastle but she'd ignored it, determined to speak to Benson before she left the party. Not that there was much of a festive atmosphere, the room was too big for such a small gathering. She stood with her back to the wall to observe the small group around Benson. One of the men kept topping up their glasses until, eventually, they had to find a chair for their guest of honour. The younger faction were gathered round the rapidly diminishing supply of rolls and cakes. Mills spent half an hour chatting awkwardly to the administrator while they waited for the Head of Department to arrive. Apparently, he wanted to give a speech before they presented Benson with a small gift, which Mills assumed was in the fancy carrier-bag tucked under the buffet table.

She was thinking it was time to approach Benson when a harassed-looking Head of Department burst into the room, apologising loudly to everyone for his late arrival. The administrator rushed over to stand beside him, clutching the gift. Mills was distracted by another message from Simon; this time she texted that she'd been delayed by a student and would let him know when she was free. The Head had started a rambling speech which had little to do with Benson but focussed on lack of funding for blue-sky research. Mills wondered if he had made any attempt to find out about the professor's career. The guest of honour himself was slumped in his seat, paying little attention to his surroundings.

As soon as the Head left, the room began to clear. It was nearly two o'clock, the plates were bare, the bottles were empty. Mills was waiting patiently for her chance to speak to the professor alone but there were still three old colleagues gathered round him. She turned to thank the administrator, who said she was off to call for a taxi to take the old boy home. Mills saw her chance.

'That's OK,' she said. 'I'm going in his direction; I can take him.'

Between them, they managed to manoeuvre Benson along the corridor and down the stairs to the main entrance. They lowered him onto a bench, where he sat with the administrator until Mills had brought the Mini round to the front of the building.

'D'you think you'll be able to manage?' the woman asked after they'd got him into the front seat. She lowered her voice. 'He seems a bit out of it.'

Mills nodded. 'It's not just the drink, he's deteriorated since his wife died,' she confided.

Benson woke when they reached his house but it took a few minutes for him to realise where he was. He called her Janine as she struggled to haul him out of his seat and down the garden path. She found his keys in his coat pocket, opening the door before helping him into the kitchen.

'Shall I make us some coffee?' she asked briskly.

He didn't answer but sat with his head in his hands. She filled the kettle, searching the cupboards until she found a jar of instant granules. There was no milk in the fridge so she placed the black coffee on the table in front of him. He was half-asleep, muttering to himself. She sat opposite, examining his wrinkled features, wondering if he could have been capable of poisoning his wife.

'Tell me about Dawn, Professor Benson,' she asked. It was worth a try.

He lifted his head. 'My wife? She's dead. She was my life.'

'I'm sorry. How did she die?'

'Cancer. Stage four cancer.' He seemed very certain.

'But Rachel said she was in recovery.'

'*She* wouldn't know. Rachel wasn't here. Her mother didn't want to worry her on the other side of the world.'

'Drink your coffee,' she urged him.

'I don't know what I'd do without you, Janine.'

'No, I'm not…' She stopped. If he thought she was his daughter he might confide in her. 'Do you think Dawn took her own life?' she asked gently.

He looked at her sharply and for a moment she thought he was growing angry but he relaxed back again, muttering that he wouldn't have blamed her.

Mills could feel her heart racing. 'There was something strange in her blood,' she said, waiting for his reaction.

He shook his head slowly. 'They couldn't find anything in the post mortem.'

'Rachel asked for more tests.'

'What?'

Mills took a deep breath. 'They found bacteria, strange microbes.'

It was a long time before he responded. It was as if his brain was booting up again, that he couldn't respond until it was firing on all cylinders. He was looking at her as he asked, 'What d'you mean, strange?'

'They were strange to Porton Down... but they may not be strange to you.'

She studied his face as his expression changed from confusion to anguish. He pushed himself to standing, making his way unsteadily to the sink, hanging on to the furniture for support. There he threw up noisily over a period of several minutes while Mills watched. He took a mug from the draining board, filled it from the tap, downing it in one go.

'I don't feel so good,' he declared unnecessarily. 'I think I'll go and lie down.'

Mills waited until he was stretched out on the sofa in the sitting room with a cushion under his head, then placed a blanket over him. She offered to stay but was aware that Simon would be getting impatient for her to reply to his repeated requests for a lift.

'Will you be all right?' she asked.

He didn't reply but was breathing gently, his eyes shut. The poor old man was evidently exhausted. Her phone pinged with yet another message from Simon, this time he said he wasn't going to wait any longer, he was getting on the train now. She replied that she would be at the station in ten minutes. Taking one last look at the figure lying with his mouth open, she tiptoed out of the room, gently pulling the front door closed behind her.

As she waited outside the station, she tried to convince herself that Benson would be fine. She was startled by Simon opening the passenger door, demanding to know why she'd taken so long to fetch him. Once he'd settled himself in, she went to start the engine then stopped.

'Listen,' she began, 'and don't interrupt me until I've finished.' That got his attention. 'I was giving Prof Benson a lift home after his leaving do. He's a bit worse for wear,' she explained.

'OK,' he said slowly.

'No, it's not. He wasn't very well. I left him lying asleep on the sofa but if he's sick again he could choke. I think I should go back.'

When Simon didn't object, she drove in the direction of Benson's house. The daylight was fading and she noticed there were now lights on inside.

Simon pointed to a car in the drive. 'It's OK, his daughter has dropped in.'

But Mills wasn't going to drive on yet. She parked in the road and jumped out.

'I need to check he's all right,' she called as she struggled with the gate.

Janine looked surprised when she opened the door,

commenting coolly that she'd asked her not to pester her father again. But when Mills explained how she'd brought him home unwell, that she just wanted to check he was safe, her demeanour softened and she invited her in. The professor was propped up on the sofa watching television.

'I don't know what's bothering him,' his daughter confided, wandering into the kitchen. 'He's becoming more and more confused.'

Mills agreed. 'He told me Dawn had terminal cancer but Rachel told us she was recovering.'

Janine shook her head. 'Dawn was very poorly but she didn't want Rachel worrying. We wanted to get her over from Japan but Dawn wouldn't hear of it. I thought it was selfish and it caused a lot of trouble between us because Rachel still doesn't understand why I didn't contact her.'

'It must've been a stressful time.'

'Tell me about it! Dawn should have been in a hospice but she insisted she wanted to be at home towards the end. Dad couldn't cope so I had to take the brunt of it. It was a terrible time for everyone.'

Someone was tapping on the front door.

'That's probably Simon,' Mills said, heading back down the hall, followed by Janine. 'Look, could we have a chat sometime. There are some things that we should probably share with you about Dawn's death.'

She opened the door, asking Simon to wait for a second while she got Janine's number.

'I'll call you,' Mills told her. 'Perhaps we could meet for a coffee or something.'

'What was that all about?' Simon asked when they were in the car.

'Dawn really was terminally ill. I'm beginning to think

241

that Benson helped speed her on her way. We really must talk to Janine again.'

She didn't catch what he said but it sounded as if he disagreed. She concentrated on the road until they were out of the traffic, heading towards Richmond.

'So how did it go in court?' she asked casually.

'Do you really want to know?'

'Of course.'

'I thought you had more important things to deal with.'

It was unusual for Simon to sulk, so she tried making light of it.

'Did they make mincemeat of you?'

'No, but they demolished any case the defence had.'

'Good.'

'Really?'

'Yes, I don't ever want to hear the name Rogerson again!'

'Ah.'

'What does that mean?'

DS Caldicott had given him strict instructions not to discuss their conversion with anyone. He considered telling Mills but thought she might tell Donna... or Nina... or Brenda, so decided it was best to keep it to himself and changed the subject back to Professor Benson.

'How come *you* gave Benson a lift home?' he asked.

'Why me? Because I happened to see him leaving Biology when I was coming to pick you up in Darlington. It was practically on the way.'

He knew she was lying because her message had said she was just ten minutes away, presumably as she left Benson's house. Mills waited for him to challenge her but he didn't bother. Instead he said she should involve Rachel Clark in any discussions she was going to have with Janine.

Chapter 31

Mills wanted to clear the air between them next morning.

'I'm going to ask Janine and Rachel for an online meeting,' she announced in the spirit of openness. 'Do you have contact details for Rachel?'

'Japan is nine hours ahead so I hope you can find a time that suits them both,' Simon replied, keeping his eyes on the road.

Mills considered the narrow window of opportunity. 'It'll have to be in the morning then. Perhaps Janine could do lunchtime or I could suggest the weekend.'

As he dropped her outside the Archaeology Department, Mills asked Simon to send her Rachel's email address. He drove round to his space in the Chemistry Department carpark and hurried into the building.

'Professor Pringle!' The departmental administrator was coming down the corridor waving a piece of paper. 'There was a call for you just now, someone called Caldicott? He wants you to ring him, I took the number.'

Simon thanked her, studying the paper as he went to his office. He had a lecture in less than thirty minutes so it could wait; it wasn't a call he wanted to make. But his curiosity finally got the better of him and as soon as he was at his desk, he dialled the number.

'Thanks for getting back, I know you must be busy.' The DS sounded serious. 'It's about what we discussed yesterday, OK?'

'Yes.' It wasn't, but he listened.

'Good. I'm progressing our plans now we know you're on board. A package will be couriered to Rogerson's on Monday but we're raising an order for them today, so they may be in touch sooner rather than later. Our request will be for a quality test under strict accredited conditions for presentation to court.'

Simon was curious. 'Will they know it's from you?'

He had a throaty laugh. 'Not a chance. Fortunately we have ways and means to make it appear to originate from an offender.'

Simon waited but the DS didn't expand.

'So we'll wait to hear from Rogerson's,' agreed Simon. 'That's if they ask us to do the work,' he added.

'Oh, I think they will. There aren't any other places left willing to work for them.'

His laugh irritated Simon. 'My colleague doesn't want *us* to work for them again.'

'It's your call but I've put things in motion so it'll be difficult to turn it round now. Just treat the work as routine but ensure that everything you do is recorded in detail. This operation will be used as evidence against their illegal practices.'

Simon ended the call after promising to let Caldicott know as soon as he received a request from Rogerson's. Mills had sent him a reminder to give her Rachel Clark's email address. He responded, adding that he would like to join the call, if that was permitted.

Mills smiled at the formality of his message, replying with a thumbs-up emoji, and immediately sent messages to the stepsisters explaining that she'd like to chat with them both about what they'd found out about Dawn's death. It would not be an easy meeting because she would be forced to disclose that she'd taken the vial from their father's study. However, she decided it was better to tell the truth and be damned than keep secrets.

To her surprise, Rachel replied almost by return, saying she was free on Saturday. She was keen to hear her news, without referring to the fact that Janine would be present. Mills was relieved she hadn't objected outright to sharing the call with her stepsister. She had to wait until that evening before she heard back from Janine, whose response was less good-natured. She was available all Saturday afternoon but only free between ten-thirty and eleven on Saturday morning, if they had to include Rachel. It sounded as if she wasn't entirely happy involving her stepsister in their discussions. Mills sent an invitation to Janine, Rachel and Simon for a meeting on Saturday morning at ten-thirty before anyone could change their mind.

Next morning Donna dropped the bombshell.

'I've just had a call from Rogerson Forensics,' she informed Mills. 'They said another sample will be delivered early next week.'

'What? No Donna, there's no way we're doing any more work for them.'

The girl looked perplexed. 'I assumed we were expecting it, the way he spoke.'

'I've heard nothing from them and I can't imagine Simon would have talked to them, not after what he's been through this week.'

She went off to find Simon, finally catching up with him in the lab with his final-year students. She signalled through the glass in the door that she needed a word and he came out into the corridor, looking concerned. To her surprise, he didn't immediately agree with her that they were going to refuse any more work from Rogerson's.

'Perhaps we should think about it,' he began. 'After all, last time it was a lack of communication, wasn't it? If we insist on following the standard, having all the checks in place, what can go wrong?'

Mills was puzzled by his change of tune. 'I think we should tell them to keep their work, it's not worth risking our reputation.'

Simon disagreed in measured tone, insisting they needed the money. They couldn't discuss it properly in the corridor and Simon wouldn't leave the students, so they agreed to disagree until lunchtime when, Mills warned, a decision had to be made. Meanwhile she was going to call Brenda to confirm her view. As soon as she'd gone, Simon rang his postdoctoral researcher to take over from him as soon as possible. He eventually arrived half an hour later, freeing Simon to slip back to his office to make a call.

Luckily, he reached Brenda first, so he explained that Mills wanted to remove Rogerson's from their customer list. He tried to persuade Brenda that they needed the income, but she argued they could lose even more business if other potential customers learned of their connection with such a shady company. The only way for Simon to convince her was to come clean.

'Can you treat what I'm going to say in the strictest confidence, Brenda?'

'What is it?'

'It's not to go any further. I haven't even told Mills.'

'What is it, pet?'

He related what DS Caldicott had said to him in the café

and more recently on the phone. Brenda listened quietly then commented that if it was a police matter it had best be done.

'This will put you in their good books, we hope,' she added. 'But I think you're unwise not to tell Mills what's going on. You'll be in her *bad* books when she finds out.'

'They said not to tell anyone but I had to speak to you before Mills does. Do you think you can persuade her to take the work?'

'I'll do my best, pet. And if it comes to a vote we are in the majority, aren't we?' She wished him luck as they said their goodbyes.

He waited anxiously to see what Mills would say when he met her for lunch. She seemed subdued and when he asked if she'd had a chance to speak to Brenda, she admitted she had.

'I think she was a bit distracted,' she said. 'I'm not sure she understood what I was talking about because she said we should be grateful to have the work, whoever it came from. I told her what they'd put you through in court but that didn't make any difference either.'

'She's right,' said Simon, biting into his sandwich to avoid her gaze.

Mills went quiet. Finally she said, 'OK, you win, but we will have to be super-vigilant every step of the way. This time we'll insist they accept all the necessary standards or we won't do their work.'

'I agree.' Simon thought of DS Caldicott's instructions. 'We'll record every tiny detail. That way we can't be criticised.'

'I hope you're right, Simon, I really do.'

Chapter 32

Mills watched the time nervously as it approached ten-thirty. She'd set up her laptop on the kitchen table facing their two chairs but Simon said he didn't want to be seen, he just needed to hear what was said. Rachel was already waiting to join the meeting. She was wearing a turquoise tank top that showed off her toned arms and shoulders. It was the sort you wore to the gym or a yoga class, although the woman was fully made up with her hair pulled up into a smooth ponytail. They made small talk about life back in Japan until Janine appeared on screen a few minutes later. Mills was struck by the contrast between the two women. She reminded herself that there was at least a ten-year age gap, but the contrast was exaggerated by Janine's straggly grey hair scraped back behind her ears, and the baggy jumper that exposed her flabby neck. Her response when Rachel wished her a good morning was cool and barely audible.

Mills pointed out that Simon was within earshot before beginning her rehearsed speech.

'Thank you both for agreeing to meet us.'

Rachel was smiling while Janine's gaze was expressionless. Mills took a breath as she glanced surreptitiously at the scribbled notes in front of her.

'Rachel, I'm very sorry for the loss of your mother,' she continued. 'I know you were searching for the cause of her death when you spoke to Simon.' She was still smiling politely.

'I was. Dad was in a state over the police suggesting it was suicide. I couldn't see why Mum would want to take her own life when she was in recovery.'

Mills looked across the screen to the older woman. 'Janine, what did you understand about Dawn's illness?'

She was fiddling with the sleeve of her jumper. 'I'm not sure… I wasn't supposed…'

Mills smiled encouragingly at her. 'Go on. It's the truth.'

'I'm sorry, Rachel,' she told her stepsister. 'But your mother wasn't going to get better. Her cancer was aggressive. It was terminal. I wanted her to move to a hospice but she refused.'

Rachel looked confused. 'I've told you before, I don't believe you. She said she was in remission. I offered to come over but she said there was no need, to wait for the better weather when she would be strong again.'

'I'm sorry Rachel, Dawn forbade us to tell you. She was adamant about it. I didn't feel I could break that promise.'

The younger woman's face was a mixture of anger and frustration mixed with tears. She was shaking her head.

'I can't believe she'd do that to me,' she sobbed. 'Just give me a minute.'

Mills watched her move away from the screen, disappearing through a door at the back of the room. Janine looked visibly shaken but remained seated. Mills turned anxiously to Simon, who was signalling for her to put herself on mute.

'Don't panic,' he said. 'Use the time to ask Janine about the vial.'

'What?'

He came over to the table to unmute the microphone again. 'Hello Janine,' he began. 'I wonder if I can clear up something that was bothering you.' The woman was waiting. 'OK,' he continued. 'So it's a little awkward because you were concerned why Mills was in your father's study, weren't you?'

'Yes, he doesn't like anyone going in. He doesn't even like me running a vacuum round.'

'Do you know why that is?'

'He says he knows where everything is, his papers and suchlike.'

'What about the locked cupboard, do you know what he keeps in there?'

She shrugged. 'No. I told you, he doesn't let me go in there.'

'I do.' Rachel had reappeared. Her eyes looked red and puffy, with dark smudges where her mascara had run. She had pulled on a grey sweatshirt. 'I know what's in the cupboard that he keeps locked.' She sounded pleased that she was the only one that knew.

Simon encouraged her to explain.

'I used to go in sometimes when he was working up there at the weekends. He would be sitting at his desk writing papers for scientific journals. He would tell me about them sometimes, and I'd pretend to understand. He kept a tiny bottle of liquid in the cupboard, high on a shelf where I couldn't reach. He said what it contained was very special because he'd made it.'

'Did he tell you what was in it?' Simon asked.

She laughed. 'We'd been reading that book by Roald Dahl, "George's Marvellous Medicine" so I believed it was some sort of magic potion. I think he might have put the idea in my head. But when I was older Mum explained it was a very dangerous substance that Dad had been working on, so I wasn't to go near it.'

Janine interrupted her stepsister. 'Can I ask why you want to know about the bottle? What's it got to do with Dawn?' she snapped.

Mills left Simon to answer. 'Rachel asked us to investigate the bacteria found in Dawn's body. We identified a very unusual species not seen before, the sort of thing your father researched in the US.'

Mills was watching the confused faces of the two women. They both shook their heads. She couldn't let Simon handle this all by himself.

She leaned towards the screen. 'I'm sorry, but we took a sample from the vial to have it analysed.' She felt Simon squeeze her hand gently. 'There is a connection between the bacteria that killed Dawn and its contents.'

There was a long silence before Janine asked, 'So what are you saying?'

'Does that mean he gave my mother the bacteria?' asked Rachel.

'We're not suggesting anything,' Simon said quickly, trying to calm them down. 'We just wanted you to know the situation before we...'

'Have you spoken to Dad about this?' Rachel asked.

'The state he's in?' Janine asked sarcastically. 'You haven't seen him recently, have you? He's hardly functioning.'

'So what are we going to do?' Rachel asked.

'I'll ask Dad about it,' Janine snapped.

'Then it's important that Professor Pringle is there too,' Rachel replied firmly.

Simon assured her that he would arrange to meet Janine and the professor as soon as possible to get to the bottom of the situation. The older woman did not seem happy, checking her watch exaggeratedly before saying she had to dash. Her screen disappeared before they had a chance to discuss when to meet with her father. Rachel was in tears again as she thanked them for working so hard to get to the truth. She now planned to get in touch with her mother's old GP to establish whether it was really true that she had been terminally ill but hidden it from her.

Mills sat at the table for several minutes after the call, trying to make sense of what they'd heard. Simon busied himself making coffee before admitting he was less clear about what had happened than before. They discussed what the women had told them, going over and over it, until their coffee had gone cold. Eventually Mills suggested they took Harris for his walk to clear their heads.

The snow of two weeks ago was a distant memory, in fact it felt almost spring-like out of the wind, even though it would be a month or so before there was much warmth in the sun. They walked in silence, calling the lurcher back occasionally, keeping an eye open for any sign of the red kite they'd spotted a couple of times in the past month. Mills was turning over in her mind how unfair it was that Rachel was kept in the dark about her mother's prognosis when her father and his daughter knew. She asked Simon what he would have done in Janine's situation, agreeing they would probably have defied the dying woman's wishes, regardless of the consequences. He began to say that he would have wanted to be told if his mother was dying, then stopped abruptly.

'It's all right,' Mills said. 'You don't have to stop talking about it because of my mum.'

He gripped her hand tighter. 'Hopefully Rachel will get

confirmation that what Janine says is correct.'

Mills sensed that if sides were being taken, he would support the younger, more attractive stepsister. But she was sympathetic towards Janine, who'd been left to cope with the dying stepmother and her father's grief, while juggling a demanding job and a family. However, there was a question that still niggled her.

'Do you think Janine really hadn't ever noticed the vial in the cupboard?'

'She's never been in the study.'

'Well I have, remember. Surely it would be thick with dust if she really never cleaned in there?'

Simon didn't argue. 'The thing that's bugging me is why she was so averse to us talking to her father about it.'

'Protecting him? Perhaps she suspects he helped his wife to a merciful release.'

'It may have been a release from her illness but it wasn't a very peaceful death, was it? He would have known that would be the case, surely.'

'Maybe all will be revealed when you meet with Benson and Janine. If not, Rachel will have to draw a line under it and get on with her life.'

They had reached the point where the track divided. Without discussion, they continued towards the top of Gunnerside Gill. It was not long before they were perched on a rock out of the wind watching Harris pottering about in the water.

'I wonder if I should call Nina. She was going to get the name of the officer who interviewed Benson when his wife died.'

Simon was fiddling with a piece of dried reed. 'I don't think it's a police matter, do you?'

'It is if he injected his wife with the bacteria.'

'I doubt they'd prosecute if he did it out of compassion. He's an old man who seems to have become rather irrational.'

'That's true. You'll probably not get much sense out of him when you do get to speak to him. But Rachel may not see it that way, she might demand justice for her own peace of mind.'

Chapter 33

If peace had not been completely restored, a truce had certainly been declared between Simon and Mills, so he now felt it was safe to point out that it was the fourteenth of February on Monday, so this was technically Valentine's weekend. Mills declared she'd forgotten to get him a card, which was a little disappointing, but he wasn't going to be put off.

'I thought we deserved a treat after everything that's been going on,' he continued.

'It's still going on.' Mills was rubbing the dog's paws vigorously with an old towel.

He persevered. 'I booked it months ago actually because they get very busy, especially this time of year.'

'Do they? What d'you mean?' she asked.

'It's a surprise but we will need to leave after lunch, so you'd better get packed.'

He wouldn't give her any clues, except to say she could dress up or down, depending on how she felt. She would need an overnight bag. She went upstairs slowly then immediately reappeared.

'What about Harris?' she asked tetchily. 'We can't keep asking Muriel.'

'Don't worry, he's coming with us!'

He followed her back upstairs to fling a pair of chinos and a clean shirt in the bag with his toiletries, then went down to tidy the kitchen and pack food for Harris. Mills was still up there half an hour later, by which time he'd packed his MG with everything the lurcher could possibly need except the dog bed, which was provided with the room. Mills appeared every so often to ask him questions, such as was it going to be muddy or cold, was the place they were staying posh, should she take her hair dryer, and so on. They finally left mid-afternoon, driving over Buttertubs Pass to Hawes, then on to Wharfedale.

'Are we stopping here?' she asked, as they approached Buckden. But Simon shook his head. They sailed past the "Buck Inn", "The White Lion Inn" at Cray,' and the "Devonshire Arms" at Cracoe. Finally, Mills decided he must have booked a holiday cottage, so they could take a dog with them.

Simon would not give in to her questions until he eventually turned onto a road signposted "The Angel at Hetton".

Mills gave a shriek. 'Not "The Angel"? You're kidding! Is it really?'

Simon gave her a smug grin. She'd been particularly taken with an article about the place, which she'd read to him months ago, pointing out that the restaurant had a Michelin star. That had given him the idea for her surprise.

'We've got a dog-friendly room booked,' he assured her, before adding, 'When we're settled in, we can take Harris for a walk before dinner at seven.'

As they waited for the lurcher to extract himself from the back seat of the car, Mills hugged Simon and kissed him. 'Thank you, it's a lovely surprise.'

Everything about their stay was perfect as far as Mills was concerned. Their room was in a converted barn with fabulous views. She assured Simon that it was wonderful as they strolled down the lane in the dusk. It was too cold to stay out for long so they retreated to the bar where the lurcher curled up in front of the fire, snoring softly until it was time for them to change for dinner.

Mills was pleased she'd packed her silk jumpsuit, despite Simon's earlier protestations that they didn't need to get dressed up. She spent time smoothing her hair back into shape, applying a little more make-up than she usually did for a night at the pub. Simon was wearing his new shirt and she commented that pale blue suited him. Harris, who had gobbled his dinner, was now fast asleep in the comfy bed provided. He lifted his head when Mills opened the door into the corridor but snuggled back down as they crept out, leaving him with the soft light from the bedside lamp for company.

When Mills later recalled the evening, it wasn't the food that featured first, despite it being "out of this world" in her opinion. No, it was that she and Simon were enjoying each other's company once again, like they had before everything that had been happening over the last few months. Simon talked about their trip to the States, the places he could take her to see, the seafood restaurants they'd go to for steamed crab. She agreed it sounded perfect but still didn't say she would go with him. When they stumbled across to their room in the barn, Harris was lying with his legs in the air, grunting contentedly.

Mills was surprised to find it was eight o'clock when she woke next morning. There was no sign of Simon and Harris, so she made herself a cup of tea before having a leisurely shower. They finally reappeared when she was about to go looking for them.

'It's great out there, blue sky, not a cloud in sight.'

'Cold?'

'Freezing! Hurry up, I've got a great walk planned after breakfast, followed by Sunday lunch.'

'Where, or don't I ask?'

'Surprise.'

It turned out not to be such a big surprise because "The Angel at Hetton" was in a favourite area of theirs for walking, so Mills soon guessed they were on their way to Linton. Simon had booked "The Fountaine Inn" for Sunday lunch, where Harris folded himself under their table in the snug, close to a roaring fire.

Two hours later, Simon pointed out white flakes drifting across the window. It was hard to tear themselves away from the cosy atmosphere but Simon reminded Mills they still had to walk back to Hetton and it would be dusk in a couple of hours. Outside the snow was falling gently, melting as soon as it touched the ground, but they hurried along arm in arm, with Harris leading the way. Simon was anxious to drive back to Mossy Bank before the snow settled but when they reached "The Angel", a layer of white covered his car.

'It would be lovely to get snowed in here for a few more days,' commented Mills.

But Simon was getting Harris onto the back seat. 'No such luck,' he said. 'But we'd better hurry if we're going to get over the tops tonight.'

The snow stopped as suddenly as it started. When they reached Swaledale, the sky was clear with a few stars already visible. The cottage was cold but Simon soon had the fire going while Mills made tea. As they sat eating toast and marmite, they agreed it had been a great weekend, the best they'd had for a long time.

*

Early Monday morning, Donna joined Mills and Simon for their lab meeting. It was scheduled weekly but somehow the practice had lapsed. However, this morning they had something important to discuss: the sample arriving from Rogerson's. It was problematic for Simon, knowing how Mills felt, because he couldn't admit that the police were behind the request, although he desperately wanted to. Donna was equally dubious about doing more work for the company and said so. Simon placated her by explaining how they were going to handle the sample.

'We've agreed that you will have responsibility for the quality assurance, as you are the most experienced in that side,' he told her.

Mills added that Donna's job was to ensure there was a chain of custody form to record every aspect of the work as it progressed, and to photograph the sample when it arrived.

'I want this work to stand up in court this time,' she warned. 'If there is anything about it that means we can't use our accredited procedures, tell me at once,' she added.

Simon smiled at her then turned to Donna. 'Let me know the moment the sample arrives. We'll get it tested as soon as possible. I've got teaching today and tomorrow morning but I'm free most of the week; at least there's nothing I can't rearrange.'

Mills was happy to leave them to deal with it, the less she was involved the better as far as she was concerned. She went back to her office, admitting to herself that it was good that the team was back on an even keel. She had to concentrate on her academic role for now, conscious that she'd neglected to prepare for a new optional lecture course on forensic archaeology. It was being offered to both departments, and she knew that catering for a mixture of archaeology students and those studying forensic science was going to be a challenge.

Nige was in and out of the office but generally she was undisturbed as she worked on her lecture notes. She only stopped to grab a sandwich, which she ate at her desk. It was a productive day which only finished when she had a call from Simon, who was waiting to go home. As soon as she was in the car, he wanted to talk about the heroin sample from Rogerson's, explaining that Donna was preparing it so he could start testing the following afternoon. She found his change of attitude towards the whole Rogerson thing strange.

'That's fine, but I don't need a blow-by-blow account,' snapped Mills. She immediately regretted sounding so touchy and added, 'I'm sure Donna is keeping notes.'

'She is. She's marvellous, isn't she?'

'Yes, she certainly is.'

Mills kept herself busy away from the lab, with the excuse that she had to concentrate on her lecture course. Simon had begun testing the heroin but said the result wouldn't be ready until Wednesday. There had been no mention of the proposed meeting with Prof Benson and Mills had forgotten about it until she had a call from Nina. It was unusual for her friend to ring her at work unless it was important so, at first, she assumed it was about Nige, who hadn't appeared in the office yet.

'No, Mills, he's working at home today. You asked me if I could find out who dealt with Mrs Benson's death?'

'Yes!'

'I've got the name of the officer who spoke to her

husband at the time. Is that who you were looking for?'

'Yes!'

'It's a Constable Arthur Young.'

She gave her a contact number, saying he was a very experienced uniformed officer. She'd informed him that Yardley Forensics was working for the dead woman's daughter and had information that might be useful. Mills told Nina about the online meeting they'd had with the stepsisters and how Janine was supposed to be arranging a meeting with her and Prof Benson.

'I'm not sure what will come out of it but I'll wait until we meet before contacting PC Young,' said Mills.

'That sounds like a good idea. You don't want to rush in making formal statements unless you are sure of the facts. Why don't you run it past me first when you're ready to speak to him?'

Mills had been accused by Nina of being hot-headed in the past, so she understood what her friend was tactfully pointing out to her: that she needed to be circumspect in this case. As soon as she finished their call, she compiled an email for Janine, reminding her of their proposed meeting, suggesting that maybe one evening in the week would be convenient?

She suspected that Benson's daughter would prevaricate, that she'd have to send reminders before hearing from her, so it was a surprise when she received a response that same afternoon. Even more amazingly, she said the following evening would be fine if they could do six o'clock at "Arcadia".

DS Caldicott was on the phone to Simon, checking that everything was running according to plan.

'So far, so good,' said Simon quietly, making sure no-one was listening. He was alone in the lab but Donna could appear at any moment.

'That's what I like to hear,' the DS replied. 'If it goes smoothly at your end, it'll be a textbook case.'

Simon wasn't sure it was a correct description to use in this situation but he agreed. The detective reminded him to record everything so it could be used verbatim in court.

'Can I ask, just to be clear,' Simon began, 'will I have to appear as a witness if it comes to court.'

'Not *if*, Professor, but *when* it goes to court.'

'Will you need me to give evidence? Just to be clear.'

'Yes, you'll be our star witness.'

Simon sighed.

DS Caldicott laughed. 'Don't worry, you'll have police backup. And won't it give your company some good publicity?'

'Hopefully it might mean some more work in future?'

He hadn't noticed Donna standing in the doorway until he'd finished the call.

'I'm sorry,' she said. 'I didn't mean to disturb you.'

Chapter 34

The report for Rogerson's was going to be ready on Wednesday afternoon as promised. Donna put the final touches on the paperwork before asking Mills to authorise it. She read it carefully, noting that the heroin had been diluted with lactose, just as before. However, this time the distribution of the bulking agent was more uniform but there was less of it. All the standards had been applied so she was happy to sign off the tests as being carried out under their accredited procedure. This time they'd not been asked to return the sample but requested to destroy it, so she told Donna to put it in the locked store room until they decided how to do so.

Once Mills had left the office, Simon told Donna that *he* would keep the sample in a special safe he used for Class A drugs back in his department. She handed him the package, asking him to sign the chain of custody form.

'Keep that form with it at all times,' she warned, before adding, 'I'll tell Mills about the change of location.'

'No need,' he said quickly. 'I'll let her know. In fact I can dispose of it safely for you as well.'

DS Caldicott had asked him to keep the sample once it was tested, since the undercover officer posing as the customer had confirmed he didn't want it back. He would collect it from Simon himself, together with a copy of the test report.

'And, Donna,' he added, 'could you send me a copy of the final report, together with your notes, for my records.'

'You can access it on the server.'

'I know but it would be handy to have it in my files.'

She went to the lab computer to press a few keys. Once he'd gone off with the package, Donna sat in front of the monitor without seeing it. She was weighing up whether to speak to Mills about Simon's odd behaviour. First, he'd taken the sample with him, promising to destroy it, then he'd asked for a copy of the report, when it was readily available on the central system which he could access in the lab any time he wanted. And she'd heard him on the phone asking whether he'd have to appear in court again. He knew that Rogerson's was a dodgy set up, yet he insisted they do more work for the company. It sounded suspiciously as if he was working *with* them as well as *for* them.

When Mills came down to the lab at the end of the day, Donna decided to tell her about her concerns.

'Do you have a minute, Mills?'

'Sorry, Donna, have you seen Simon? We're supposed to be meeting Prof Benson in half an hour.'

Mills eventually found him leaving the Chemistry Department.

'I'm so glad the work for Rogerson's went well,' she commented as they drove towards Darlington.

Simon agreed. He'd already sent the report to DS Caldicott, arranging for him to pick up the sample in the morning. He hoped that would be the end of his role in the police operation.

'So what's the plan for this evening?' he asked.

They'd had little time to prepare for their confrontation with Professor Benson.

'Keep it simple, I guess,' replied Mills. 'Tell them what

we know, see what they say. I imagine Janine will have spoken to her father about what we told her, so he'll be prepared.'

She didn't feel as confident as she hoped she sounded; in fact she was beginning to feel nervous now they were approaching the house. At least the outside lights were on and the door was opened by Janine as soon as they knocked. Her father was seated in the kitchen as before but this time there was no sign of the usual wine bottle on the table, it had been replaced by a teapot, four mugs and a plate of shop-bought Bakewell tarts.

They removed their jackets before sitting opposite the old man.

'Good evening, Robert,' Simon began. 'How are you?'

He responded that he was bearing up, sounding a little more coherent than at their previous visits, which Mills put down to the absence of alcohol.

Janine poured the tea. 'Help yourself to a Bakewell,' she insisted.

Simon took one, placing it in front of him, untouched. 'Thank you for letting us come to see you,' he began.

Mills concentrated on eating her cake.

Janine looked serious. 'I told Dad about our meeting with Rachel on Saturday. He was surprised to hear what you told me about the bacteria that killed Dawn because there was no mention of it on her death certificate. He's been quite upset, haven't you Dad?'

Her father had been trying to remove his cake from its foil, unsuccessfully. He put it back on the table and looked up.

'I don't understand it.'

Mills had a question. 'You did know that Dawn was

terminally ill?'

He nodded. 'Yes. She didn't want people to know, especially Rachel. She thought it would upset her. She was always a sensitive little girl.'

Janine smiled as if satisfied that she had been proved correct.

'So do you think she might have wanted to end her life?' Mills continued.

He shook his head. 'No. The police asked me that. I told them, she was a strong woman, she wouldn't want to seem weak. And she would have known I wouldn't have helped her either.'

Mills looked at Simon for the next question.

'Robert, may I ask you about the vial that you keep in your study?' he asked.

'Vial?'

'There's a locked cupboard containing a small glass ampoule of liquid.'

He looked at Janine with a puzzled expression. 'Is there?'

She shook her head. 'I don't know, I don't go in there.'

'Don't you?' He thought for a moment. 'I don't recall but if you say so. Janine can check.'

Simon continued. 'It appears to contain a bacterium which could be lethal.'

Mills offered to fetch it to show him. Benson nodded, still looking puzzled. Janine seemed annoyed, picking up their mugs without a word and taking them to the sink to begin washing them up. Mills returned with the vial, placing it on the table in front of the old man. He picked it up, holding it to the light to examine the liquid. His daughter remained at the sink.

He nodded. 'This must be very old now. I'd be surprised

266

if it's viable.'

'Do you know what it is?' asked Simon.

He shrugged. 'Can't remember the details now, my memory's shot. Piece of work I did a years ago, I suppose.'

'Was it for the US?'

'Probably. It can't have been successful or I wouldn't have it in the house.'

'Well, we believe that it *is* viable, probably responsible for your wife's death.'

The old man sank back in his chair seemingly unable to accept what he was being told. 'I don't understand what you're saying.'

'Did Dawn know about the vial?' Mills asked.

The professor was shaking his head in response. 'No.'

Now Janine turned from the sink. 'You're wrong,' she said. 'Dawn knew what was in there, she told me herself. It's morphine.'

Benson turned to stare at her. 'Morphine? Don't be daft, girl.'

She came across to the table, her eyes were brimming with tears. 'She told me it was morphine! Why would she think that?' She was staring at her father, waiting for a response. 'Why would she think that?'

He sat with his elbows on the table, his head in his hands, until finally he looked up. 'I really don't remember,' he said.

They sat in silence. Simon, who appeared to be at a loss for words, looked anxiously at Mills, who was trying to make sense of what had just happened. Had Dawn really told Janine the vial contained morphine, and if so, why? Benson seemed to know it held a toxin and Dawn had even warned Rachel it was dangerous. Everyone was at her,

267

waiting, so she finally took control by asking if there was any objection to her contacting the police officer who interviewed them when Dawn died. The professor shrugged, indicating he had no problem with that, while his daughter stared at him as if she thought he should have.

Mills picked up the vial. 'D'you mind if I take this?' she asked casually.

The old man shook his head. Janine followed them as they got up to leave and, once they were in the hall, she asked if it was really necessary to involve the police.

'My father's an old man. As you can see, he's not dealing very well with Dawn's death. Wouldn't it be better to leave him be?'

Mills muttered something about seeing what they say, while Simon thanked her for the tea and cake, which sounded incongruous in the circumstances. As soon as they were outside, Simon asked how Mills was going to find the officer who interviewed Benson.

'That's easy, I got his contact details from Nina.'

'And what are you planning to do with the vial?'

'Nothing. But we now have a legitimate reason for having it in our possession, when we tell the police what it contains.'

They soon discovered their impressions of what had occurred during their visit to "Arcadia" differed considerably and they spent the entire journey home discussing their points of view.

'At least you agree that neither Benson nor Janine knew what was in the vial?' asked Mills.

'I'm not convinced. Robert must have some inkling, even if he doesn't remember exactly where it came from. He said himself that the contents were probably no longer viable, which suggests he knew what it was originally for.'

'So why did Dawn think it was morphine?'

'You don't want to tell your family that you make cocktails that can be used in biological warfare, do you?'

'But I remember Rachel saying her mother told her it was a very dangerous substance *that Dad had been working on.*'

'Well, Janine certainly doesn't want her father to be investigated any further. So are you really going to contact the police, Mills?'

'I'll call PC Young tomorrow. I can explain that we've been working for Rachel, to find the cause of her mother's death. We can also give him the results of the tests on the vial.'

'I'd better warn Rachel, so it doesn't come as a surprise.'

'I'm sure she'll be delighted with the news, after all it was her that started our investigation into Dawn's death, wasn't it?'

Chapter 35

Mills was trying to concentrate on a grant application despite Nige having a noisy discussion with a student about late submission of his coursework. She was relieved when Donna rang to say there was a policeman in the lab asking for Simon.

'Don't worry, it'll be for me. I'll be right over.'

She'd called PC Young first thing in the morning, when he'd promised he would come as soon as he could, but she hadn't expected to see turn up so soon. As she hurried to the Chemistry Department, she rehearsed what she would say to him. The vial was in her bag and she would ask Martin to explain what it contained, if she could find him.

Donna was talking to a middle-aged man who looked exactly as Mills had imagined him, a rather weary-looking figure who'd been in the job a long time but was still only a constable, without ambition for a more senior rank. She was surprised he wasn't in uniform but grateful since it would cause less consternation within the department.

'PC Young, thank you for coming so quickly,' she said, offering her hand.

'No, Miss, I'm Detective Sergeant Caldicott. I'm here to see Professor Pringle.'

She looked at Donna, who was standing beside him but she shrugged.

'OK, but we are both dealing with the Benson case.' She turned back to Donna. 'Can you get Simon, please?'

Her technician rushed to the phone.

'Shall we go into the office?' she asked, leading the way.

Once they were seated at the table, Mills offered him coffee, which he declined. He didn't remove his raincoat but sat with the collar turned up, as if he was cold.

'I think there may have been some confusion,' he said. 'Unless Professor Pringle has told you how he is helping us with our investigation.'

'What investigation?'

'I'd prefer to speak to Professor Pringle.'

There was no way Mills was going to sit with him in silence, so she left to find Simon herself. Closing the door firmly, she took Donna to one side.

'Is he coming?'

'Yes, he was in his office.'

'Do you know anything about this?'

Donna hesitated. 'There was something I wanted to ask you about. Did Simon tell you he took the heroin sample? He said he could dispose of it but he hasn't done so yet or he would've returned the chain of custody form to me. And he asked for a copy of the report for his own files, which I thought was odd. I know I shouldn't have listened but he was on the phone and...' She broke off as Simon rushed in.

'He's in there,' said Mills, pointing towards the office. 'He won't tell me what it's about.'

Simon didn't answer but went in and shut the door. 'DS Caldicott? You'd better come to my office. We need to go back there for the sample anyway.'

He held the door open for Caldicott to follow him into the lab. Mills and Donna watched him lead the DS out into the corridor.

'It's not far,' Simon explained. 'If you'd called, I would've

271

met you at the entrance.'

'It's not a problem, Professor Pringle, no harm done.'

That's easy for you to say, thought Simon. He'd seen the look on their faces as he left the lab and he wasn't relishing the debrief that would follow Caldicott's visit. The policeman, on the other hand, seemed in good spirits when they reached the office.

'Everything has gone according to plan, I'm pleased to say. Fortunately Rogerson's have followed our instructions to the letter, including our guy's directions to get him a "good" result, if you get my drift.'

Simon did his best to sound pleased, reminding himself that he'd done nothing wrong. He unlocked the drawer in his desk to retrieve the heroin sample, handing it to the DS.

'Thanks, Professor. And for the report, it was an impressive set of notes you provided too. I'll keep you informed of progress. Unfortunately for you, this may mean the end of work from Rogerson though.'

'We won't be sorry. But do you think there is a chance that your people might be persuaded to use our services in future?'

'You never know, although it's not my call.' He pulled an evidence bag from his pocket, placed the heroin inside and shoved it into his raincoat pocket.

'You'd better take this as well,' added Simon. He quickly signed the chain of custody form before handing it to Caldicott.

'Good call,' he replied. 'Don't want the case collapsing over something trivial like that.'

There was something Simon needed to know before he left. 'Will you still need me to appear at the trial, now you've got everything?'

'It depends whether they plead guilty. If not, you'll be our star witness.'

Simon didn't like the sound of that but Caldicott reassured him as they walked to the front entrance together. Simon watched him leave before making his way reluctantly back to the lab, where Mills and Donna were waiting for him.

'I know, I know, I owe you both an explanation.' He held up his hands in submission. 'But can we discuss it over a cup of tea, please?'

No-one spoke as Donna boiled the kettle while Mills put teabags in the mugs. Simon sat at the table, waiting.

'So what's going on?' asked Mills when she finally placed the mug in front of him. 'What was he doing here?'

Donna joined them quietly at the far end of the table.

Wondering where to start, Simon sipped the tea but it was too hot to drink. 'OK. DS Caldicott introduced himself in the café after I'd done my bit in court. He was involved in the case because he's investigating Rogerson's. He asked me to help him to expose the company for their dodgy dealings. The heroin we were sent by Rogerson's actually came from the police working undercover. All he wanted us to do was test it as usual but follow all the correct procedures, so they can prove it was tampered with before we received it.'

'You mean diluted like the cocaine they sent us?' Donna asked.

'I presume so.'

'So why didn't you tell us?' demanded Mills.

'He told me to tell no-one.' He tested the tea again before admitting that he'd spoken to Brenda so she could persuade Mills to let him go ahead with the job.

Mills seemed lost for words but Donna looked relieved. 'So that's why you wanted the paperwork and the sample?' she asked.

'Yes,' he replied. 'The DS was here today to collect it.'

Donna was smiling at Mills. 'That's a relief then.'

But Mills didn't look pleased. 'What happens now, Simon? Is our name going to be dragged through the courts yet again?'

'Only in a good way. We've been helping the police remember; that could mean working for them in the future.'

Mills muttered, 'Fat chance.'

But Donna agreed that it was an advantage for them to be seen to be helping the police, suggesting it would be good publicity if Simon appeared as a witness for the prosecution. Mills finished her tea in silence before announcing she'd be in her office if anyone needed her.

She didn't mention that she intended to call Brenda to apologise for the way Simon had involved her in his deception. But when she spoke to her, she discovered that her old boss was surprisingly supportive of Simon's decision to help the police investigate Rogerson's shady dealings. She told Mills she was proud of the way he had handled it, despite keeping it to himself.

'But he told *you* what he was up to,' objected Mills.

'Ah well, pet, he knew he could trust me to keep it to myself.'

Mills objected strongly to the suggestion that she was a gossip.

'The fewer people in the know, the better though, isn't it, pet? He definitely made the right call. And it all came right in the end, didn't it?'

'I hope so.'

'Don't be like that, Mills. Treat it as your first job for the police, one of many, hopefully. Meanwhile, I hear that Harry is sending more work your way.'

'Really? Where did you hear that?'

'Oh, I was chatting with him the other day. I expect that was it.'

Mills suspected that Brenda was working hard behind the scenes to help them keep afloat. She thanked her for her help as she said goodbye, promising to keep in touch. Perhaps Brenda was right. Simon had made the right call, as she put it. But she still felt aggrieved that he hadn't confided in her.

Mills was at her desk early next day, working on her emails. The previous evening had not gone well and she knew it was her fault for not accepting Simon's apology gracefully. He'd tried to explain but she'd over-reacted, telling him if he didn't trust her what hope was there for them. While she shouted at him, he just looked dejected as he admitted he'd made a mistake.

'What's up with you today?' Nige was looking across at her from his desk. Then he said something in Welsh.

Hoping he hadn't seen her eyes misting up, she replied that she knew the phrase now but she did not have "a face like a wet weekend", and hunched over her keyboard. There was a message from PC Young, asking if he could come over at two o'clock. She replied immediately, copying Simon in, so he knew she was directing the policeman to his office in the Chemistry Department. Half an hour later, Simon called her to ask if she'd told Martin about the meeting. Of course, she'd forgotten.

'Don't worry,' he said. 'I'll check that he's in and get him along. See you later.'

She was surprised how cheerful he sounded, acting as if she hadn't been behaving like a teenager in a strop.

'Thank you, Simon,' she said, but he'd already gone.

Her colleague, who must have been listening to her conversation, was looking at her enquiringly.

Mills sighed. 'Not that it's any of your business, Nige, but we're meeting PC Young. Nina gave me his name so you can thank her for me if you like.'

With that she went to join her second-year students for a tutorial.

The police uniform caused quite a stir as Mills accompanied PC Young through the building. She was amused to see Martin, who had already joined Simon in his office, jump to attention when they arrived. Once they were seated, Mills asked Simon to introduce himself and explain why Martin was present. Meanwhile, Mills studied the constable from across the table. He was overweight, if not obese, she decided, and his hair needed a trim. He didn't look particularly interested as he sat clicking the end of his ballpoint pen. She suddenly realised they were all looking at her expectantly.

'This is rather awkward,' she said, looking at Simon.

'We'd better start at the beginning,' he said, launching into an explanation of how Professor Benson had come to see him after his wife's death, requesting he attend the post mortem.

The policeman was shaking his head as he riffled through his notebook. Eventually he found the page he was searching for and studied it intently while Simon related how Mrs Benson's daughter then asked for further tests to be carried out as she wasn't satisfied. Young scribbled in his notebook without looking up.

'Tests on the sample provided by the hospital raised some questions that weren't covered in the post mortem report,' Simon added.

'What questions?' the PC demanded.

Simon told Martin to explain. Mills listened as the microbiologist launched into a long discourse that even she couldn't follow. Young had begun to make notes but soon put his pen down noisily.

'Sorry, mate, but you lost me after the first couple of sentences. Just cut to the chase and give me the bottom line.'

Poor Martin looked deflated as Simon jumped to his assistance. 'In a nutshell, we concluded that Mrs Benson had died from an unidentified bacterium that had destroyed her organs.'

The PC was busy writing again. 'Thank you, I'll pass that information on,' he said, closing his notebook.

'No, that's not all,' Mills insisted. 'We believe the bacterium came from Professor Benson's study.'

She hadn't meant it to come out like that. It sounded ridiculous. The policeman was staring at her, then looked round the table at the others, as if questioning her sanity.

Simon stepped in as the voice of reason, once more. 'What she's trying to say is that this unusual bacterium appears to relate to the research work that Benson has been doing. He had a vial in his home with contents very similar to the material we found in the hospital sample.'

They waited for Young to digest this. 'Are you really

277

suggesting that Professor Benson administered poison to his wife?' he asked eventually, clearly incredulous.

Silence. When no-one responded he put his notebook away.

In view of his dismissive attitude, Mills ignored the vial in her bag. She needed a more direct approach. 'Actually, I thought you might want to talk to Professor Benson's daughter, Janine.'

'And why should I speak to *her*?' he asked standing up to leave.

'Because at first she said she didn't know about the vial, but later she admitted that she did.'

Chapter 36

They didn't stay long after the police constable left. Mills offered to see him out but he said he would find his own way. He wasn't very communicative, just saying he would speak to his sergeant. Once he'd left, Martin expressed concern that the police might want to question them again but Simon assured him that it was probably the last they would hear from him.

'Do you really think that?' Mills asked Simon when they were alone. 'That he won't talk to Benson or his daughter.'

He shrugged. 'To be honest, I rather hope they don't.'

'Well *I* hope they do,' she muttered under her breath.

They left at four o'clock, telling Donna she could go home early. They went back to the cottage but only to collect Harris before heading over to "The CB Inn", where Simon said they were going to cheer themselves up. They didn't pass a soul as they drove across the moors to Arkengarthdale in the dark.

'It's been quite a week,' he commented when they were seated with their drinks. 'I'm so looking forward to a nice quiet weekend.'

The bar soon began to fill with locals and visitors arriving for the weekend. They decided to order food and make a night of it since the lurcher was happy, asleep under the table as usual. Mills relaxed over a second glass of wine, telling Simon that he didn't need to worry now that Rogerson's and Prof Benson were being dealt with by the police. She changed the subject to their plans for the weekend, pointing out that it might seem dull after spending the previous one at "The Angel in Hetton".

Simon laughed. 'Dull suits me fine.'

Mills had a bit of a headache in the morning. She admitted it was probably due to the amount of alcohol consumed the night before. She was sitting in the kitchen, still in her dressing-gown, drinking coffee and scrolling through her phone, while Simon walked the dog. When he returned, she gave him the news.

'I've just had a text from Janine. The police are going round to her father's this afternoon.'

'Oh dear.'

'It's worse than that; she wants me to be there.'

'Just you?'

'It says will you be there please.'

'Will you go?'

'Of course. Should I ask if she wants you there too?'

'No.'

So he really doesn't want to be involved any further, Mills thought. 'That's fine.'

'I'll drive you over but wait outside if you like.'

'OK.'

Mills took two paracetamol and went back to bed for a couple of hours. After a quick snack, they set off in good time, arriving outside Benson's house with fifteen minutes to spare. There was little conversation during the journey but, once they were parked, Simon warned Mills to say as little as possible during the police interview. She assured him she would remain silent throughout.

Five minutes before the allotted time, she walked slowly up the path. Janine opened the door before Mills reached it. She ushered her into the sitting room, where a man in plain clothes introduced himself as Detective Sargent Stringer, showing her his warrant card as he did so. When Mills explained who she was, he nodded, as if he had already heard about her from his PC. His expression suggested it was not all good.

'Janine asked me to come,' she added, to explain her presence.

'I see,' he said as he lowered himself back down into the large armchair.

Janine was wearing a skirt and co-ordinating sweater. Mills could see she'd taken care over her make-up and hair. She looked down at her own jeans as she took a seat on the sofa, wishing she'd dressed more smartly. When the DS asked after Professor Benson, his daughter went to find him, leaving them in an awkward silence that Mills felt compelled to fill.

'I'm representing the forensic service that carried out the tests on Mrs Benson's sample.' She felt that sounded suitably professional.

He made a kind of harrumphing noise while continuing to consult a file he'd produced from a slim briefcase.

'Would that be Yardley Forensics?' he asked without looking up.

'Yes, have you heard of us?'

'I made some enquiries. There was something on file.'

Oh no, thought Mills, that will be the Rogerson investigation. Fortunately they were interrupted by Janine returning, closely followed by a shuffling figure hardly recognisable as the professor. His stained shirt was hanging out of brown cords that may have fitted him before he'd lost a considerable amount of weight. The detective stood up but the old man ignored him, making for the armchair on the opposite side of the fireplace. Janine joined Mills on the sofa, whispering that her father had been having a nap. Mills, who didn't know what to expect, was pleased that DS Stringer took control by reflecting what PC Young had learned on his recent visit to the university. They listened in silence. When he'd finished, he asked if they had any further information to add. What he said was largely accurate so Mills wasn't going to interfere; Benson had his eyes closed; Janine looked as though she was going to speak then shook her head.

'Good,' said Stringer. 'I'm here to tie up some loose ends, that's all.' He paused to consult his notes. 'Dr Sanderson, I understand you took a vial from here.'

Mills could feel the colour rising in her face. 'Yes, it's still…' She picked her bag off the floor, opened the zipped section inside and retrieved the vial, handing it to the DS. To her surprise he produced an evidence bag and popped it inside.

'I'll hang on to this for the moment,' he said. Then he looked at the sleeping professor before turning to Janine. 'Did you know what was in this bottle?' he asked, holding up the bag.

The woman was fidgeting with her wedding ring, turning it round and round on her finger. She coughed and rocked back and forward a few times before answering.

'We thought we did,' she said quietly, looking over at her father. 'Dawn was under the impression it was morphine.'

The detective turned a page in his file. 'Your father's research work on biological weapons, what do you know about that?'

She looked puzzled. 'Weapons? No, not weapons, he's an eminent biologist.'

He looked over at the old man, still asleep, slumped across the arm of the chair. 'I will need to talk to your father about his work and this bottle, if only to clear up any confusion over how it's connected to Mrs Benson's death.'

'He definitely wouldn't have hurt Dawn. He was devoted to her.'

He gave her a sympathetic look, 'It's possible he was being a compassionate husband. Unfortunately we must investigate.'

Janine seemed to be on the brink of tears. 'You can see how frail my father is. Dawn's death has hit him really badly. His memory is failing, he hardly eats, he can't take much more. I'm a nurse, I've seen how the elderly can deteriorate after a bereavement.'

The DS closed the file. 'A nurse?'

'Yes.' Her face was pale despite the makeup.

'And you were told this bottle contained morphine?'

Her eyes darted round the room, settling on her father. Mills watched her tears welling up.

He persisted. 'This bottle is designed for use with a syringe, isn't it? Not something everyone can handle but you must be used to injecting patients?'

Tears were smudging her mascara as she wiped them away. Mills could feel the sofa shaking as the woman sobbed silently.

After an agonising wait, she began to respond hesitantly. 'She was in such pain... I knew it would help her rest, so he could get some sleep too. It was killing him to see her like that. She told me it was morphine but I only gave her a tiny amount because I didn't know how much… and it seemed to help, honestly.'

There was a long silence broken only by Janine's sobbing. Mills put out a hand towards her but withdrew it again as the detective eventually stood up.

'I think we'd better get you to Northallerton as soon as possible, so we can complete a formal statement,' he said, zipping up his briefcase.

Janine looked horrified. 'But what about Dad? I can't leave him in that state.'

They all turned to look at the old man, slouched in the large chair, a line of dribble on his chin.

'I can stay,' Mills told Janine, then turning to the DS she asked, 'How long will she be there?'

The policeman shrugged. Janine said she'd get her coat, so they followed her into the hall. Mills took her phone from her bag to message Simon and by the time Janine was leaving, he was at the front door. They spent the next half an hour going over what had happened. There was a lump in her throat as Mills wondered aloud what the outcome for Janine would be.

Benson was rousing slowly. He sat up and asked politely whether he'd had his tea, apparently unaware that Janine had gone. They left him in his chair while they went into the kitchen to find something for him to eat. He was clearly not capable of looking after himself: the waste bin was overflowing with half-empty tins and there were dishes floating in dirty water in the sink. Mills ordered Simon to look for a meal they could concoct for the old man while she tidied up. He found plastic boxes of meals stacked neatly in the freezer, the contents of each described and dated, presumably by Janine. He selected a cottage pie, heating it through in the microwave. Mills put it on a tray, with a glass of beer, before carrying it through to the sitting room.

Benson had turned the television on and was watching a quiz programme. He took the tray without taking his eyes from the screen, continuing to shout the answers in quick succession.

'There's certainly nothing wrong with his brain,' commented Mills, when she returned to the kitchen.

'Do you think he's pretending to have dementia?'

'No but he could be suffering from depression over the loss of his wife, like Janine said.'

'Particularly if he thinks his daughter was the cause.'

'I don't think she was,' said Mills. 'It was Dawn who told her it was morphine. I believe she knew it contained something connected to her husband's work so it could be dangerous.'

Simon went out to get fish and chips while Mills finished tidying the kitchen, then remembered to message Muriel asking her to feed Harris and let him out for a wee. When Simon returned, they sat with plates on their laps, watching the evening news with Robert. Finally, after four hours of listening for footsteps on the gravel drive, Mills heard voices outside but when Janine came in, she was alone. She looked pale and drawn but held her head up as she addressed them.

'I apologise for leaving you to look after Dad,' she said. 'It's been a long day; I expect you want to get home.'

'Robert has had his tea,' Simon offered. 'Is there anything we can get you?'

She seemed grateful for his sympathetic tone. 'No thank you. I think I should get back too; they'll be wondering where I've got to.'

She told her father she was off, turning away quickly and making for the door. Mills followed her into the hall.

'Janine, call me when you're ready. I want to help you, we both do.'

The nurse was pulling on her coat, wrapping a wool scarf round her neck.

Mills tried again. 'Anything we can do…' She trailed off, uncertain what they could offer.

As Janine went to open the front door, she turned to face her. 'I'm not worried for myself but I'm scared of how my family will take the news.'

'Will it help if I come with you?'

The woman smiled wanly. 'Thank you, but I was actually thinking of Professor Pringle… he might be able to explain things better?'

When Mills and Simon finally arrived back in Mossy Bank it was well past Harris' bedtime, so there was no excitable welcome for them. He raised an eyebrow when they appeared in the kitchen but remained in his basket. They sat together for another hour, drinking hot chocolate, going over the events of the day.

'She was adamant she wanted you to go home with her,' Mills told him.

'You were lucky. It wasn't anything you'd have wanted to experience. Her husband seemed a nice enough guy but I guess the shock of hearing it all for the first time was too much for him.'

'How did he react?'

'He shouted a lot at first. She was in tears much of the time. I don't know how she thought I was going to help.'

'So what did you do?'

'Kept my mouth shut, hoping it would quieten down. Eventually I suggested she made us coffee, so I was left alone with him.'

'How did that go?'

'As well as could be expected. I tried to explain in simple terms about the business with the vial, assuring him his wife wasn't a cold-blooded murderer, that it was all a horrible mistake. He calmed down then. When she came back in, we went over it again, so he got the whole story, including what happened when she was taken off to Northallerton.'

'What did the police say?' Mills asked.

'They took a statement. She said they understood that she thought she was helping Dawn.'

'So they believed her?'

'I think so but they'll need to consider what the next step will be. I assume they will have a new inquest to record death by misadventure?'

'I imagine so. But technically the new verdict would be accidental death since it was not caused by a voluntary risk.'

'So hopefully it won't come to court.'

'There's a possibility she could be charged with involuntary manslaughter, if the police think she was negligent in not confirming the contents of the vial.'

'Like a drug dealer selling heroin or fentanyl that results in someone's death.'

'Exactly.'

'I hope we don't get involved in that one. It's bad enough waiting to hear if I'm going to be called for the Rogerson case.'

When they finally got to bed in the early hours, Mills lay awake going over how an apparently good deed could turn out so badly. She thought Robert was really to blame by keeping such potentially hazardous material in his house. But Dawn, who had been her husband's secretary, would have had a pretty good idea of what the vial contained. Mills was certain that she had deliberately misled her stepdaughter into ending her life, unable to do it herself. Janine clearly didn't plan to kill her stepmother or she wouldn't have been so careful to inject her with only a tiny dose, aware that too much morphine would be lethal.

Chapter 37

Mills sat in the public gallery of Newcastle Crown Court, surrounded by members of the press, anxiously waiting for Simon to give evidence. A week earlier Mills had been sitting in the Coroner's Court in Darlington to hear the new inquest on Dawn Benson deliver a verdict of accidental death. Janine, who was now free of any charges, had come over to thank Mills personally for her help. Simon had stayed away, having dealt with the fall-out from Rachel Clark, who continued to accuse her stepsister of deliberately administering the bacteria that killed her mother, despite his protestations. Thankfully that case was finally over.

Unfortunately, a few days after the dust had settled on the Benson case, Simon received news that he was required to give evidence at the trial of the three men from Rogerson's. Derek MacDonald, Damien Pawson and Alan Rogerson were accused of various crimes associated with drugs, including tampering with evidence. During the days leading up to the trial, Simon became increasingly anxious about his performance on the witness stand. He spent weeks going over the details of their involvement in the police operation.

Now on the third day of the trial, Mills was concerned that it was dragging on longer than she'd anticipated. She hoped to see Simon giving evidence that afternoon so it would be his last day of worrying. Also they had received more work from Harry Fraser and, although Donna continued to cope wonderfully, Mills didn't want her to feel abandoned. She needed to allocate more time to her students because her inbox was filling up with requests for help, particularly from the first-years.

The morning had been spent on the forensic evidence provided by the police. The original heroin had been carefully analysed by the Wakefield laboratory before an undercover officer had taken it to Rogerson Forensics. He had requested they get it tested, implying that he needed the result to come back as low quality. Mills was amazed by the price the company had quoted to him, a great deal more than any normal rate for forensic work. Presumably customers were willing to pay to get the result they wanted. There was much legal wrangling in court about the legitimacy of the "honey trap", as the defence barrister scathingly referred to the police operation.

Simon was finally called in the afternoon. He looked self-assured as he stepped up to the witness box but Mills could tell by his demeanour that he was far from comfortable. He took the oath then looked across at the defendants. She was glad she'd persuaded him to wear his blue tie, it looked less sombre than the ones he'd selected, making him appear at ease. She tried to view him as a stranger would: a university professor, an expert witness who had tested the drugs forensically and found they had been tampered with. He described the work exactly as he had when she'd gone through it with him. Unlike in his last court appearance, this time he was a witness for the prosecution, which made the cross-questioning far easier. The defence lawyer couldn't fault his credentials or how he had carried out the forensics; his only way of attacking him was to ask whether he'd worked for Rogerson in the past. He agreed he had. When the barrister asked him why, Simon said he hadn't known at first that Rogerson's tampered with forensic evidence but now he did. Mills smiled at him, although he was busy observing the jury. Soon he left the witness box to join Mills in the public gallery. She squeezed his hand, whispering that he'd done a good job.

They'd agreed that they couldn't spare any more time to watch the rest of the trial, so as soon as the court adjourned for the day, they left. As they stepped out into the entrance hall, DS Caldicott came over to join them.

'Thank you, Professor Pringle. I think we can be confident of a safe conviction for all three by early next week. Will you be back again tomorrow? It should be interesting to hear their explanation of what went on at Rogerson's.'

When Simon explained he wouldn't be around to hear the verdict, Caldicott promised to contact him as soon as he knew the outcome, adding that it was a foregone conclusion anyway. Simon said he hoped so. As they parted, the detective gave them some good news.

'By the way, your contribution hasn't gone unnoticed, you know. My superiors have been asking me about your laboratory. I suggest you send me some literature so I can pass it to the relevant people.'

They thanked him and ran through the March winds to the coffee shop that Simon had discovered during his previous disastrous court appearance.

When the clocks went forward that weekend, Mills declared that she was glad winter was over. It had been a long, miserable time worrying about the Rogerson business and Professor Benson's family.

Simon was hunched over his laptop. 'You do realise they're both a result of the running the forensic lab.'

'What d'you mean?'

'I'm just saying, maybe it would be less stressful if we didn't have to worry about the business, that's all.'

Mills didn't reply. There was no way she was going to give up now. They had a steady stream of work from Harry Fraser, thanks to Brenda, and a promise of police work following successful prosecution of the Rogerson three. Samples were due to arrive from the Cleveland Police imminently, according to the email she'd received in the week. When she called Nina to give her the good news, her friend was delighted for her, offering to spread the word around *her* relevant colleagues in the North Yorkshire Police.

'It'll be like when you were down in Harrogate with Brenda,' she'd said. 'I've been missing our chats about body fluids!'

After the call, Mills turned to Simon. 'Perhaps we should consider taking on a junior technician.'

'Why do we need another technician?' he asked, concentrating on his laptop.

'Because Donna will need help to keep on top of the work.' He didn't respond. 'Particularly if we're both going to America in the summer,' she added pointedly.

Finally she had his attention. He looked up quickly with a nervous grin.

'That's if you still want me to come with you,' she added with a smile.